MY LORD

TRACIE PODGER

Copyright

Cover designed - Francessca Wingfield PR & Design

Editing – Lisa Hobman

Proofreading – Joanne Thompson

CHAPTER ONE

Visiting a sex club wasn't what I was expecting, but it was certainly what I needed. Accepting the invitation from a rather vile client of mine presented, unknowingly at the time, a huge and unexpected opportunity.

I was in my office and had just taken a call from Lord Patrick Stanton, a 'name' at Lloyds and one of only a handful of clients I had managed to switch over to my own company that I started in preparation for my departure. It was clear that Lloyds was about to fall from a great height, and I expected to get the boot. Obviously, because of my title, being a Lord of the Realm myself and coming from a renowned family, I was able to attract some nice clients without any trouble. I hadn't liked Stanton when he'd been thrust onto me a few years previously, and I disliked him more as time passed. He was a cretin of gargantuan proportions; sleazy, and part of a very undesirable ring of 'all male club' types that like to abuse women.

However, the invitation to the sex club would potentially give me that snippet of evidence I needed to get rid of him as a client without retribution. No one wanted to be associated, publically, with prostitutes. Since it was mostly rumour that he was violent with them, reporting him to the police was a futile exercise; the women didn't come forward. It also appeared that some members of the police force were also part of his little club, it was a done deal that he would be protected.

"Alex, did you hear me?"

I turned from the floor to ceiling glass windows in my plush corner office. "Sorry, Daisy, I was miles away. What did you say?" I smiled at the elderly lady that saved my bacon every day of the week. She was about the best personal assistant one could wish for.

"You have a meeting in a half hour, I wanted to remind you because I'm sure you need to get moving," she said, returning my smile.

"I do and thank you."

I pushed myself away from the desk and rose. It was time to get my arse into gear and not spend so much effort on Stanton. I wanted to pitch to a new client, one I'd been after for a few years. Mackenzie Miller was a venture capitalist with cash to invest. He was also the most intriguing person I'd had the pleasure to meet. Well, when I say *meet*, it had been at a dinner, and briefly. He'd had a woman on his arm that I could have instantly fallen in love with. So much was my attraction to her that I had to keep my distance in case I physically salivated and offended them both. I never got her name, but her blonde hair and elegance, coupled with her Southern American accent, just blew me away.

Maybe I'd ask after her, simply so I could discover her name.

I'd spent a lot of time researching Mr. Miller over the years. He was American with businesses both in the UK and stateside. Although he seemed to spend the majority of his time flying back and forth, I'd heard he had recently purchased a house in London. His UK headquarters were in Canary Wharf and from what I was able to ascertain, he owned a lot of real estate there. The most interesting thing that came from my research was most of his CEOs, or at least significant employees—although I hated that term—were women. It went against the 'old boy network,' of course, and he was ridiculed in the gentlemen's clubs for it.

"Pussy whipped, I bet," I remember Stanton saying, and then confessing to have never met Miller.

I wasn't sure that was the case. He was an extremely confident man and although he was often pictured with the blonde, he seemed to have a stable of beauties to accompany him when she couldn't.

I hailed a taxi and slid into the back seat. I flicked through the file I'd retrieved from my briefcase, stopping at a photograph of Miller. Although he was smiling in the apparent corporate shot, he had steely eyes and his fixed expression and strong jaw gave the impression he didn't suffer fools gladly. I'd been surprised to be granted the meeting after making many attempts over the past year.

I hadn't noticed the taxi was out of the city until we stopped at a checkpoint. I watched as security officers peered through the side window and ran their mirror under the car, before waving us through.

"Security still tight, then?" I asked the driver, who stared back through his rear-view mirror.

"Yeah, not a bad thing. Don't want my cab blown up, I'll lose my livelihood," he replied, smiling at me.

I smiled in return. There was nothing like a good conversation with a London taxi driver. They were a law unto themselves and full of knowledge and opinion. An institution, he had reminded me when we'd spoken.

We pulled up alongside the entrance to one of the many towering, vast glass and steel office buildings. A metal sign stood beside the revolving door listing all the businesses inside. I knew that Miller either owned them outright, or had interests in each one. That day, I was heading to the top floor and his personal offices.

After signing in and receiving a visitor's badge, having my briefcase X-rayed and walking through a metal detector, I was shown to the lifts. A security guard accompanied me but stepped back to allow me to exit the lift alone. However, I wasn't quite alone. As the doors slid open, I was face to face with the blonde that, yet again, took my breath away.

"I...erm...I have a meeting," I stammered through my sentence as I stepped out of the lift. She gently chuckled and I felt as though she'd set my insides on fire. "I'm sorry," I said, straightening myself and pushing my shoulders back. "I'm Alex Duchoveny, and I have a meeting with Mackenzie Miller."

She held out her hand. "I'm pleased to meet you, Lord

Duchoveny. My name is Gabriella Collingsworth." She didn't offer her position within the organisation, but I had no doubt she wasn't his secretary or personal assistant. I frowned in confusion, I hadn't mentioned my title and wondered how she knew it.

She had a firm handshake and when she turned to lead the way, as much as I tried, I couldn't stop my eyes from travelling down her back and over the tight arse covered in a cream pencil skirt and legs encased in cream stockings—not that I knew for sure they were stockings but I could dream, I thought—ending in impossibly high heels. I wanted to clear my throat or take a moment to adjust my hardening cock. Her perfume left a trail and I was like a bear with a honey scent. I could have followed her with my eyes closed.

By the time I looked up, Mackenzie Miller was leaning against the frame of his glass office door. He raised his eyebrows and I felt my cheeks flush at being caught. He stepped to one side. I got the distinct impression that, although she was in front of me, she knew I'd check her out. She knew the effect she had on men, for sure. I chuckled quietly.

"Lord Duchoveny," Mackenzie said, holding out his hand. Another one that knew my title.

I nodded. "Alex, please. It's a pleasure to finally meet you."

Mackenzie waved his arm allowing me to walk ahead of him. Gabriella had already taken one of the seats and I was shown to the other.

Mackenzie strode behind his desk to sit. "Let me introduce you to my right-hand woman, Gabriella

Collingsworth. She runs UK operations alongside me, and alone when I'm not here."

"It's a pleasure to meet you, also, Ms. Collingsworth."

Gabriella's lips twitched before she smiled. She cocked one eyebrow. "Gabriella, please. We're all on first name terms here." She purred out the words in a voice like melted chocolate being drizzled over me and I found my pulse rate had increased.

"Alex, I'm impressed with your handling of the Lloyds disaster. I understand that it has affected your family greatly, and I'm sorry for that." Mackenzie said, cutting straight to the chase, which startled me; it threw me off track if I was to be honest.

I cleared my throat. "Ah, yes, greatly. Not the best time for my family." I wasn't sure how much to divulge.

"I lost a parent, as did Gabriella, although not in the same circumstances, but we can empathise with you, Alex." His words were kind, yet the meaning behind them suggested he had really done his homework on me. Obviously, that's where he and Gabriella had learned of my title.

Lloyds of London had been bankrupted due to spiralling asbestos insurance claims from the US and my father had taken his own life after losing the majority of the family's fortune. It happened a couple of years back but the pain was still as excruciating as the day I had discovered my father hanging.

Gabriella placed her hand on mine, gave it a squeeze and then let go. My skin continued to tingle even when her contact was withdrawn.

Mackenzie leaned back into his seat and smiled. "So,

you're here to tempt me to invest in, what? Your business or a deal you have knowledge of?"

I smiled at his candour. "You know, I believe I have underestimated you. I don't think, I, nor my company, can actually offer you anything you can't do yourself. Perhaps it was foolish of me to assume otherwise," I said, reclining in my seat to mirror his action.

Mackenzie looked to Gabriella. "Well, that's a first. How about lunch?" He turned his attention back to me.

I shrugged. "Might as well. I booked the whole afternoon out of the office." I laughed as I spoke.

Mackenzie rose and buttoned up his suit jacket. "Gabriella?" he asked.

"Thank you, but I have a rather important date with your accountants. I'll have to take a rain check, maybe another time?" She looked at me when she asked, and I flustered again. She chuckled and patted my cheek before she nodded to Mackenzie and left the office.

"I think she likes you." Mackenzie said, leading the way back to the lift.

"I might be mar—"

"You're not. As much as I'm sure you've investigated me, I've done the same."

I had been about to say that I might have been married. Instead, I laughed again. I liked Mackenzie Miller, a lot.

"I'm really not sure what to say," I added, and I wasn't. Mackenzie was so very forthright and yet again, I was dumbstruck.

As we travelled down, he described the businesses in the building. He also explained that, as tenancies came to an end, he was looking to bring all his companies under the one roof. I wanted to know more about Gabriella and what she did for his organisation.

Mackenzie didn't have an obvious southern accent, although every now and again I'd hear a slight twang.

Curiosity got the better of me. "You're from the same place as Gabriella, are you?" I asked, as we exited the lift to be met by a driver.

"We were born on ranches next door to each other. We've been friends since childhood. I moved away, hence the loss of accent," he replied with a chuckle.

His driver opened the rear door of a sleek silver Mercedes and we climbed in. I welcomed the air conditioning and loosened my tie.

"Do you mind?" I enquired, opening the buttons of my jacket.

"Go ahead, no formalities with me," he replied, and I slipped off my jacket. He eyed me for a moment. "You're not going to be all British and talk about the weather, are you?"

I turned abruptly to face him. "Well it is rather hot, but no," I replied.

Mackenzie chuckled. "Thank fuck for that."

I liked Mackenzie even more at that point.

Lunch was in the private dining room of a very exclusive back of Knightsbridge restaurant and, although I'd lived in London all my adult life, I'd never heard of it before. It was a Michelin starred menu and I was in my element with the wine list alone. I could have scanned for hours had Mackenzie not just ordered water for himself. I followed suit, we chose our dishes and the waiter took the menus away.

Mackenzie rested back and studied me. "Tell me, Alex. What's it like being a Lord?"

"If I had a pound..." I answered, and then laughed. "It opens doors, sometimes. It closes more, for sure. There's a huge misconception that, since I'm a *toff*, I like buggering boys and I can row a boat."

It was my turn to cause Mackenzie to splutter; so much so that he had to dab his mouth with his napkin since he'd just taken a mouthful of water.

"Jesus, Alex. That's about the funniest, and the first, thing I thought of as well."

I held my hands up as if to prove my point. "Well, never done either. Not interested in boys and too tall for the boat." I picked up my glass of water and raised it to him in a toast.

We chatted back and forth over lunch, mostly about our lives and where we came from, our childhoods, and then about business. Although candid in some areas, Mackenzie was quite forthcoming discussing his many companies, and there were many.

"Where do you see yourself in five years, Alex?" he asked as we waited for the plates to be removed.

"I'd like to build my business, obviously. Pay off the family debts, I guess, and start living my own life, not the one intended for me." It was as blunt a statement as I'd ever given, and I surprised myself with my honesty.

He nodded thoughtfully. "Before you came to see me, I'd decided that you and I should have a discussion. I'm not interested in using your investment firm. As you said, I'm more than capable of dealing with that myself, although sometimes, I do distance myself from a deal. But I had planned to headhunt you. Seems that you have saved me the trouble by scheduling our appointment first. I want you to run one of my companies."

For a moment there was silence. I shook my head; had I heard correctly? I'd only known Mackenzie for a couple of hours. "I'm sorry, you want me to do what?"

He grinned, clearly amused by my reaction. "I want you to run one of my companies. I'm about to buy one of the largest communications companies in Europe. Obviously, no one knows about it yet. I intend to merge it with a smaller one that I own. What makes me want you, is that the new company has some very lucrative military contracts and I think you would be the best person at the helm, rather than some redneck from the United States."

I was so taken aback I wasn't sure how to answer so I did so stupidly. "So, you just want my Lordship?" I asked, laughing to ensure he realised it was humour. Although I wasn't sure it worked.

He pondered for a moment. "Partly, yes. A Brit in charge is probably better for liaison than me. You might think we don't know each other, but I've been researching you for a while."

"That sort of sounds illegal," I said, again laughing.

That time, he joined in. "Alex, we're businessmen, we do what we have to. Obviously, I don't expect an answer now, but Gabriella has prepared a proposal that we'd like to send to you," he said.

I reached into my jacket pocket and pulled out my wallet. I handed him a personal card with my home address. "Okay, it wasn't what I came to see you about, obviously, but I can't say I'm not interested to learn more."

"I think you'll find the proposal attractive and the benefits are enormous," he added.

"I'll be interested in reading it."

Mackenzie insisted on having the bill sent to his office, despite my protests, and with promises of the proposal being sent by courier, something I found rather old fashioned, we parted ways.

I hailed a taxi to take me back to my office and he stepped into his car. He had offered a lift, but I'd declined. It had been the strangest meeting I'd had in a long time and I really just needed to clear my head before getting on with my day.

My phone buzzed in my pocket and I pulled it out to see Stanton's name displayed. Bile rose to my throat at the thought of spending the evening socialising with him, but I reminded myself it was for the greater good.

I took the call. "Stanton," I said, clipped and with authority.

"Just checking on this evening, old boy. I've sent you the address. No phones, no cameras, and you're there as my guest. Arrive about eight, yes?"

He had tried to mimic my clipped tones and authoritative voice, but he couldn't match them. Mine was an inherited title, his was given for services rendered and it most certainly made him feel inferior to the rest of us. He was a short man with an excessive love of port that showed in his bulbous nose and rotund frame. In addition, his sweaty body gave him a slimy look. His reminder that I was to be there as his guest was his way of pretending he was superior to me in some way. I smiled to myself as I clicked off the call.

Evidence, that's all I wanted.

CHAPTER TWO

A large white envelope with a small embossed insignia in the corner sat on my table. When Mackenzie had said he would courier over the proposal, I had assumed it would be to my home address and in a day or so. I removed my jacket and placed it on the coat stand, leaving my briefcase beside it. I didn't intend to stay long; I had returned simply to gather some work for the evening. After I returned from the 'club,' I had every intention of catching up with a client in the Far East.

I picked up the envelope wondering whether to take it home or not. However, I could smell a faint hint of familiar perfume and knew that Gabriella had put it together. I smiled as I slid my fingers under the flap and shook out the contents.

I picked up a summary and read halfway, pausing to gasp at what I was reading.

It appeared I was being offered a one-off payment to clear my family debt; a figure very close to what was owed was mentioned. In addition to this, a salary three times what I was currently earning would be offered with a six-month review, the usual pension and medical insurance, first class travel, accommodation when in the States was also on offer. As far as I was aware, the position was UK based but I wasn't averse to travel overseas if necessary.

"Wow," I whispered.

Daisy popped her head around the door. "I'm off now."

"Yes, thank you. I'll see you after the weekend," I said, smiling at her.

With the office quiet, I read the summary again. It was an offer that would be extremely hard to refuse, however, I needed to know the catch; there had to be one. The offer was simply too good.

Stanton had instructed me on the dress code for that evening. Unbeknownst, I hoped, to him, I was a member of a very exclusive 'club' in London. I knew exactly what to wear. The thought of sex led me straight back to Gabriella.

She was going to plague me, I was sure. I laughed as I showered and couldn't help but think what she would look like naked as I pleasured myself. I hadn't had a lover for a few months, and I hadn't had a long-term partner for a few years. I shuddered as I came and also at the thought of being straddled by the Lady Elizabeth, someone my mother thought a good match. The girl dissolved every time I was close to her, and the one time I had taken her on a date, a brief kiss to her cheek had almost caused her to orgasm. She was too needy. As much as I wanted a woman to succumb to me, I needed a fight first.

Driving out to Hertfordshire was both relaxing and anxiety ridden. As a car fanatic, I loved being behind the wheel of my Bentley Continental. Just the smell of the bespoke interior and the calf leather clad seats eased the tension in my body. But the thought of whose company I was to spend the evening with caused my stomach to knot.

All I needed was to see Stanton in one compromising position or situation and I could use that to dissolve our business arrangement. It was one I had partly inherited. When the Lloyds scandal was brought to the public domain, I had no idea of my father's involvement. I had only cared that I had seen some very shady dealings and cover-ups that the investors should have known about. Money was being taken even after the company had started to crumble. Having lost the bulk of his fortune, my father had been persuaded by a small group of investors—of which Stanton was the instigator—to borrow money from them. It was at a ridiculous interest rate and even years after his death, the estate was still beholden to them. Stanton liked to remind me of that fact, and it was the only reason I kept him as a client. Initially, I wanted to make money for him, forfeit my commission in lieu of the debt. Stanton and his cronies just made it harder and harder. If it were just me, I'd have taken the bull by horns and ousted them, but I came to learn there were a few old 'names' that had also lost everything they had under their control. So, I kept him close until I could find something of substance to have him crawl under a rock for many years to come.

Without realising, I came upon a driveway with a pair of large iron gates that I recognised. There was an intercom on a stand at window height and I pressed the call button.

"Lord Dochoveny, guest of Lord Stanton," I said when it was answered.

"Please drive to the main house, a valet will wait for you."

The gates opened without a sound and I followed the drive that cut through the most perfectly mown lawn. The gardens were magnificent and reminded me of my childhood. I shook my head in surprise. I'd visited the house that appeared before me many times as a child.

I left my car in the care of a valet and walked up the stone steps towards the large, ornate wooden door.

It was opened and I heard a squeal.

"Oh, my God, darling, whatever are you doing here?" Veronica said. She wore a black suit; her blonde hair was pulled tight and high in a ponytail. She wore ruby red lipstick and a red bra showed through the suit jacket as she moved.

"I'm meant to be visiting a sex club at the request of a vile man—"

"Stanton?" my cousin enquired.

"Yes, I'm assuming you know him. And you really need to tell me what is going on. This is all rather embarrassing, Von." I reverted to the nickname I'd called her as a child. Veronica had been a tomboy and always up for any challenge, it seemed fitting to shorten her name to a more masculine one.

She grabbed my arm and pulled me towards another door. "Come quick before he knows you've arrived. I'll have someone get him drunk, or something," she said.

We stood in her office and she closed the door behind us.

"Oh, Alex, it's so lovely to see you. Why has it been so

long?" She strode over to me, and placed her palms on my arms.

"I don't know. Life, shitty life, I guess."

Both our fathers had lost money when Lloyds collapsed. Her family had, thankfully, retained the family home and had managed to keep a hold of it. I had lost mine.

"Sit, I think I have some explaining to do," she said, waving her hand towards a chair. "Whisky?"

"I think I ought to," I replied, and then laughed.

Veronica poured us both a large glass, added some ice and for a moment we just sat in silence staring at each other. It had been at my father's funeral that we'd last seen each other and I cursed both the length of time we had been apart *and* my apathy for keeping in contact with family. It was, at the time, both painful and embarrassing. One simply doesn't just lose all their belongings overnight and smile the following day.

She took a deep breath. "So, I needed some money to stop *the olds* from selling the house, and, well you know me, my darling, I do love an adventure and sex, of course. So, I thought, what to do with this monstrosity?" She took a sip of her whisky and stared at the ceiling. Plaster was peeling and some of the original coving was missing.

"You set up a sex club?" I frowned and tried hard not to laugh.

She smirked. "I did, but a high-end, exclusive one. Nothing cheap or nasty here, I promise."

"You're a pimp, Von." My voice rose in amusement.

She gasped. "Not exactly, I don't take money from the girls, whatever extra they earn, they keep. They're paid a salary, Alex. I keep proper accounts." Her voice rose in mock indignation.

"And what have you registered your 'business' as at HMRC?" My eyebrows furrowed and I pursed my lips to contain the snigger.

"A gentleman's club, of course. Whatever else? You won't dob me in, will you?"

I rubbed my chin and paused before replying. "Of course not, but, Veronica, I'm a little worried about you being involved in this. It's not a safe environment and it's your home."

"Darling, you came here not knowing where you were coming to, and you might have boxed for Eton but I have always been able to defend myself as well."

I sighed. She was my cousin, and being an only child, her father turned her into the boy he wanted. She could fence better than her club captain, horse ride, she undertook martial arts when she disappeared to Thailand for a while. I had no doubt she could defend herself, but owning a sex club? Surely that was on another level.

"This is high class, Alex. Out there are some very familiar faces, you'll struggle not to chuckle. Some are spouting off in parliament about the poor and disadvantaged during the day, then heard fucking the brains out of a lovely male submissive in the evening."

I held up my hand. "Am I going to compromise myself, Von?"

"No, it's a quiet night. There's only Stanton and Jeremy Daughton in the bar just now. Do you know Jeremy?"

I shook my head not recalling the name. Needing more

information on what I was letting myself in for, I asked a question I hoped I wouldn't regret. "What happens here?"

She went on to explain that she had some bedrooms available for patrons to use either with other patrons, groups, or sex workers. She told me that every girl there had a full medical check and was willingly employed, some were old school friends who, like Veronica, lived a hedonistic lifestyle, loved the sex, and wanted the money.

I held up my hands in a kind of surrender. "Okay, I'm only here to see if I can get some dirt on Stanton," I confessed.

She tilted her head. "I can imagine. And had you asked, I could have helped with that a while ago."

"Let me go and meet with him in the bar. Can we chat later? Or maybe tomorrow?"

She smiled and nodded, then slid a card over her desk. It contained her personal mobile number, something I didn't think I had. I pocketed the card and then rose.

"Alex, if this place isn't for you, you know, for now..." She gave me a wink. "I can provide you whatever you need. Stanton released my family from his shady fucking group because he knows I have images of him. All I have to do is walk in there later and pretend I hadn't seen you come in."

I thought for a moment. I wasn't there for the sex, and it would certainly solve a problem. I nodded. "Give me ten or so minutes."

I left her office and walked slowly across the vast hallway. It was a shame to see the ornaments gone, the chandelier missing, and all the glorious things that made it a grand home, sold to pay taxes and debts. It was shabby but, thankfully, in a still chic way. It wasn't a high-class gentleman's club, though. I had been to many, and even just that walk to the bar had me thinking.

I could hear Stanton from outside the room. His booming voice reverberated around the mostly empty, former library. To one side was a bar with an immaculately dressed barman who was polishing glasses, and I wondered just how many stories he had to tell. The man acknowledged me when I entered, alerting Stanton that I was there.

"You're late, old boy. I began to think you'd chickened out." His raucous laughter was echoed by his other guest.

"No, not at all." I turned to the barman. "Glenfiddich, with ice."

Stanton's guest didn't introduce himself; although he had no need as Veronica had already told me his name, not that I recognised him at all. He was shady looking, kept quiet, but with a permanent smirk. Stanton babbled on, telling his guest all about my business. I began to realise this visit wasn't about sex but about being introduced to Jeremy Daughton. I had a feeling I was being interviewed. When Daughton spoke, it was with a heavy accent, possibly Russian and I then doubted his name was really Jeremy.

There had been one thing that kept me from trouble my whole life. It was a gut feeling that was indescribable but not to be ignored. I got that feeling the minute I spoke with Jeremy. He explained that he was looking to invest heavily in the UK and his friend, Stanton, had thought I might be able to help.

Stanton looked between us, licking his lips as if he were about to eat a meal. Or expect a fat commission and finder's fee from us both.

"Perhaps, Mr. Daughton, I'll take your details and we can arrange a meeting. I'm sure you don't want to be doing business on such a pleasant evening as this. However, I should add, I'm not taking on any new clients just yet, another opportunity has arisen that will keep me busy for a while. But I might have another avenue for you," I said.

Stanton clapped me on the back. "You could do a lot worse than have Daughton on your books, old boy," he said. His touch made my skin crawl. "And you're right, why spoil this evening when this place is full of sexy and very compliant women?" He winked at Daughton who returned the wink.

A voice came from behind us. "Alex! My darling, how absolutely wonderful to see you here."

I smiled as I turned to see Veronica striding across the room. Her staggeringly high heels clip-clopped on the wood. Stanton visibly shrank. Jeremy seemed impressed.

"Veronica," I said, as she closed in. She held my biceps and kissed both my cheeks.

"Do you have all you need, gentleman?" she asked. "And Lord Stanton, please adhere to my previous warning."

She held such an innocent look on her face, her eyes were wide, and her lips curled into a smile. He swallowed hard.

"Warning?" I asked.

"Yes, my darling. Your friend here can be a little too rough with my ladies and he's on a yellow card already," she explained.

"Stanton, how terrible of you," I said, with mock disgust.

He tugged at his collar. "How do you know each other?" he asked, stammering slightly through his question.

"We're cousins. Our fathers were brothers," she said, brightly. "Now, my darling cousin, be sure to catch up with me when you leave, and I'd be delighted to meet for lunch tomorrow. We have so much to discuss." She looked pointedly at Stanton as she spoke to me.

She left and I asked for the barman to refill our glasses. Stanton made a point to check his watch and spluttered a, "Good gracious, look at the time." I chuckled as he made excuses to leave.

"And then there were two," I said, raising my glass to Jeremy.

"And then there were two," he replied, doing the same.

From then on, it became an interesting evening. It was very early on established that my business wasn't a match for what he wanted and although I was very unsure on where the money he wanted to invest had come from, I was able to pass him on to others that I knew would do all the relevant checks. Money laundering, especially money laundered from Russia was a hot topic and highly investigated. Either Jeremy was aware of that and still wanted to take the risk, or I had misjudged him. Either way, he was a friend of Stanton and, therefore, not someone I wished to do business with.

"I think this evening hasn't gone to plan, yes?" he said, placing his glass on the bar.

"Yes, poor old Stanton thought he had one over on me. Seems he just realised that he hasn't," I said, not minding for one minute if he knew that.

He nodded. "I think I know what. Good luck, Lord

Duchoveny," he said as he slid from his stool and patted my shoulder before leaving.

"Pour us some drinks," said a voice from behind me. "In fact, just leave the bottle, we'll shut up shop early. Please let the girls know to go home." Veronica was back in the room.

"How did you know?" I asked.

"Camera's everywhere," she smiled.

We proceeded to drink the bottle of rather fine whisky, talk about our childhoods, life after my father's suicide and her father's recent death, and get drunk.

The following morning, I was woken in a strange and very sumptuous bedroom by a knock on the door.

"Are you decent?" Veronica called out.

I looked under the sheet to check since I had no idea how I'd gotten to bed the previous evening.

"Yes, just about," I replied.

She giggled as she opened the door while holding two mugs of coffee.

"What a wonderful evening, Alex. Just like the old days. We will stay in touch, won't we?"

I shuffled up the bed and she sat on the edge. She handed me a coffee and I took a sip, wincing as the hot liquid burned my lips.

I nodded. "Absolutely," I replied.

As much as I wasn't sure about her chosen profession, I did appreciate that the need to keep her ancestral home was so overwhelming for her that she'd do anything she had to.

Once I'd finished my coffee, I shooed her from the room so I could dress. I'd shower when I got home. We then sat with pastries and more coffee chatting for a good couple of hours. She told me all about her plans for the club and the more I listened, the more interested I became. She didn't want to keep the girls, and I was grateful for that, she wanted to have a high-end facility with rooms designed for play by consenting adults. She wanted a great restaurant, a spa, some outbuildings converted into cottages for mini-breaks and she wanted to charge a fortune in membership to ensure she got the right people. What she didn't have was the capital to do it.

"I might know someone," I said, reluctant to give over any names in case I was way off the mark.

I had been a member of various clubs over the years and although there were plenty of women on offer, paying for sex wasn't my kind of thing. However, a club where partners could indulge in their fantasies, where couples could hook up with others, did entice.

"I have a couple of people I'd like to approach, not that I know how to. If you're *someone* isn't suitable, maybe you'd help me?" she asked.

"Absolutely."

We said goodbye and I climbed into my car confident I was clear to drive after the copious amounts of coffee and pastries, and headed home. I lived in an original art deco apartment block in Kensington, not far from the restaurant Mackenzie had taken me to, one of the reasons I was so surprised not to know of its existence. I enjoyed my own space and although I missed company, the apartment suited my needs.

I walked into the kitchen and switched on the coffee machine. I probably drank way too much, but I certainly felt the need for another cup. I chuckled as I recalled the conversation I'd had with Veronica and Stanton. And I wondered who Jeremy really was. Sitting on my table was the envelope from Mackenzie and although the scent of perfume had diminished, I could imagine it. Not knowing anything about American life in the South, I could picture Gabriella spraying a little of her perfume over an envelope as if it were completely normal.

I visualised her. Her walk, so slow and seductive when she showed me to Mackenzie's office even though she could have simply pointed. She knew what she was doing, she was playing a game, and I liked it.

The first smell of a chase, the first whiff of sexual desire is what stirred me. The thought of a challenge enticed me, what excited me more was that she might be forbidden. Mackenzie had referred to her as a childhood friend and not his partner; although I was sure he wouldn't divulge such private detail. I wasn't the kind to steal a woman from another man, but that gut instinct was playing havoc with me and I smiled, looking forward to discovering who she really was.

I once again tipped out the contents of the envelope. As I read, thoughts of Gabriella were pushed to one side. The contract was very tempting indeed. I knew of the company, Trymast, which Mackenzie was buying. As he'd said, one of the largest communication's companies in Europe. It might just be a change in career I could get my teeth into.

CHAPTER THREE

I played a round of golf the following morning with two old work colleagues. The only two left that were still able to talk to me without fear of being persecuted. I had been classed as a whistle-blower but if I saved just a few lives or the devastation of bankruptcy, they could call me whatever they wanted. Grudges were held for many years in the city, unfortunately. I was simply buying time at the recently formed *new* Lloyds. It wouldn't have looked good on them if they had kicked me out straight after I'd brought world attention to their shady cover-up.

"I hear you lost the Stanton account?" Len said as he teed up his ball.

"I hope so," I replied, pulling my cap down to shield my eyes from the sunlight.

"Horrible slimy fuck, he is," Pete added.

Len and Pete played golf every day, mostly in Portugal where they owned villas. Although retired, the two still dabbled in investments and the golf course, once a week, was where they shared their wins and losses. It's also where they swapped tips.

"He hasn't actually told me, but I'll be glad to see the back of him," I said.

Len grunted as he swung his club in a semi-circle and clouted the ball straight down the fairway. "You'll have to tell me how you did it."

"About the best shot you've played in a long time," Pete said, shielding his eyes to watch where the ball was heading. The two were like a couple of old women, always arguing.

We continued our round, chatting and teasing each other. Applauding a good shot, and ribbing poor ones mercilessly.

"What do you know about Mackenzie Miller?" I asked, as we'd done our nine holes and headed into the clubhouse for a coffee.

"Venture capitalist, wealthy, got an eye for a deal. Not afraid to get his hands dirty if he has to, though," Pete said, while also asking for three coffees by sign language.

Len and I had taken seats at a table.

"Why?" Pete asked.

"I wanted to pitch to him, he ended up offering me a job."

"Blimey, what did you say?" Len asked.

"Nothing, yet. I'm tempted, for sure. I just don't know a lot about him."

Len said, "I don't know that anyone knows a lot about him. I've heard he's a good chap to have on your side, but not necessarily one to cross." Pete nodded as if in confirmation.

"How did he get started?" I asked.

"Rumour has it that he bought a business, built it up, lost it, I think, then started again. Found out his father-in-law had shafted his father, so he spend the next few years buying up the father-in-law's businesses and ousting him. Something like that, anyway." It confirmed what I had read about him in my research.

"Someone who has worked from the ground up then?" I asked, impressed. I admired men, and women, who did that. I disliked those that fell into the family business and then acted as if it had taken blood and spit to get to the top.

I'd used my name and family connections when I'd had to, but I hadn't been handed the proverbial silver spoon.

We drank and we ate a hideous bacon sandwich, complained, as we did every single Saturday, and vowed to cancel our membership, not that we ever did that, either. We laughed as we headed to the car park and then on with our days.

Sunday morning came and I sat in my kitchen with the financial papers spread over the table. I read an article about Mackenzie who had attended a dinner with the Prime Minister. It appeared she was keen to have him on board as some sort of business ambassador. The UK wanted American investments and trade deals, maybe she thought he could be a great intermediary. Gabriella was beside him and had her hair pinned with tendrils just caressing the side of her face. She wore a diamond choker style necklace on her elegant neck, and I wondered if she was from money; not that I really cared.

The slinky silver dress that she wore showed off her thin waist and slightly rounded hips. The neckline plunged to near her navel. I wet my lips and then shook my head.

"Get a grip, Alex," I said to myself.

I couldn't remember the last time I lusted after someone as much; in fact, I don't think I'd ever done so. There was something *siren like* about her. A need for her crept over me. A want that I hadn't experienced before. I grabbed my laptop and researched. I couldn't find anything to suggest that she and Mackenzie were partners. In all the articles I found, she ran his UK operations on a day-to-day basis while he went back and forth. There was an interview that confirmed they had known each other from childhood, and I was very impressed with one or two of the, obviously female, interviewer's questions.

She had asked why Mackenzie deliberately chose women over men. Gabriella had responded that he employed the best person for the job and sex didn't come into it. He had simply found that the women he had employed had been far better than their male counterparts. It was suggested that he embraced women, and that perhaps he liked to empower them. Gabriella had shrugged her shoulders in response, according to the interviewer.

I got the vibe from our lunch that Mackenzie wasn't like a lot of businessmen who were, in actual fact, threatened by successful women. They didn't seem to do well in the workplace because men didn't allow them to. As old fashioned as it seemed to me, men put up the barriers and as much as women fought for equality, in the city, in the money markets especially, they had a long way to go before they were on equal footing. It had saddened me. I remembered Alice, an amazing trader that I'd met. She had lasted a couple of years before she quit not being able to stand the abuse, constant sexual innuendos, and inequality in pay. I folded my papers, the news did nothing but depress me of late.

For the third time, I read through the contract, studying it, analysing it, and then scanning and emailing a copy to my family's lawyer. Even though it was a Sunday, George rarely had anything to do other than work. It wasn't even an hour later that he replied with some points to consider and in capitals wrote:

THERE DOESN'T APPEAR TO BE A CATCH, WHICH COULD BE THE CATCH. YOU'D BE MAD NOT TO TAKE UP THIS OFFER.

In addition to running his business, Mackenzie was allowing me one day a week to use his facilities and continue to run *my* business, should I wish to. I knew next to nothing about communications and even less about military contracts, so to keep that one day, in case I should decide Mackenzie's company wasn't for me, was a wise idea.

I picked up the business card attached to the summary. Instead of Mackenzie's details, I noticed Gabriella's.

I reached for my phone and dialled.

"Hello?" I heard in a delightful southern drawl.

"Hi, I'm sorry to call on a Sunday—"

"Alex, it's good to hear from you, even on a Sunday," she said, cutting me off.

A pang of want formed in my stomach at the sound of her voice. "I've been through your very generous contract, run it past my lawyer, and I'd like to discuss it further."

"I'm delighted to hear that, Alex. Perhaps we should meet. Would you like to schedule now?"

A thought ran through my mind and I shut it down super quick. I knew what I'd like to schedule to do. I coughed to clear my throat.

"Do I make you nervous, Alex?" she asked, and that threw me for a loop.

"No, I..." She laughed so softly I felt it in the pit of my stomach. I fought to gather my composure. I sat upright and forced my voice to be stern. "No, Gabriella, you don't make me nervous. Yes, I'd like to schedule a meeting now."

"Now?" Gabriella asked.

"Huh?"

"How about now? You can take me to dinner, Alex."

I don't think, in all my adult years, a woman had asked me to take her to dinner. No, not *asked*, but *demanded* by her tone of voice.

Determined to stay business-like I said, "Fine. Please text me your address, I'll collect you at, say, seven?"

"Seven is just fine. Gives me plenty of time to fix my hair."

I relaxed into my chair. "I don't know what to say," I said, and then chuckled.

"I like you Alex, I think you like me, and I'd like for us to have dinner." Her voice was soft, and her words strung out. "And I'd like for you to collect me. I'm not a feminist, I also expect you to pay."

Just the tone of her voice made me laugh, and had we been face to face, I was sure she might have added a wink.

"My lady, I wouldn't dream of letting you pay," I said. I then cut off the call.

It wasn't that I was being rude, but I wanted control, I

wanted her coming to me, not the other way round. It had been a conversation of push and pull for sure. I smiled and nodded as the ping of my phone showed up her address and a heart emoji. She was going to be a challenge; I had no doubt.

I deliberated over which restaurant to take Gabriella to. I wanted somewhere private and quiet so that we could chat. The perfect location came to mind. A wine seller in London had an intimate dining room where one could not only taste wines, but also have a meal. I held wine in their cellars. I called and although it cost me another case of wine, a table was found for me.

The sat-nav took me straight to a Georgian house near Hampton Court and I parked on the driveway. As I walked up the steps to the front door, she opened it. She stood in a white lace summer dress that skimmed her curves. I could see glimpses of smooth tanned skin beneath the lace. She smelled divine and I leaned in close to kiss her cheek. She made me laugh when she turned to kiss my other cheek and I'd already leaned back.

"Sorry, two kisses," she said, and chuckled as well. "Would you like to come in for a drink before we leave?"

I glanced at my watch. "I think we have time for that, yes."

She stepped back and allowed me to walk through, although my arm brushed against hers as I did. The hairs on my skin stood to attention. I was sure my cock would at the slightest prompting too.

I let Gabriella pass and followed her through a kitchen

to a wonderful and surprisingly large garden. A bottle of white wine was chilling, and two glasses were set aside on an outdoor bar.

She poured and handed me one. "A Californian Chardonnay," she said. "Not one of my favourites, but the only one that was cold." Her voice sent a tingle up my spine.

I raised my glass to hers. "As long as it's cold, it's fine," I replied before taking a sip.

"Please sit," she said, indicating to a bar stool. "Do we have time?"

"Yes, the table is reserved for half past seven but they'll hold it for as long as we need. This is a lovely house," I said, admiring the garden.

"Thank you, I only rent. I wasn't sure how long I was going to be in the UK, so I never bought."

Something ran through me; a sense of dread. I hadn't thought about her not being long term in the UK. "Do you think you'll be heading back home soon?"

She shook her head. "Not for the foreseeable future. Things are just getting interesting here." She smiled at me over the rim of her glass and I watched her tongue dart out to lick at it.

"Indeed, interesting," I said, mumbling into my glass.

Her startling blue eyes held my gaze in a dare, who would look away first? I felt my blood pump faster when she submitted and lowered hers. She was coy, but I knew underneath that expression was a woman who knew exactly what she wanted and how to get it.

I smirked in victory and then placed my glass on the table. We chatted about London life and how it compared to America. I detected a nostalgic tone to her voice when she spoke of home. She told me of her favourite *haunts and boozers*, as she called them, mimicking her friend's British accent and it made me smile.

"I think it's time to leave," I said, as I stood and held out my hand.

She took it and I helped her to slide gracefully off the stool she was sitting on. "I need to grab my bag."

I left her to do so and headed for the front door. I was grateful for the moment alone so I could adjust my rigid cock to a more comfortable position. I stood beside my car and held the passenger door open for her. There was no scrambling to lower herself to the seat, she had it down perfectly and I chuckled.

"It's a southern thing, or rather it's my southern mother thing. All ladies must know how to enter and exit a vehicle," she said, exaggerating her accent.

"Then I owe your mother a debt of gratitude and wonder if perhaps she might offer online lessons to some of the British mothers I've encountered." As the words left my mouth, I regretted them. "Not that I've met that many, of course," I quickly added.

"Alex, a gentleman as handsome as you won't be short of dates, I'm sure," she replied as I gently closed her door.

I wondered just how surprised she would be to know her statement was way off the mark. I was still musing on her comment as I opened the driver's door and climbed in.

Gabriella adjusted the air vents so cool air blew over her, fanning her hair gently and, more importantly, wafting her intoxicating scent around the car.

"I have to ask, what is that perfume you're wearing?" I said.

"Do you like it?"

"Very much so."

"It's a special blend, made for my grandmother initially by her great friend, Coco. It's only sold in the States now, and in one boutique not far from my hometown. I have to buy in bulk, but I'll be sure to decant some for you." She offered a sexy smile as she finished her sentence.

I'd never had the desire to own women's perfume before, but to be able to keep her scent alive when she wasn't there was rather tempting. I didn't reply, obviously, it would be a little creepy to accept her offer, I thought.

I stole glances as I drove. I highly doubted her pouty lips were that way from cosmetic surgery. She had high cheekbones and clear, fair, flawless skin. It was hard to see if she wore much make-up, it was so expertly applied.

"Great genes," she mumbled, and she opened her handbag to retrieve a compact mirror. I frowned and she nudged me lightly. "Lord Duchoveny, you've been checking me out since we left my house. I'm just saying I have great genes. You should see my mother; she has flawless skin and I'm rather envious."

I don't think a woman had ever called me out as much as she had already, and I liked it.

Dinner was fantastic. It was great to talk and simply enjoy each other's company. We spoke about the appointment at Trymast and it thrilled me to see the change from Gabriella the friend, to Gabriella the businesswoman.

"If I take up the appointment, and I'm very tempted, you'll be my boss," I said, smiling.

She tilted her head and eyed me inquisitively. "Does that bother you?"

"Not at all, although it's a shame in one way."

Dinner had been eaten and we were sitting with a

glass of fabulous red wine. She was running the tip of her finger around the rim and before she spoke, she placed that finger on her lower lip and transferred the wine to it. I watched as she licked her lip and I didn't think it was necessarily in a flirtatious manner, it was something she did unconsciously.

I wondered how many men came simply by watching her. I was sure I could without even touching myself.

"And why is that a shame, Alex?" Sultry Gabriella had replaced the business version.

"I'd like to get to know you more, on a personal level, but I don't date colleagues."

She laughed. "Then I guess it's a bonus that we aren't actually colleagues. I'll have nothing to do with Trymast when you're CEO. I might manage the UK side of Mackenzie's businesses but even I can't manage them all on my own. So, let's go back a step and talk about this *personal level*, shall we?"

All I wanted to do was to push the table aside, grab her hand and drag her from that building. I wanted to wrap my hand in her hair and force her head back, tilting it so I could kiss her. My desire for her built. I didn't speak, however, I simply stared, and it pleased me immensely to see her cheeks flush, her lips part a little, and her breathing accelerate.

I glared at the waiter as he interrupted the moment to place a folder on the table. Without even looking, I signed it. Then I stood and held out my hand. She took it and without further words, I led her back to the car.

The sexual tension in the car was palpable, the air thick and heady with the scent of desire. She glanced at me regularly, particularly down to my crotch. I had no wish to hide the hardness; I wanted her to see the effect she was having on me.

It wasn't long before we were pulling up outside her house. I turned off the engine and swivelled in my seat to face her.

"Alex..." She started to speak but trailed off.

I reached up and ran my fingertips down her cheek, then over her plump lips. Her tongue darted out and she closed her eyes as if it was the most decadent taste.

"I want to fuck you, Gabriella, but I won't. Not yet." Her eyes flew open and I expected a retort to my bluntness. She opened her mouth to speak but I didn't give her an opportunity. "For now, I want to get to know you. I will take up the offer for Trymast, it would be my pleasure to be on board."

"But—"

"I've laid my cards on the table and I believe you want the same. I expect honesty and I need to tell you something about me, Gabriella. I don't do equal in the bedroom, that's *my* domain."

My heart thumped rapidly in my chest. My need to dominate sexually was why I didn't have many partners. I wasn't a Dom in the traditional sense; I didn't want that in everyday life. I just needed to be in control where sex was concerned.

I watched a pulse beat rapidly in her delicate neck, her cheeks flushed further, and I'd gambled she would accept what I'd said. I held myself rigid until I saw her slowly nod and lower her gaze.

I opened my car door with shaking hands and walked around the car to hers. I pulled it open and held out a hand. She took it and slowly slid from the car. She was close enough for me to feel her breath on my face and she stared directly into my eyes.

"I'll top from the bottom, Alex, isn't that what they say?" Her whispered words blew my mind. Then she turned and walked away.

Leaving the car door open, I strode after her. She kept her back to me, facing her front door, and I placed my hands on the wood at either side of her head. I pushed into her back and she stilled. She leaned back into me, resting her head on my chest.

I leaned down, blowing gently on the side of her neck and inhaling the intoxicating scent of her. "Never. I'll allow you to believe that, though," I whispered. Her gentle moan was all I needed to hear. She tilted her head and I kissed her neck. "You are going to drive me insane, I feel."

I stepped back removing my hands from the door and her hands shook as she placed her key in the lock. Without looking back, she opened her door and gently closed it behind her. I walked to my car knowing she was watching me from the glass pane. It wasn't until I had left that I had to pull over near the park and take a deep breath.

"Fuck me," I whispered, and then laughed.

I took great delight in handing in my notice the following morning. Although it was accepted with the obligatory, *sorry to see you go* comments, both my boss and I sighed with relief. I was the problem they had many a late night meeting about and kicking out the whistle-blower would have made them look bad. The fact I was leaving voluntarily suited us all.

CHAPTER FOUR

Mackenzie called the following day to congratulate me on taking up his offer. We arranged to meet at the office he intended for Trymast's base. There was much to discuss, especially since he would be ousting most of the upper management. Hostile takeovers weren't something I would shy away from and I wasn't sure, until I spoke with Mackenzie, how he came to purchase the company. Growing excitement coursed through my body and along with that, the anticipation of a second date with Gabriella, although I didn't expect to see her until the next weekend.

Hello, Alex. I've thought a lot about you since last weekend and I would like to meet up. I have tickets to the opera, and I wondered if you'd accompany me. Gabriella.

I didn't answer immediately; I wasn't playing games or expecting her to come to me, it was more that my time was taken up with things I needed to get in order. I needed a conversation with Daisy about the offer I'd accepted and was grateful that she hadn't wanted to move with me but wished to retire instead. She had been working with me since I'd joined Lloyds and was an absolute treasure. I wasn't sure how she would cope in a large corporation. She was set in her ways, didn't want to work long hours and didn't like to travel too far from home, especially on dark winter nights. I understood that and so we said our good-byes over a wonderful meal where her husband joined us.

Hello, Gabriella. I'm sorry for not replying immediately. I had a lot to do today. The opera sounds wonderful. If you'd like to call with the details, I'd enjoy listening to your voice. Alex.

I read the text a couple of times hoping that it wasn't too cheesy. I did want to listen to her voice. I'd imagined it so many times while lying with my cock in my hands but as the days wore on, it was beginning to fade from my memory. It was being replaced with imagined moans and cries of ecstasy, of course.

I pressed send and then waited. It wasn't long before the phone rang.

"Gabriella, it's so lovely to hear you," I said, seeing her name pop up.

"Alex, you've programmed me into your phone, that's simply delightful," she teased.

"Of course, I didn't want to waste time with the obligatory *hellos*."

She chuckled and the sounds trickled straight to my balls. "I have a box at the Royal Opera House and my usual date has informed me he can't accompany me now."

I bristled at the 'usual date' comment and was desperate to know more. "So, I was second choice?" I asked, not quite teasing her back.

"Darling, you would have been first choice had I known you a year ago when I got these tickets. Now, don't be jealous. Mackenzie needs to skip town, heading back the US for a few days so I'm dateless."

I breathed a sigh of relief. "Then I'd be delighted to accompany you."

"Wonderful, I can email you the details. I'll be lunching with a girlfriend that day and will dress at her flat, so perhaps I could meet you there? I'll be the blonde propping up the bar." She chuckled, and I could just imagine the smirk that would accompany that statement.

"Mine's a pint and I'll see you there," I said.

I could hear her laughing as she ended the call. I held the phone and smiled at it. Daft as it was, I didn't want to let it go since it was the most current connection with her.

For the second time I arrived outside the impressive glass building in Canary Wharf owned by Mackenzie Miller. On that occasion he was in reception waiting for me. He strode over with his arm already extended. I shook his hand firmly and he patted me on the back as we walked to the lifts. I appeared to have moved on from *visitor* phase and was greeted warmly by security using my full title. Once I had corrected him, requesting he just use my first name, the lift door was opened and we stepped inside, leaving the security chap outside.

"Does that get boring?" Mackenzie asked.

"What?"

"The, *just call me Alex* bit?"

I laughed. "Sometimes, and to be honest, it's so automatic now that I say it even when I hadn't wanted to."

We travelled up to a floor below the previous visit. It was a large open plan space already occupied by builders and carpenters arranging workstations and erecting a glass office in the corner.

"The new UK headquarters for Trymast," Mackenzie announced. "And your office."

"How many staff are moving here?" Although large, the floor didn't seem big enough to house a whole company.

"About three quarters. I think there are a lot that can work from home and I like to promote that."

We walked around the space and Mackenzie told me more about the company he had just acquired. Once inside the office, although only furnished with a desk, a chair, and a sideboard, there was a folder that he picked up and handed to me.

"I know this is an *in the deep end* situation, but I need to head home for a couple of days."

I nodded. "Yes, Gabriella mentioned you were returning home," I replied, immediately wondering if I should have said anything. I wasn't sure how Mackenzie would feel knowing I wanted to date his... I wasn't sure *what* she was to him, other than a childhood friend.

"She told me you recently went for dinner," he said.

I placed the folder on the desk. *Might as well address that.* "Do you mind? I wasn't sure of your relationship at first. I'm not keen on the working and dating thing, but I'm very attracted to her," I said, thinking that I should be honest.

He grinned. "I don't mind at all. She's big and bad enough to look after herself."

I responded with a wide smile of my own. "I'm getting that impression."

He leaned in conspiratorially. "Let me tell you one thing about Gabriella. She has the heart of an angel and the balls off the devil. And she'll juggle those balls just to remind us men how tough she can be."

I laughed so hard at the comment; it wasn't one I'd ever heard but knew it to be totally appropriate.

He continued. "She's my best friend and, obviously, I don't want to see her hurt in any way. However, I know both you and her will keep it professional when needed."

I nodded and smiled. It seemed I had his approval, for which I was grateful.

I pursed my lips and took in a breath. "I actually have something rather strange and maybe a little delicate to discuss with you. I can't think of a better man to pitch this idea to, to be honest."

"Mmm, sounds intriguing. How about we do that over a pint. I'm quite partial to your British beer."

Mackenzie and I departed for a local pub, a faux *authentic* Irish pub but one that had a great atmosphere and an amazing garden that overlooked the Thames.

"So, she's your cousin?" he asked after I'd explained about Veronica.

"She is. And I know this is a strange idea of hers, but I can tell you now, no matter what that woman has done, she's profited from it. She wants a high-end gentleman's club that caters for men and women with certain sexual tastes."

I had already explained what had happened and what Veronica hoped *could* happen.

"She doesn't have the cash, I take it?" Mackenzie asked.

I shook my head. "I don't have that cash without liquidating some assets, either. Otherwise, I'd have jumped straight in myself."

"Well it certainly sounds interesting. What do you know about the clientele?" I reeled off the names that Veronica had given me and he raised his eyebrows. "Lord Stanton? This is sounding even more interesting," he said, and then shook his head with amusement.

I couldn't help sneering when I thought about the oaf. "I loathe the man, personally, but I do know he's rather influential within the Home Office."

"Trymast, military contracts, the Home Office, and an exclusive gentleman's club. What could possibly go wrong?" Mackenzie said, smiling. "Set up a meeting, will you? I'll be back at the end of next week. Also, Alex, unless there are more than two of you with the same name, I'm assuming it's your uncle, but I had some dealings with Veronica' father. I don't know if she is aware of that."

Although I was *Lord* Duchovney, the surname being the same as my uncle's, obviously, he was generally known as *Viscount* Duchovney. It wasn't a common surname and I wondered if Mackenzie's prior dealings with the family had been a factor in him headhunting me.

"She certainly didn't mention anything. Can I ask what dealings?" I didn't need to know, of course, but I was certainly curious.

"He needed to free up some money, so I bought some shares in a manufacturing company. I never met him, but I understand that the cash might have kept him afloat for a while. I turned them over pretty quick and made a profit, she might not like that idea."

I shrugged my shoulders. "I don't think she knows that."

The more time I spent with Mackenzie, the more I liked him. I had no doubt his closet was full of skeletons, but he was honest with his answers. It seemed the feeling was mutual. I wondered what his social life was like. I knew him to be a member of a few ex-pats clubs and that he often attended some of the many events for one society, charity, or another. It felt as if I'd found a kindred spirit but was yet to discover exactly in what.

Mackenzie raised his pint glass to me. "I'm pleased that you've decided to come on board, Alex. You're exactly the kind of man we need."

Sitting with him chatting about London life, business, and our families was like catching up with an old friend. We clicked instantly and that was a first for me. I had friends, of course, acquaintances more like, but there was something easy with Mackenzie and I knew we would have a meaningful friendship.

We watched the river taxis make their way up and down the Thames. Canary Wharf was the new business hub of the city and housed a lot of the financial sector. Suited men and women bustled around, and there was a general buzz in the air. The money markets were doing well, wealth was on the up, and I picked up on Mackenzie's enthusiasm for the progression of Trymast.

When I left the pub, I came away with the distinct impression that Mackenzie loved business. He wasn't in it just for the profit, but his desire for the success of any company he bought was infectious. His ideas were radical and progressive, for sure. He encouraged working from home, *bring kids to work* days, he had the idea that if employees had a better work/life balance their productivity increased. I was sure he'd brought those ideas over from the US and whether they would work in practice in the UK, I didn't yet know. I also didn't want to have a group of children running about the place.

I placed a call to Veronica that evening and told her about Mackenzie. At first, she was a little hesitant, not necessarily wanting a partner on board. I explained that Mackenzie didn't invest unless he was actively involved in some way, that ensured his investment was well looked after. I also told her that he had helped her father.

"Really? I wasn't aware. To be honest, darling, I haven't touched any of his paperwork. I've left that to mother to deal with. What did he do?"

"He bought some shares and sold them on for a profit. It seems your father needed a quick cash injection."

"Ah, okay. Well, I don't think that has anything to do with me, or does it?"

"No, but I guess you should know so that you can go into this with open eyes."

"Well, if he helped my father, then he is definitely the man I want to help me as well."

"He seems quite keen to do so."

"And he knows exactly what I do here?" she enquired with surprise in her voice.

"Yes, I told him everything. I highly doubt he'll be interested in your *girls* but the idea of an exclusive club where people can indulge in a certain lifestyle seemed to intrigue him."

"How about you, my darling? Have you met anyone *special* yet?"

Veronica and I were more than similar in our tastes and had only discovered that when we'd bumped into each other, rather embarrassingly, at another *exclusive* club in London some years ago. I remembered that I had been mid fuck when she'd walked into the room to watch. Of course, my cock deflated instantly and the woman beneath me furiously stomped off leaving me naked in front of my laughing cousin. A vow had been made that we never frequented the same venues again. I wasn't into fetish behaviour but sometimes, I just wanted sex with no strings attached. It was while at those clubs, however, that I'd discovered my like for certain elements of the BDSM scene.

"I may have. Well, someone I'm rather attracted to. It's going to be complicated, however," I replied.

"In what way?"

"Well, technically she's my boss." I laughed, and she joined in.

"Yes, awkward, but rather hot, don't you think? All that forbidden love," she said. "Anyway, I have to go. We open shortly. And I'll email over some dates for Mr. Miller. Let me know which one is best."

I disconnected the call, placed the handset on the arm of the chair and sighed. Sitting in my home office I looked around thinking of all the places I could fuck Gabriella. There was a rather handy picture rail with hooks still attached, perfect for restraint. I shuffled in my seat at the thought and wondered whether she'd allow me to do that to her.

Such was my attraction to her however, I think I would choose vanilla if that was all that was on offer.

For the next few days I fantasied about Gabriella and it distracted me from my work. I was winding down and had a weekend visit to my mother planned before I could see Gabriella next.

The thought of my mother caused my shoulders to tense. She was a bitter woman, but in some ways I didn't blame her. She had lost so much, and even after pledging her support to my father after he lost their fortune, she lost him too. She wasn't bitter about losing the house, the cars, the staff, the lunches with friends and she wasn't concerned when she was ostracised by her *clique*, even. She was, however, devastated and scarred by Dad's suicide. She could not move on from the belief that he had taken the coward's way out leaving her to cope with it all. Still, I did my duty and spent one weekend a month with her. As time had passed, that weekend had lessened from being Friday to Sunday, to only overnight on a Saturday. Even then, I usually arrived later in the day.

My father was a victim of fraud, lies, cheaters, and scoundrels, and even though he was dead, I idolised him. I struggled to sit through her tirade of abuse about him for any length of time.

It was midday on Saturday that I opened the front door to my mother's apartment. It was quiet, which was strange. Mother normally had the radio on for company, she'd say.

"Mother?" I called out, there was no reply.

The apartment was within a stately home that had, like

many, been split up into spacious and extravagant apartments. Mother's was on the ground floor. I walked through to her kitchen and noticed her French doors open. There was a communal garden and as I stepped out onto her patio, I heard the tinkle of her laughter. It was the first time in years I'd heard her do that and I frowned.

"Darling? We're over here," I heard her call. I looked towards the tennis court to see my mother in her whites wielding a tennis racket. I also noticed an elderly gentleman on the other side of the net. He raised his racket in greeting. "This rascal is cheating," she added with further mirth.

I sat on the bench outside the fence that surrounded the court and watched as she finished the set, winning her the match.

As he left the court, my mother's opponent said, "Your mother is amazing. I've lost every game." He strode over and tucked his racket under his arm then held out a hand. "Duncan Windsor," he said. It was odd, the surname was familiar, of course but, and I chastised myself for my snobbish thought, *Duncan* didn't sit well as an upper-class first name in my mind.

I shook his hand. "It's a pleasure to meet you. I must say, I haven't seen my mother so animated in a while."

Mother slapped my chest with the racket. "Oh, Darling, don't be so silly. Tomorrow, Duncan, same time?" Duncan nodded and left us. Mother slumped onto the bench and I sat beside her. She huffed the air through her puffed cheeks. "Phew, Alexander, I'm pooped."

"I'm sure you are. When was the last time you played tennis?" I asked.

"Yesterday, and the day before. In fact, every day for

the past two weeks. I decided I couldn't live the way I was, and I know you've delayed your visits to me in the past because I was always so sour. I found my racket, I even, and you won't believe me I'm sure, bought a pad thingy, got online and ordered these rather attractive clothes."

I scrunched my brow but couldn't help smiling. "A pad thingy?"

"Yes, I forget its name. Anyway, I can order all sorts online." She laughed as she stood. "I was quite shocked at what one can find on the interweb."

I opened my eyes wide and joined in. She linked arms and we walked back to her apartment.

"I don't think you should leave the doors open, Mother," I chastised.

She waved a dismissive hand. "Oh, the folks here are so old even I would catch up with them if they decide to smash and run." She placed her racket on the kitchen table.

"Smash and run?"

"Isn't that what it's called? Anyway, tea?"

I allowed her to make tea, there was absolutely no way she would ever accept a cup of tea made by anyone else. She set out her china, silver strainers and spoons. She carefully measured tealeaves into a matching pot and waited for the water to boil.

"This seems a rather rapid change, Mother. Are you sure you're okay?"

She smiled brightly. "Of course. As I said, I was sick of being sick, so I decided not to be anymore."

As if it was ever that easy to shed layers of grief and misery, I thought. I let it go, though. The woman making the tea with the precise number of stirs in a certain direction was my mother of old, and I welcomed seeing her.

She brought the tray to the outside table and we sat. "Now, tell me what's happening with you?" she asked.

I told her all about the job offer and about meeting up with Veronica. Of course, I omitted the part about the sex workers.

"How utterly delightful. I'm thrilled for the girl; please pass that on, will you? She was a wild card, that one. I remember many a time your father and uncle traipsing London to find her after a call from her school to say she had skipped out again. They used to find her in the most undesirable places. Strip clubs, Alex. She'd be front row pushing money down panties, so I was told. God knows how your father found out about those places." She gave me a wink and I laughed.

Mother sat and reminisced on days of old and she did so with a smile. There was a part of me that wanted to check her medicine cupboard; I didn't believe she could have changed so dramatically in three weeks. It was lovely to hear how fond of Von she still was, though. I remember as a child, Veronica being the daughter my mother never had. They were very close.

"I should have said, I'll have to leave early in the morning. This isn't me skipping out, before you say. I have a date at the opera in the evening," I said.

"Oh, Darling, do tell?"

I gave a very brief description of Gabriella. My mother would have wanted her over for tea and inspection in the old days. Any possible girlfriend had to be assessed for worthiness, and to ensure she wasn't likely to *swan off with the family jewels,* my father used to say, mocking my mother's belief that all my friends were from the criminal fraternity. I made a promise to bring her for a visit when the time was right.

"Let me put my bag in my room, and then I need to take a shower. Where would you like to eat this evening?" I asked. It was a done deal that Mother wouldn't cook. There was a restaurant within the house, but we usually dined out together. Mother always had a new place that she'd read about and wanted to check out.

"I've booked us a table in a lovely little Italian. I love Italy, your father and I had plans to retire there one day." She sighed wistfully at the memory, one I wasn't aware of but also highly doubted since my father hated anything foreign.

I left her to rinse the cups—again, something she would never allow anyone else to do should they chip the china—and I took my holdall along the corridor to one of the four bedrooms. I placed the bag on the bed and moved my toiletries to the en suite. Although the family's ancestral home had been sold, Mother had been able to keep many of the furnishings, all of which seemed to clutter the bedrooms. She had often wanted me to take some, but my apartment wouldn't suit a fourteenth century masterpiece. I had told her time and time again to sell it all.

We had a pleasant evening and the restaurant she had found was rather nice. So much so that I took a card and made promises to return.

"How did you find this one, Mother?" I asked, expecting her to tell me it had been advertised in a local magazine.

"Duncan brought me here last week. Rather annoying that he'd forgotten his wallet, though."

I stopped walking and stared at her. "Did *you* pay?"

"Of course, I'm hardly the type to offer to wash the dishes and I really didn't want the annoyance of the police arriving."

Red flags sprang up in my mind. "How often have you been out on dates with him?" We started to walk towards the car again.

"On dates? Only the once, although we've played tennis nearly every day. We're going to *date* again next week," she replied.

"Let me know how that goes, will you?"

"Alexander, is there anything wrong? Do you dislike Duncan?"

"I dislike anyone foolish enough to leave a wallet at home when entertaining a woman, especially one as classy as you, Mother." I gave her a wink.

"Oh, you daft thing," she replied, chuckling as she spoke.

My mother wasn't *worldly* although she had travelled it. However, her first-class experiences did not allow for fraudsters to take advantage of her, or so I had thought.

A little digging on Duncan was in order, for sure.

CHAPTER FIVE

I straightened my bow tie before I left the taxi outside the Royal Opera House in Covent Garden. It was a vibrant area of London that attracted diners and street artists. Tourists made a beeline for the squares to admire the architecture and the mix of nationalities and colourful people. I made my way into the foyer and collected the ticket that had been left for me. From there, I headed to the bar where I knew Gabriella would be waiting.

As I walked in the door, I paused. She was facing away from me and was chatting to a man. Her back was rigid, and I wondered if she was uncomfortable. As if she'd sensed me, she slowly turned. There was no smile initially, until she caught my gaze. I strode over and she reached for my hand.

"Darling, you made it. I heard the traffic was simply awful," she said. She then turned to the man. "Thank you for keeping me company but my husband will take over from now." She gave him a smile, although it was forced. He nodded his head in my direction and moved on.

"What an odious man. Honestly, Alex, I'm so glad you arrived when you did, I was about to let the '*southern*' be released." She shuddered and leaned up to kiss both my cheeks.

"I'm glad to be of assistance, and if he was rude to you, I'll also be glad to punch him."

"My knight in shining armour. Whatever would I do without out you?" she said, waving her hand in front of her face in mock fluster. "Champagne?"

Before I could reply, she took the bottle from the cooler and refreshed her own glass before filling mine.

"So, wife, was he really annoying you?" I asked, looking to see the man had moved onto his next conquest. She laughed and, once again, the sound travelled straight through my stomach to my crotch.

"Rather like a mosquito, needs swatting," she replied.

I asked about her lunch and she told me about a couple of her American girlfriends and how sad she was today when she learned one was heading back home.

"It must be hard being away from your family?" I asked. "Do you have any siblings?"

She paused and I saw her jaw tense. "I miss my momma, for sure." She didn't answer my second question.

The bell rang and it was time to leave the bar for our box.

Perhaps cream or white was her colour, she wore a silk dress that clung to all her curves and as much as I checked, I couldn't see a panty line at all. The thought of her naked under her dress aroused me, uncomfortably so.

Gabriella sat with her ankles crossed and her hands on

her lap as she looked around, she reminded me of a debutant, so very proper. She was delicate on the outside, but I knew, tough as steel inside. I didn't believe the *ladylike* behaviour was for effect, it was part of her upbringing.

"So, tell me, how did you first meet Mackenzie?" I asked.

"I was in love with his best friend when we were younger, and maybe a little bit him. We are the best of friends now and have been since we were children." She laughed when I raised my eyebrows. "We grew up together, we lived a short distance away until he moved away after..."

I turned to face her. She didn't explain further but kept her focus on the stage ahead. However, I didn't fail to notice her furrowed brow and her rapid blinking to, perhaps, clear her eyes of tears.

I changed the subject. "And how do you find working in London?"

The question brightened her; she faced me and smirked. "I get to meet one or two handsome Lords and an awful number of frogs." She batted her eyelids and I knew she was teasing. "Seriously. It's bad enough in the States with men's egos the size of stadiums and, somehow, I thought it would be different here. Present company excepted, there aren't as many gentlemen in business as I was led to believe. Still, I know how to play the dumb blonde and still get my own way."

"Are you doing that now?" I asked and my voice lowered slightly. "Are you playing now?"

Her breath hitched and I watched her pupils dilate. She opened her mouth to speak but before she could, the lights lowered, and the opera began.

Gabriella and I sat through the first act. I watched her mouth the words and clutch at her heart at one death scene. She clearly knew the story and loved it. She smiled and frowned, shuffled, and slumped. I believe she could have acted every scene.

We sipped our champagne during the interval, and she asked me lots of questions about my childhood. I feared that I was too blunt when I told her how my father had killed himself. She grabbed my arm and squeezed. As much as I enjoyed any contact from her, I didn't want pity. Any earlier *playing* had gone, and I enjoyed us getting to know each other a little more.

"Would you like a coffee somewhere?" I asked as we left the opera house.

Gabriella shivered slightly as we paused on the pavement. I removed my jacket and placed it over her shoulders.

She smiled her thanks. "I'd love to, yes."

Covent Garden was a hive of activity, as usual, and it took a little strolling to find somewhere that had a spare table. Had we wanted dinner, I would have suggested The Ivy. Although a little clichéd, the food was good. Instead, we found ourselves in a small courtyard coffee house sitting outside in the square under a parasol with a heater. We people watched for a little while. A juggler was throwing batons into the air and catching them while blindfolded. A circus artiste walked around on stilts, and a busker sang to entertain us all.

"I shall miss London if I ever leave," she said, sighing wistfully as she spoke.

She had mentioned before that she wasn't in a rush to leave and I wondered what would cause her to.

As if reading my mind she continued, "Mackenzie gets a pull to head home every now and again. As much as he loves being here, he's a homeboy for sure. I was rather surprised when he asked me to accompany him here. Initially it was just for a year, but he keeps doing business," she said.

"Well, I'm glad you *both* decided to stay," I replied.

We paused our conversation for a little while, sipping our coffee. "Do you feel it, Alex?" she asked, looking at me over the rim of her white cup.

I instinctively knew what she meant. "Yes."

"Is it odd?"

I contemplated my answer. "I don't know. I guess, if you want it to be odd it could be."

She placed her cup back on its saucer. "I don't want it to be. I feel a connection with you, an attraction, and yet, I've met you three times."

I reached out, placed my hand over hers and ran my thumb over her knuckles.

"See," she said, "I feel that inside me."

"Good," I replied.

"But I think this is all way too fast," she added, and I deflated a little.

I took in a long slow breath. "Yes, I agree, sort of..." I laughed and called for the waiter. I ordered a bottle of wine. "Let's slow it down a little."

Mackenzie had left me a list of instructions, things he wanted my input on, as well as figures and projections to study. He assured me that he was at the end of the phone if needed and would check in regularly. He expected to be away no more than a few days but was a little vague on specifics. He was also excited to know that Veronica wanted a meeting.

"Its not my usual type of investment but I do like to diversify occasionally," he had said.

The more I thought about the club, the more lucrative I believed it could be. And the more attractive it became, considering the use. There were clubs in London and surrounding counties that catered for various sexual tastes but nothing as high-end or exclusive, and nothing that didn't involve paid women. It wasn't that I was averse to escorts; I'd used one myself on occasions when the event called for a *plus one*. The side benefits were, obviously, great, discrete, and expensive!

I settled down in my new office and went through the plans. Trymast wouldn't be relocating for another week or so but the removal companies and some of the staff were back and forth with favourite desks or personal items. I made sure to introduce myself to every individual. Although I had been presented by Mackenzie to the main players in Trymast, and I'd walked around and smiled and nodded, I hadn't had the time to talk and get to know the staff. I wanted an open-door policy; I wanted them to feel free to share their fears over the move. I wanted them to know I was approachable, and I respected them for taking the plunge and coming on board.

What I didn't want them to know was that there was any kind of relationship between myself and Gabriella, beyond professional.

"Hi, are you free for lunch?"

I looked up to see Gabriella leaning against the doorframe. In the background a few of the guys were staring and I glared past her at them.

"I'm not, I'm sorry," I said, probably too abruptly.

"Oh. Okay, I'm sorry for disturbing you," she replied, and it was clear she was confused by my response. She straightened up and looked around her as if embarrassed.

I sighed as guilt niggled at me. "I'm sorry, that was probably a little sharp. Yes, let's go and grab a quick lunch," I said, retracting my earlier response.

I also made sure to leave a gap between us as we walked to the lift. When the lift doors closed, securing us from prying eyes, Gabriella turned to me. She placed her hands on her hips and I knew I was in trouble. I smirked.

"Please don't do that, Alex. We don't have a policy here that says you can't date the staff. So, as long as it's kept professional it's fine. I also saw you give those guys the death stare. Although I rather like that little jealous streak you have," she said, letting her hands slide from her hips.

I took one step; it was the one needed to have her pinned to the wall. "Yes, I get jealous. Since I'm CEO of Trymast, it will be my rules we'll adhere to, not yours. I sincerely apologise for embarrassing you in any way, and those *guys* were checking out your arse."

I was centimetres away from her. She looked up and her breath fanned my face. I breathed it in, along with that perfume that was so fucking intoxicating.

"I like the way you say *arse*."

"You'll like the way I spank it as well."

Her eyes widened and for a split second I thought she was going to have a fit of rage. Her cheeks flushed a deep red and her hands balled into fists by her side.

I hadn't meant to say it. It was her, the minute I was

near her all the things I dreamt of, all the things I had done, came to mind and I wanted to experience them all again with her.

"I'm sorry, I shouldn't have..." I took a step back, giving her some space.

She glanced to the digital display and then back to me. "If we had another few floors to travel..." she didn't complete her sentence but she licked her lips slowly.

"I think you're going to be the death of me," I said, chuckling as I turned to face the doors that were about to slide open. I felt her small hand reach to touch mine and I clasped it.

Fuck the staff and my rules, I wasn't letting go.

I led her from the lift, and once in reception opted to take the small door to the side that led to the stairwell down to the car park. I pushed open the door and walked through. I then held her against the wall and cupped her chin in my hand to raise her face.

"I'd rather do this anywhere but a stairwell, of course," I whispered before I lowered my face.

I wanted to taste her lips and, placing both my palms on her cheeks, I held her face still. I pushed one of my legs between hers ensuring she couldn't move if she wanted to and was pleased to feel her writhe against it.

I ghosted my tongue against her lips and she opened her mouth, her tongue met mine in a slow dance. When I was done with slow, I tightened my fingers in her hair tilting her head back further. She gasped and I sucked in that breath.

"Alex," she whispered. I was about to pull back when she gripped the lapels of my jacket and scrunched them in her hands.

My tongue explored her mouth, lips slid against each other, and breaths were stolen. As my cock hardened, I pushed against her. I needed for her to feel how aroused she made me. She moaned so softly, and it was like a cascade of butterflies in my stomach. My heart rate increased the deeper I kissed her. I couldn't breathe, I dragged in air through my nose and she did the same.

The toot of a car horn echoing from below reminded me where we were. It wasn't that I was bothered but she deserved better, for sure. I slowed the kiss, gently pulling back despite her not wanting me to. Eventually, I closed my mouth and just allowed my lips to linger on hers for a few seconds more.

"Alex," she whispered, again.

I softened my hold, removing my leg from between hers and stepped back. She stared at me and I licked my thumb to run under her lower lip where lipstick had smudged. She did the same to me, wiping mine with her fingers.

"Wow," she said, and then smiled. "That was some kiss, my Lord."

My stomach flipped as she spoke. "You deserve that, and more," I replied.

"I only asked if you wanted lunch." The sassiness was back, and I laughed.

I looked at my watch. "Do we still have time?"

She took my hand and we descended to the car park. We walked to a nearby deli, ordered sandwiches and coffees and sat outside in the sun.

"I think I'll send you the cleaning bill for my suit if you don't mind," she said, straining to see the back of her jacket.

"I'll gladly pay it."

Although we texted and called, I didn't see Gabriella for a few days. We were both busy, and with Mackenzie due to arrive back in a day or so, I was excited about the prospect of discussing the club with him.

CHAPTER SIX

"This is her ancestral home?" Mackenzie asked as we waited at the gate for it to open.

"Yeah. She's a...a *colourful* character, shall we say. Spent most of her youth running away, pissing off her parents, doing every Full Moon party around the world, and getting high." I laughed at the memory of some of the letters I'd received from her with graphic details of the life she was leading.

"She sounds very intriguing."

The gates swung open and we followed the drive. Veronica, in her usual attire of business suit and hair pulled tight in a ponytail on top of her head, stood at the door. Her smile was broad when she watched us come to a stop and open the car doors. Mackenzie buttoned up his suit before allowing me to walk to her first. I kissed her cheek and introduced her to Mackenzie.

"It's a pleasure to meet you, Veronica. Alex has told me a lot about you and your project here," he said.

For the first time in years I saw a change in Veronica. She didn't seem the ballsy woman I knew. Instead of reaching out and shaking his hand firmly, as I expected, she seemed... *compliant* I guess is the word I'm looking for. Whether Mackenzie saw or not, I couldn't tell, but he certainly didn't act upon it.

"Welcome, please come in. Would you like to sit in the bar and have a cool drink, or the office with coffee?" Veronica asked eventually.

"A cool drink would be good, I think," he answered.

I might have well been invisible, and then I realised. She liked Mackenzie, *a lot*. In the few minutes they had met, it seemed she had connected with him. I chuckled quietly to myself and received a scowl from her and a frown from Mackenzie. With a smirk, I raised my eyebrows at her and widened my eyes. Behind Mackenzie's back, she scowled again.

"This way," she said.

Veronica led us into the bar and even though I'd been there many times, it was an impressive room that took one's breath away on each visit. The walls were half panelled in rich coloured wood, and there was red velvet covering above. A fireplace took up most of one wall and the bar, I feared, had been fashioned from the once grand bookcases. I seemed to remember, in an act of defiance one time, Von and I had scratched our names in the oak. We had been sent to do schoolwork in the library with Von's private tutor, even though it was the summer holidays. I scanned the top to see if I could see our graffiti.

We sat on a collection of wingback chairs set around a small coffee table.

"Tell me, Veronica, exactly what goes on here and what is it you want this place to be?"

Veronica slid the folder that had been sitting on the table towards him. He ignored it, staring intently at her. I called the waiter for some cold drinks since it appeared Veronica had forgotten.

Mackenzie left the folder untouched on the table. "I'd like to hear it in your own words, if I may," he said.

She took a deep breath and wetted her lips, she seemed nervous and there was no wonder. It's not every day one has to promote a sex club to a potential investor.

"My mother needs to sell this house," she told him. "I don't want her to, obviously. It should be passed to me. I have an idea, a means for it to earn money and, potentially, so I can keep it, and that's where I'd like your help. Before Alex mentioned you, I had you listed as someone to approach, and that wasn't because of my father's dealings with you, I wasn't aware of that, but simply because I thought you were open-minded enough to listen to me, at least."

"So explain," he said. She did.

She first told him of her lifestyle and even I had to screw my eyes closed at a couple of points, with embarrassment. She was my cousin, and although I was more than aware of her hedonistic lifestyle, I didn't really want to hear it. However, it appeared Mackenzie was enthralled. He leaned forwards, placing his elbows on his knees and rested his chin on his fists.

I sipped the iced spring water that had been placed on the table and tried not to listen. I thought her father would be turning in his grave. Then I had to chastise myself; Von and I weren't that dissimilar in our preferences.

I perked up when Von started to detail her vision. Mackenzie and I both chirped in with suggestions and excitement built. Not only that, but when Mackenzie detailed some of the *activity* rooms possible, we believed he was on board with the idea already.

We decided to take a walk in the gardens. I'd had the idea of lodges to let for short breaks, and Mackenzie liked the idea of a fully functioning spa. What we ended up with was an exclusive hotel complex that allowed members to use the facilities just for an evening, for a few hours, or a weekend.

Veronica was tasked with redrafting her proposal and to cost what was needed. Mackenzie would put her in touch with teams of designers and builders, Veronica would know where to purchase the necessary equipment. We also decided a very discrete CCTV system was to be installed for two reasons. We wanted to be sure of the safety of our guests and, like the case with Stanton, we all had enemies and we would benefit from learning a little about their private lives.

It wasn't that Mackenzie was shady in the least; he was a very astute businessman who knew how to protect himself. It led me to think he had been in battle many times; perhaps he'd lost a lot also.

We had toured the building and were heading back to our car when Mackenzie stopped and turned to face the front elevation. He looked up at the turrets and the broken windows, the crumbling chimneystacks and the torn and battered flag that once displayed Veronica's coat of arms.

"I know the system here is different than the US. Y'all willingly pay taxes your whole life, and then again when you die, and I find it sad when heritage is left to crumble as if it doesn't matter and no one wants to pay for it anymore," he said.

Veronica glanced up too. "I agree, although I also think we are complacent. This house isn't that old in terms of heritage. There are far older ones. And we're surrounded by it, so we don't necessarily appreciate it. How many times do we walk past the Tower of London, for example, and don't give it a second glance?" she replied.

Mackenzie nodded slowly. He turned to her. "I'm not going to propose that I simply invest, Veronica. I want to own this business. I don't want to own your house, you keep that, but the business will rent the property from you, which should allow you to pay off any debts. You run it; I won't interfere unless I need to. Part of my deal will be a loan for you to repair your home to its former glory."

Both Von and I stood silent and looked at him. "Do you know what the repair of this type of building will cost?" I asked.

He shrugged his shoulders slowly. "We'll get some experts in, but ten million. Ish?" I suspected he wasn't that far off.

"I don't know that I can pay that back," Veronica said.

"You will. This business is going to be so successful, the fees high enough to ensure only the right clientele are members, and then with all the add-ons, I expect to see a profit within a year. And if you really can't pay it back, we'll come to some arrangement." He stared at her intently and she wilted, again. On that occasion he was fully aware, and without acknowledging I was still standing there, he seemed to grow in stature.

We left then, climbing into the car and welcoming the air conditioning.

"What do you think?" he said, not looking at me but over his shoulder as he turned his Aston Martin around on the drive.

"About you and Von, or about this project?" I teased. "She practically melted in front of you. I've never seen her like that."

"Would it bother you to hear that I find her attractive?" he asked.

"No, not at all. As long as you know what you're getting with her."

"I think I do." He laughed as we drove away. "Now, what do you think about this *business*?" He smiled, emphasising the word.

"I think she should snap your hand off. I've visited some of the clubs in London, frequently, I guess, and what she has on offer here is unique and desperately called for. If I had the cash, I'd have done the same as you."

"You are more than welcome to come on board as a partner. We can arrange a share scheme and you can buy in whenever you want."

"I'd like that," I said.

My relationship with Mackenzie changed that day. We weren't employee and employer anymore. We became more than that. We became friends, best friends, even. We were confidants and he learned to trust me more and more.

"You've done what?" Gabriella asked.

The three of us were sitting in a restaurant for dinner. She had likened us to the three musketeers, and I was glad to be included in their very tight circle.

"Bought a very high-end gentlemen's club," Mackenzie said, taking a sip of wine.

"That's not what you just said, is it, Alex?" She looked at me.

"It's going to be a high-end gentlemen's facility that will also accommodate their sexual habits in a safe environment," I said, pleased I might have come up with a description.

"Isn't it rather sexist and old fashioned to call it a *gentlemen's* club considering, I'm assuming, there will be women there?" she asked, pouting her lips and widening her eyes at us.

"Tax purposes, Gabriella. We can hardly call it a couple's sex hotel. Gentlemen's club is a more palatable title for the stuffy old gits at the tax office," I replied.

Gabriella laughed. "Oh my, Alex, you must absolutely take me there when it's all done. I saw that movie, I forget its name, and I want to try that cross thing."

I screwed up my eyes and pinched the bridge of my nose.

"Something you want to tell me?" Mackenzie said, slowly while smirking at my discomfort.

"I think your best friend should learn that not every thought needs to be verbalised," I said.

"That's not what I'm talking about," he said, looking pointedly at her.

She raised her eyebrows. "We're dating, there, I've told you. It's new, we're finding our feet, so no teasing."

I hadn't, until that point, realised we were actually *dating*. We had been on a few dates, I had kissed her, and told her I wanted to fuck her, badly, but that was it.

"Dating huh?" Mackenzie said.

I shrugged my shoulders. "Yes, we're...dating." I stumbled over the word to Gabriella's mirth.

"Don't hurt her, Alex," he said, his voice had lowered, and I perceived the threat concealed beneath the words.

"I can't promise that, but I'll do my best not to, intentionally," I replied.

"Boys don't do that alpha crap, please. I'm still here. You are my best friend, and you are soon to be my lover," she said, just as a waiter poured more glasses of wine.

I slumped. "Jesus, Gabriella. Don't you think before you speak?" I chuckled to let her know I was teasing.

She gave me a smile in return. "Now, can we eat? I'm famished. You know, Alex, I heard a phrase a friend said: 'I could eat a scabby monkey's arse.' It sounds perfectly awful but is that a saying?"

I guffawed loudly. "Not from my neck of the woods, it isn't!" I replied, appalled at the thought.

We chose our meals and talk returned to Trymast. We had all gone through the lists of employees and Mackenzie was amused with an elderly lady called Mary. She had apparently told him that she wasn't leaving, and she was to be his PA. She was due to retire and would continue to work until then. She left no room for argument, according to Mackenzie. I couldn't wait to meet her.

"Well, I think I'll leave you two alone, I have a hot date myself," Mackenzie said, removing his napkin from his lap and placing it on the table.

"Anyone we know?" Gabriella asked.

"Nope, I hope not." He gave her a wink and a laugh. He patted my shoulder as he passed and left.

"Ugh, I hate it when he does that," she said.

"You're protective of him, aren't you?" I said.

"I am. He needed me when he was young, my momma took care of him, we all did. He'll tell you his story, Alex, but it wasn't pretty for a while." She let out a sad sigh. "I wish he'd find someone and settle down again."

"Again?"

"Oh, he was married to the bitch from hell. Awful woman, Alex...I don't want to talk about it now, it will turn my delicious dinner sour," she said with a dramatic shudder.

"She sounds delightful," I added.

She rested her elbows on the table and her chin in her hands. "Mmm. Tell me again about this club."

A very small part of me wanted to swipe her elbows from the table, such as had been done to me many times as a child. I chuckled at the thought.

"You seem very interested, Gabriella," I replied.

"I am. The thought excites me. I haven't been as... experimental as I think you have. I'd like to be, though."

"Are you trusting enough to allow me to teach you?" I asked and I wanted to hold my breath as she thought about it.

She fixed me with a sincere gaze. "Yes, I do trust you."

"Trust is a major factor, a big deal. If there's no trust, it can't happen." She nodded slowly, so I said, "Then I would like to take you somewhere."

I signalled for the waiter only to be told the bill had been paid. I cursed Mackenzie as I took Gabriella's hand and we walked from the restaurant. I hailed a taxi and gave an address.

"Where are we going?" she asked, nervously.

"I just want you to see some things, that's all."

We slid across the black seats and were silent for the journey.

"Sure this is it?" the taxi driver asked. Gabriella looked down a cobblestoned alley, following his gaze.

"Yes, thank you." I left some cash in the tray in the divider and we climbed out. I took her hand and walked, slowly so her heels didn't catch, to a large wooden door with metal studs.

"Oh, it's looks rather Dickensian," she said with a nervous giggle.

"I imagine this building is that old," I pressed the intercom and was greeted with, *"code."* I gave it and waited.

Eventually the door was opened and I was asked for my membership card. In the time it had taken for the bolts to be released, I'd retrieved it from my wallet. It was a black card with just a small logo in the corner and my name printed across the front. A small silver chip at one end allowed the doorman to scan and verify my details.

"Welcome, Lord Duchovney, it's good to have you back," he said, stepping aside. "Would you like the cloakroom?" he asked Gabriella.

She turned to me. "Erm, do I?"

"Yes, leave your handbag there. It's perfectly secure."

She did as advised, and we walked along a corridor adorned with photographs of sixties icons. I explained that the photographer, a rather famous gentleman, was the owner of the club. Like Veronica, he wanted somewhere to indulge in his fantasies and since he couldn't find a suitable environment, he created one. The club had been in operation since the sixties and its patrons ranged from rock stars to film stars with the odd prince, or princess, thrown in.

She paused beside a rather raunchy photo of Princess Annabelle, the Queen's sister. Although sadly deceased, she had been nicknamed the *Party Princess* in her day.

Another door was opened for us and Gabriella paused. I squeezed her hand. We entered on a mezzanine level and below us was a dance floor. The music was pounding so hard the floor vibrated. Writhing bodies in various stages of undress were dancing to sounds produced by a famous DJ usually found in the clubs of Ibiza.

"This way," I said. I led her around the mezzanine, stopping on odd occasions to greet an acquaintance but never introducing her. She enquired why. "Trust me, you don't want half these people to know your real name. Think of an alias, quick."

She giggled and I loved the sound. I pulled her along behind me as she reeled off some names.

"I know, Henrietta, that's a posh English name, isn't it?" She even added a *posh* English accent.

"It's perfect, I can just see you as a Henrietta, although they generally have buck teeth and live in jodhpurs."

We came to another door and I paused before opening it. "I just want to show you what happens here. That's all, okay?"

She nodded enthusiastically and I opened the door. There were rooms with glass-panelled walls on one side of a long corridor. We stopped at the first to see a St. Andrews Cross. The room was empty, not in use.

"What happens there?" she asked. I explained that someone would be secured by their ankles and wrists.

The following room had racking against one wall. In the centre of the room was a bed and a blindfolded naked woman was lying face down. Her male partner, also naked, was straddling her legs and rolling a pinwheel over her back.

"This is sensory play," I whispered, although knowing they couldn't hear me.

"I don't know that we should be watching," she replied, nervous again.

"They can't see us."

Beside the woman was a range of toys, a feather tickler, and skin scratcher. Her back was peppered with small red marks and yet she writhed on the silk sheet enjoying every second.

"Is that painful?" Gabriella asked.

"Yes and no. I find it boring to be honest." I smiled, and we moved on to the next window.

A couple were fucking rather vigorously, he was behind her, kneeling, while she rested on all fours. He looked over to us and smiled, and Gabriella darted back out of view.

I chuckled. "You're meant to watch," I said, pulling her back to my side.

I moved her to stand in front of me and held her wrists at her side so she couldn't cover her eyes. She leaned back, resting against my chest. The man watched her and while he pumped into his partner, I could feel her breath quicken.

I leaned down slightly, my mouth to her ear. "Can you see his cock, Gabriella? He pulls out so far because he wants you to see it. She's slick with her orgasm, his cum."

The man pulled at the woman's hips ramming her back onto his cock with every thrust. She threw back her head and, with her eyes closed, panted. Sweat beaded on both their foreheads, his chest was wet, and strands of her hair had stuck to her face.

"I can't...I don't..." Gabriella never finished what she wanted to say.

Instead, she fell silent as she watched the couple orgasm. She gripped the material of my trousers as she tried to catch her breath. When the couple were done, the woman slumped to the bed, stretching like a cat, and the man sat back on his heels smiling with satisfaction. He wrapped his hand around his cock and gently massaged the last of his cum, letting it drip on her thighs.

The glass frosted over, the show over. Gabriella stayed silent for a moment.

"That was erotic," she whispered.

I kissed the side of her neck, licking up towards her ear. "Are you ready for more?" I asked. She nodded.

The next room contained a man in a bondage suit strapped to a bed while two women tortured him, all in the name of sexual pleasure, of course.

"I'm not sure..." she said, and I could see her wince as his bollocks were whipped.

"No, not for me, either," I said, laughing.

We skipped a couple of rooms until we came to another. Two men were pleasuring a woman, the three were on a large bed with no toys. One was licking her pussy, the other, from the side, was sucking her nipple, biting and causing her to arch her back.

"Please hold me, Alex," Gabriella whispered, although it was more of a whimper.

I did as before, I stood behind and placed my hand on her lower stomach. I splayed my fingers gently sliding down to below her navel. I wanted to her to feel the heat of my hand through her clothes. With the other hand, I gently held her throat, keeping her head in position to watch. I'd seen these guys before; I knew what was to follow and I wanted to be sure she didn't move.

When the biting and the licking had brought her to an orgasm, the men switched positions. One moved to be on all fours over her and the other kneeled behind him with his legs either side of hers. They fucked each other while she lay underneath. She reached for a cock and slid down until she was able to take it in her mouth.

"Oh," Gabriella said, breathlessly.

Gay sex wasn't my thing in the least, but I was aware of how many women found it a turn on. I wanted her aroused, her panties wet, and I needed her to be desperate for my touch. She covered my hand with hers and gently pushed is down a little. Although a barrier of clothing was between where she wanted me to be, I was still able to massage her. She moaned gently. While I held her throat, I kissed her neck. She curled her hand over mine and dug her nails into my skin. I licked her jawbone and bit down on her earlobe, and she whimpered some more. I could feel her body tremble against mine. As she orgasmed, so did the man. He pulled from his partner and his cum spurted. A stream of milky fluid landed on his partner's back.

I released Gabriella from my hold and her chin slumped to her chest. She breathed in deep.

"Do you want to watch more?" I asked; the threesome wasn't done yet.

She shook her head. "I think I need a drink," she said, straightening herself. "And the restroom."

She turned and I held her hips. She gripped my shirt and rose up on her tiptoes. "Thank you for bringing me here. I'm sure you haven't shown me most of what goes on, but I like what I see. Teach me, Alex?"

Her kiss was fierce and took me by surprise. There was desperation in her tongue, it was demanding attention from mine. Her teeth bit down on my lip and I tasted blood. I wanted to grab her thighs, have her legs wrap around my waist, and fuck her hard as a punishment. It was against the rules, however. Book a room or head to the bar, no fucking in corridors.

Instead, I squeezed her backside forcing her to feel my hard cock before I gently pushed her away. She was panting, and I was trying to control my heart rate. I grabbed her wrist and she struggled to keep up with me. She jogged alongside my long-stridden walk back to the main door. She collected her bag and we headed out into the night air. We didn't speak as I hailed yet another taxi, and before I could give an address my mobile rang. I wanted to ignore it until I looked and saw my mother's name. She never called me on my mobile, hating modern technology. I asked the taxi to wait.

"Hello, Mother, are you okay?" I asked.

"No, darling, I think I've been scammed," she said, and I could hear the anguish in her voice.

"You think you've been scammed?"

I looked up to Gabriella who stared back with a quizzical look on her face.

"My friend, he said he would have some of my paintings valued and he seems to have disappeared. Oh, darling, I've been a terrible fool," she said, and then hiccupped as she fought to hold back tears.

"You need to go to her," Gabriella whispered. I nodded.

"I'll be there as soon as I can," I said.

I disconnected the call. "Take this taxi, I'll get another," Gabriella said.

"No, I'm not leaving you here on the roadside. What's done is done. Come with me?"

I surprised myself by asking her to accompany me. It probably wasn't the best way to meet my mother, but, being the Eton education *toff* that I was, emotion was something I was still learning to do.

"Only if you're sure," she answered. I didn't reply but guided her into the taxi. I gave my address.

The taxi deposited us outside the apartment block, and I held Gabriella's hand while we walked to the lift. I was a little gutted to not be in the slowest lift in the world or for the apartment to be on the top floor. I could smell her dampness and it was driving me mad.

"Can I use your restroom quickly?" she asked as we entered the apartment.

"Of course. I'm loving the smell of you, but you're driving me insane."

"I'm driving *me* insane, too, I think it's going to be a frustrating evening for all concerned." She smiled sweetly and so very innocently.

I pointed to my bedroom with an en suite. The thought of her wiping her pussy in my private bathroom was pleasing.

While I waited, I grabbed my car keys and a phone charger. Mother wouldn't have one and my battery was getting low.

"I have something for you," Gabriella said huskily, as she walked back to the living room. I frowned. "Will you close your eyes just for a moment?" she asked.

I complied and felt her fingertips on my lips. I didn't just feel them, I tasted them. I grabbed her wrist and sucked them in, tasting her orgasm. I licked, wanting as much of her as I could. I moaned and opened my eyes. Hers were hooded and I just couldn't help myself. I walked her backwards to the wall and slammed her against it.

"I want you, now," I said. I nipped at her neck and she fought to lower her panties. I wrestled with my belt and zip to free myself.

I grabbed one of her thighs and lifted, she guided me into her still wet pussy. I bit down hard on exposed skin and pumped hard. She rose and fell against the wall with every thrust, but I wasn't deep enough. I grabbed her other thigh and she wrapped her legs around me. Only then was I satisfied. I held her backside, squeezing hard, holding her up until my arms shook. She wrapped her arms around my neck, digging her nails through my shirt, scrunching and tearing it across the back as her arousal peaked. As she came, she cried out and tightened her legs around me, tilting her hips so I could feel her muscles ripple against my cock. I exploded inside her.

It was short, sharp, and oh so sweet. "Fuck," I said, panting to regulate my breath.

"Yes please, but after we've seen your mother, yes?" she wheezed out.

I rested my forehead on hers. "I'm sorry, that was rather abrupt," I said, gently pulling out and letting her legs down.

"It was perfect. And as for *that* conversation, the one we should have had before, we'll have it later." For a second I was lost for words, until she made a cradle with her arms.

"Shit!" I said. Having children wasn't on my agenda.

She patted my cheek and gently kissed my lips. "We're all good, don't panic," she said. "Now I need your restroom again."

I found a clean shirt recently back from the dry cleaners, and I used the guest toilet to clean up. I met her at the door. She looked crumpled and I chuckled. We headed to the underground car park. I waved to security as I passed the hut and we were soon on our way.

I called Mother as I drove. "Hi, I'm on my way. I was in London and I needed to get my car. Are you okay? Oh, and I have a friend with me."

"I'm okay, just feeling very foolish. How much of a *friend* is this friend?" Mother asked.

"A very good friend," I replied with a smile.

"Then I shall get the good china out. I'll see you and your *friend* soon." She disconnected the call.

"I've had quite a fractious relationship with my mother since my father died, but only recently, and I mean within the past month, she's changed. She had a friend who I assumed lived in the complex but I'm wondering if that's the conman she's referring to. It would be a huge gamble on his part if he were, of course. I think my mother believes he's a distant cousin to the monarchy."

"Would someone of that standing be a fraudster?" she asked.

I shrugged my shoulders. "I guess so, plenty of Lords in prison," I said, laughing at the thought.

"Oh, what a super house," Gabriella said as we made our way up the gravelled drive.

"Not Mother's, sadly, she has an apartment. A lot of these old mansions were sold off to developers. It's a shame, and one of the reasons I'm pleased Mackenzie wants to see Veronica's house restored." I parked the car and helped Gabriella from her seat.

"To think, less than an hour ago you were fucking me against your wall, now I'm meeting your mom."

"Did I tell you that my life is a little complicated?" I chuckled but then righted myself, it wasn't the occasion for jokes and flirting.

Mother opened her door and it was clear she had been crying. I couldn't recall the last time I'd seen her cry. Not even when we buried my father.

She held a handkerchief in her hand and waved it about her face. "Come in, my darlings. It's a pleasure to meet you...?" She paused so Gabriella could introduce herself. "Gabriella, although I wish the circumstances were different. Have I interrupted your evening? And please call me Henrietta."

I smirked at Gabriella as she widened her eyes and her mouth formed a perfect O in shock.

I kissed my mother's cheek. "No, Mother, it's fine. Now tell me what's happened."

As we followed her to her sitting room, Gabriella pinched my side. I grabbed her hand and linked our fingers. As promised, the family china was laid out, and before she spoke Mother bustled off to fill the teapot.

"Is that your crest?" Gabriella asked, studying the tea plate.

"Yes. I was meant to have this when I bought a house, I declined."

She raised her eyebrows at me. "Why? It's gorgeous and part of that heritage you are so keen to protect, remember?"

I rolled my eyes in response.

"You won't be mad at me, will you?" Mother asked as she returned with the hot tea.

"When have I ever been mad at you?" I asked, confused by her question. I made a second mental note to check her medicine cupboard since I hadn't done it the first time.

Mother took a deep breath. "Duncan said that he thought I ought to get a couple of paintings revalued for insurance purposes." I sighed; my fear had been confirmed. She continued, "I let him take the small Van Gogh—"

I closed my eyes in exasperation that she even had it on display. "That was meant to be in the safe," I said rather sternly. I softened when I saw her eyes fill with tears.

Gabriella scowled at me. "Why have such exquisite art if you can't look at it?" she said and then took my mother's hand in hers. "Carry on, Henrietta."

I wanted to correct Gabriella. The piece was one of Van Gogh's pencil drawings of a blacksmith and rather dour and depressing. Hardly exquisite.

"I thought he was taking it to be valued but he hasn't been seen since. I've knocked on his door and I've asked the estate manager to open it because I was worried something had happened to him. It appears he has cleared off."

"Cleared off?" I asked.

"Yes, his closet is empty, no toiletries but... Oh, darling, you really are going to be cross with me." Her cheeks flushed bright red. "His wig was still there."

I stared at her for a moment. "His...?" Then I chuckled. "Oh, Mother. Okay, have you called the police?"

"No, I only saw his apartment just before I called you. I don't know what to do."

"I'll call the police. Gabriella, would you pour Mother some tea?" Her hands were shaking, and I wasn't sure the family crockery would survive; not that I wouldn't be happy to see it broken, of course.

I walked into the sitting room and picked up the landline. I called the police who agreed to send someone over, although we had no idea when that would happen. I assured them that Mother was elderly and living on her own, but once the gated community address was given, I didn't hold up much hope of them giving her priority. I got it. Not even a stolen Van Gogh commanded the same attention as a hit and run, or a knifing in London. The quicker they were notified of the suspect, however, the quicker they could get on to tracking him down, I'd told them. This was a half a million-pound theft I had to remind them. It was agreed an officer would come by within the hour.

"Now dry your eyes, Henrietta. I'm sure Alex will have it all sorted in no time. There aren't many places a Van Gogh can be sold without raising some eyebrows, is there?" Gabriella said as I rejoined them.

I didn't want to burst either of their bubbles and inform them that Duncan—if that was his real name—would have a long list of buyers lined up from all around the world. Art theft was commonplace among the wealthy. Once in a private collection, it was doubtful it would be found until the owner died.

I told the ladies I wanted to speak with the estate manager and left them to chat. Mother would be sure to grill Gabriella on how we met and what our future plans were. The estate manager lived on-site and since it hadn't been that long ago Mother and he had entered Duncan's apartment, I hoped he hadn't retired to bed. I knocked on the door and was grateful it was answered.

"Lord Duchoveny, I was expecting a call from you. Please, come in," he said.

"If you don't mind, do you think we might look at Duncan's apartment together? I won't touch anything but if there's a photograph handy that I can give to the police, that could be useful."

The one thing with being a Lord—an inherited title rather than a bestowed one—was it did, literally on this occasion, open doors. I followed the manager to the apartment, and he shuffled keys to find the correct one. Once inside we walked from room to room. It was quite clear to me that it wasn't a permanent residence, there didn't seem to be any home comforts.

"Was he a chancer?" the manager asked.

"I'm guessing so. Do we know his real name? I highly doubt it's the one he gave my mother."

"I was a little confused when she called him Duncan Windsor. The paperwork has him as Duncan Winters."

I raised my eyebrows not in the least surprised, though. I didn't bother to ask if he was a Duke, or whatever it was my mother thought him to be. We were both loathed to touch drawer handles and there were no photographs to hand.

"I don't suppose you're able to take a screenshot from CCTV are you?" I asked.

"I am, but I think I'd need permission or a request from the police for that. You do understand, don't you? I'm more than happy to give up whatever is needed, I don't want to hinder any investigation."

"I understand. The police are likely to be here in an

hour. Please don't think you need to stay up, I'm sure they'll contact you at some point," I said, noticing that he had stifled a yawn.

I left him and walked to the front door. A thought had occurred. Duncan's apartment was on the ground floor, same at Mother's, which meant he had a patio with furniture outside his French doors. He also had a small storage unit for bikes and whatnot. When I got close, I had to use my phone to light the lock of the unit, it was a simple key lock in a very flimsy door. Without wishing to leave any fingerprints I pulled my shirt over my head and wrapped it around my hand. I pulled at the door and it sprang open way too easily. It was empty save for a small holdall on a shelf. I lifted it out and placed it on the floor. When I looked inside I shook my head. It appeared Duncan was a regular *Pink Panther*. Everything a burglar needed was there, short of a striped top, a black mask, and bag marked 'swag.' Clearly, Duncan had hit the big time and wasn't in need of the tools of his regular trade. I placed them back on the shelf and closed the door. I would tell the police that the lock was already broken but I had opened the door to see what was inside. I replaced my shirt and walked back.

When I returned to the apartment, I was told that Mother had gone to lie down. I sat beside Gabriella and she took my hand in hers.

"What a day, or rather a night. We've watched some erotic pornography, had sex, and are now on the hunt for a missing Van Gogh. I'm not making light of things, but my momma would be thrilled with this evening if I told her."

"You'd tell her about the club?" I asked, shock causing the pitch of my voice to rise.

"Okay, well not *everything*. How are you feeling?" she asked.

I scrunched my brow and sighed. "I actually feel partly responsible. I come and stay every month but my visits have gotten shorter and shorter because I didn't want to be around my mother. Her depression and grief made her bitter...or maybe it was me, I just wasn't tolerant to her pain. Anyway, I walked past that painting in the hall. I've told her to put it in the safe. I could have put it away for her. But as you said, why have art hidden?" I thought back to my initial reaction to Duncan. "There was something about that man that made my hackles rise when I first met him, I should have acted on that."

"That's a lot of *should haves* there," she said, gently.

We sat in silence for a while reflecting, or at least I was. Not just on my relationship with my mother that had so drastically changed but the speed at which I had developed one with Gabriella.

I had no issues with sex on a first date. If I wanted sex without even knowing names, it wasn't hard to find. But it was different with Gabriella and I was sad that I had fucked her against a wall. I wanted to woo, to court her. I wanted it the old-fashioned way no matter how sexually frustrated that would leave us. I just didn't know if I had the strength to keep that up for any length of time. She could leave in a month, a few months, a year. I could spend all the time slowly building a relationship to have it ripped away. Confusion on how to proceed littered my mind. I wasn't aware of how long I'd stewed in my thoughts but when I turned to look at her, she was asleep. Her head lolled to one side and rested on the wing of the sofa. She looked so peaceful and content. Her lips were very slightly parted. I shifted away and reached for a blanket and placed it over her lap, then headed for the kitchen. I was thirsty.

I grabbed a bottle of water from the fridge and leaned against the counter. An hour had passed, and I was tempted to call the police station again. I wasn't going to be fobbed off that a poor old woman had been conned by a lover, something they'd seen time after time and would deal with when they had a spare moment. I wasn't sure they believed me when I said a Van Gogh had gone missing.

Eventually Mother joined me. "I'm sorry, I needed to rest a while."

"Don't apologise, I'm sure you've had quite the shock. I checked out his apartment, it didn't look like he was staying around for long and there was a bag in his outdoor cabinet that looked like tools for picking locks."

I saw her shoulders slump. "What a silly fool I've been. It was just company, darling, that's all. I miss having company, someone to dine out with, or see a show. The old fuddies here aren't up for outings anymore." She waved her arm upwards to indicate her neighbours upstairs. "Let's talk happy things. I very much like your *friend*," she said with a smile.

"Thank you, so do I."

"Is it a long-term thing?"

I retrieved a glass of water for Mother who only insisted on tap water despite having numerous bottles of spring in the fridge. "I'd like to think so but I'm hesitant. She could move back to the States anytime soon and that worries me."

"In what way?" she asked.

"I don't want to fall too deep and then she leaves." I

turned to hand Mother the glass to see Gabriella by the door. She smiled, albeit a sad one.

"I didn't mean..." I started but there wasn't much to follow up on really. Gabriella waved her hand as if to dismiss my words.

She smiled and walked over, kissed my lips and took my hand. "Henrietta, I think we need to teach your boy to live for the moment, don't we?" she said, giving my hand a squeeze.

Maybe that's what I needed to do. Perhaps I needed to forget the wooing and just live one day at a time.

Eventually, the police arrived, and although it was early hours of the morning by that point, they did perk up when they realised they were dealing with a *real* lady of the realm, particularly when my mother informed them she had been one of the Queen's Ladies in Waiting. Moreso when they realised it was a real Van Gogh that had gone missing. I had all the insurance documents to hand, all the registration and authentication papers, as well as some copies of Mother's bank statements. I was sure the first suspect would be her. Once everything was documented, they left promising to call.

Gabriella and I left on Mother's insistence. I had offered to stay but she shooed us out citing a headache from the stress.

CHAPTER SEVEN

"Shall we get the elephant out of the room?" Gabriella asked, and I frowned at her. We were driving along the motorway heading back to London. Seeing my evident confusion she continued, "I have no plans to leave the UK unless something happens to my momma, Alex. Especially now."

"What do you mean, especially now?"

"You, business," was all she said.

"I'm happy to hear I came before the business," I said, smirking at her.

"You're not only jealous but insecure, aren't you?" she asked, gently.

"I didn't think so before now," I replied. Was I insecure? I hadn't thought my jealousy could be that.

"You have a choice to make, Alex. You either live for the moment, and that needs to include me, or you dither and woo or whatever it is you want to do."

"So you don't want me to *woo* you?" I asked.

"It's called dating where I come from, it's simple. You invite me out, or I invite you out. We do fun things, and we either head off to one or the other's house for sex, or not sex but sleep, or sex and sleep, or we go home to our own houses until the next date. It's quite a modern concept, I'm sure you've heard of it," she teased.

"Anymore teasing and I shall spank you, Gabriella," I said.

She turned in her seat to face me. "Do you know how your voice changes when you speak that way? I like it. I feel it inside."

"And if you continue with *that* kind of talk, I'll pull over at the next appropriate place and take the risk of fucking you in the car and getting a ticket."

She laughed and righted herself. "As much as that is very tempting, I'm pooped and ready for my bed."

I smiled and drove her home. I walked her to the door, and she stood before me sighing. "Will you come in?"

"No, my darling. Not because I don't want to, but because I'd keep you up all night and neither of us would be of any use tomorrow." I glanced at my watch "*Today*."

I leaned forwards and kissed her lips, she parted them to invite in my tongue. I cupped her face with my hands and kissed her slowly before pulling away.

"Tomorrow," she said, and then smiled.

I waited until she had walked into her house and closed the front door before leaving.

All the way home, I kept my hand on my erect cock, gently massaging through my trouser material. "Live for the moment," I said, quietly to myself.

I didn't sleep well that night at all, and I was usually one to sleep like the dead. It left me feeling grumpy the following morning and even moreso when I walked into the office to see Mackenzie and a very bright and breezy Gabriella.

"Is your mom okay?" Mackenzie asked. I assumed Gabriella had relayed the evening's events.

"She is, I spoke with her on my way in. The police have been again. I think they're taking this a little more seriously than the constables sent out last night. I'd like to get my hands on Duncan, I can tell you that."

"Well, maybe we can do some investigation ourselves," he said.

I stared at him and a knowing look passed between us. I nodded. I hadn't kept a clean slate throughout my young adulthood, and I doubted he had, either. I'd love to catch up with Duncan and I would hand him over to the police, but only after I'd dished out the *right* punishment to him.

"Anyway, the deal with Trymast is complete and they need to move from downstairs up here. I have plans to merge another communications company I'm after, but I think we're about a year from that yet. In the meantime, I have some interesting thoughts on the club," he said.

"Can I make suggestions?" Gabriella asked.

"Of course, what do you have for us?" Mackenzie asked as we moved into my office.

I liked his use of 'us.'

"I had a thought about the spa and the lodges. I'll leave the sex rooms to you two." Mackenzie raised his eyebrows at me. He smirked.

I coughed to conceal my discomfort. "She appears to tell you everything, or at least put me in a position where I have to, I took her to a club I've visited, to show her what it's all about," I explained. The last thing I wanted was to detail our sex life to Mackenzie.

She tilted her head and addressed me. "Actually, I wasn't referring to that, I was simply suggesting that since this is a *gentleman's* club, you might be best placed to decide what goes on upstairs."

Mackenzie burst into laughter and eventually, after swallowing down my mortification, I joined in.

Just to twist the embarrassment knife a little more, she added, "I have to say, it was super interesting, though."

Mackenzie shook his head in mirth. "You most certainly need a good spanking, always have." Then he turned to me. "You might want to keep that in mind, Alex."

"I'm starting to believe that myself," I replied. "Anyway, can we get back to the point and allow me to pretend my faux pas didn't happen?"

Gabriella reached across to squeeze my hand. "Right, I have a contact at Elmis and although I highly doubt they'd like to take over the spa, I thought it might be good to have them design it. No disrespect intended, but that spa is generally going to be frequented by women so it should be a woman that's involved." She sat back tapping her chest to confirm *she* was the woman in question, as if there was any doubt. "As for the lodges, would Veronica get planning permission in such an old house? Did you tell me there were outbuildings? Could they be converted to cottages?"

"That I don't know until we have the architects take a look," Mackenzie replied.

We chatted back and forth some more, Mackenzie took notes and our excitement built further. I knew it was going to be Mackenzie's business but his offer to buy in was still on the table and it was something I was definitely going to do.

"Can I buy in as well?" Gabriella asked.

"Do you want to?" Mackenzie replied, frowning at her.

"Well, I'm staying here for a while, so why not?" She looked at me when she spoke.

"I have a feeling you two need to get a room. Take the rest of the day off," Mackenzie said, with a laugh.

"Absolutely not. This is exciting. We have plenty of time," Gabriella said, and I agreed with her.

I shrugged my shoulders. "I can't help it if she wants to constantly flirt with me." I grinned at her as she rolled her eyes. Then I turned the tables back on Mackenzie. "How was your *hot date* by the way?"

"A cold shower in the end." Mackenzie laughed, but it was clear to me, and I'm sure Gabriella as well, that it was a forced one.

I thought it prudent to speak with Gabriella; I wasn't sure Mackenzie was entirely happy in his private life and I didn't want to make our budding relationship so blatant to him.

With the frivolity over, we got down to business. Mackenzie delegated and Gabriella left for her office. Mackenzie and I walked down to the Trymast offices to give them the good news. He was officially their new owner. Some would be happy and some, I thought, wouldn't be. It all depended on whether they thought their jobs were on the line. I'd told him I felt there were certainly a lot of spare bodies that were unnecessary. As horrible as it sounded, a streamlining process was about to start.

We talked to the staff and I helped carry a box or two

to the trolleys. We then called everyone together. Mackenzie gave his speech, they knew he had bought their company, and he formally introduced me for a second time. I did my best to allay any fears, answer a few questions, and assure everyone, although we would be streamlining, it was business as usual.

From then on, it was exactly that, business as usual.

It was nearly a week later before I managed to spend any time with Gabriella. She had been on out of town meetings, overseeing some of the many businesses Mackenzie owned. We had spoken regularly and one evening was particularly interesting.

"Hello, how are you?" she said as she answered the FaceTime call I'd placed to her. She wore a towel around her head and one around her body. "I've just showered. I had an awful day traipsing around a factory that was filthy. Honestly, Alex, the working conditions were appalling. I'm surprised that hasn't been picked up on before now."

"Did you give them hell?" I asked as I sat on my bed propped up against the headboard.

"I sure did but they're hard work. All men, you know the kind. Don't take to a female boss. Anyway, are you in bed?" she asked.

"Not in, but on."

She shuffled up the bed and rested against her headboard. In doing so, the towel had slipped a little.

"I'm missing you," she said as she pulled the towel from her hair. Her blonde locks were wild and just cried out to have my hands wrapped in them.

"Show me," I said with a huskiness to my voice.

She tilted her head in that way she always did. "Are you asking me to expose myself, my Lord?"

"I am, now do so." I kept my tone even but forceful.

Slowly she released the towel so it fell open. I hadn't seen her naked until that point. As she sat, she moved her mobile down her body. She parted her legs a little and I could see her pussy.

"Should I pleasure myself?" she asked, her voice a breathy whisper.

"Yes," was all I responded with.

Using two fingers she parted her lips, her clitoris glistened with arousal and she stroked gently. Her mobile shook slightly.

"Are you nervous?" I asked.

"A little," she replied.

"Good. Nerves are good. Finger yourself for me," I demanded, and as she did I stripped off my jeans until I was naked too. "I have my hand around my cock, Gabriella. I'm stroking it in time with your fingers. I'm imagining it's your hand, and it's going to be coated in your juices."

She moaned a little and I saw her stomach tense. The hand holding the phone shook a little more. She sped up, and I kept pace with her.

"Show me, Alex," she breathed out.

I angled my phone so she could see what I was doing. I could see her face watching me. Her cheeks were flushed and she wetted her lips frequently. She breathed heavily and parted them when I pleasured myself harder, faster. She threw her head back and dropped her phone. It landed between her legs and I got to see her orgasm. I got to see her fingers curl inside her as she forced them deeper. I saw her wet knuckles and when she pulled her fingers out, I got to see the slickness that I so desperately wanted in my mouth.

"Alex," she moaned, reaching for her phone. "I need to see you come."

As she sucked on her fingers I pumped my cock hard, I squeezed, running my thumb over the head and spreading my pre-cum for lubrication. I breathed as hard as she had. My stomach tensed, defining my muscles and I raised my hips a little as I came. Strings of white coated my hand and I milked until every last drop was extracted.

"Oh, God, that was so hot," she whispered.

I chuckled. I brought the phone back to near my face. Her eyes were bright, her cheeks flushed. She placed her fingertips on the screen.

"I want to taste you, Gabriella," I said, my voice hoarse.

"I want that too."

We didn't say anything for a moment, and I watched as her eyelids began to droop a little.

"Sleep well, my darling, and I'll see you soon," I said.

"I miss you, Alex," she repeated. "I'll see you soon," she echoed my words.

Once we had disconnected the call, I slid my legs from the bed and headed for a shower.

Despite ejaculation, I was still hard. It wasn't my hand I needed and whether it was to delay gratification, or not, I refused to give myself any further release. I had yet another uncomfortable night.

The following morning I decided I needed to throw myself into work as a distraction. Not only was the move full on for Trymast, I decided to think about the *playrooms* for the club. Recalling what I'd seen at the various clubs I'd attended I made a list.

Wet room for food or messy play.

Bondage room with hooks and pulleys.

A bedroom with a one-way glass wall so voyeurism could be accommodated.

I then thought of some of the more extreme play. I highly doubted we would want any form of blood play but perhaps a dressing up room. I remember coming across my first adult baby and finding it extremely difficult to contain my laughter. Even more so to learn the *baby* was a judge. However, it was a *thing,* so it needed to be added.

Of course, Veronica would be best placed to know what was current and lacking in other clubs. I decided to call her.

"Hi, cousin," she said, answering my call.

"Hello. I was just thinking about the proposal Mackenzie made. Have you decided what you're doing?"

"I'm going to take him up on the offer. I'll rent the house to the *business* and I'll run it for a salary. I think that makes a lot of sense. And you? What will be your part?" she asked.

"I'm going to buy in at some point. I've been thinking about various playrooms." I then listed off what I'd written down.

"Other than the wet room, which is a wonderful idea, we pretty much have most of that in one form or another. I like the idea of the one-way glass between two rooms, however."

She told of the shock the architects had received when they came to do their survey and saw some of the existing rooms. She laughed as she detailed the shake to one's hand while drawing a sketch.

"What do you know about Mackenzie?" she asked, abruptly.

"In what way?"

"Is he single?"

"Yes, I believe so. Why?" I asked.

"No reason, he intrigues me, that's all."

"Sure that's all, Von?" I asked, chuckling.

"Okay, so I'm attracted to him. He's very dominant and I don't suppose he knows it," she said, and I heard her sigh.

"Well, I'm not going to get involved in that, I have to work for the guy, and you're my cousin," I said, cringing at any further conversation.

She laughed. "I'm due to meet him tomorrow, I'll let you know how it goes," she said.

I said goodbye and wondered if Mackenzie had mentioned a meeting or not. I didn't expect to be invited to every meeting he attended, it was his business, but I wasn't sure if I should be a little protective of Veronica. Knowing her, however, I wondered if it was Mackenzie I should be protecting. I chuckled to myself.

A voice said, "Something funny?" I look up to see him standing there.

"No, just a conversation with Veronica. How are things going upstairs?" I asked. He was meant to be in a meeting with another business owner.

"All done. Can I come in?" he asked, and I frowned.

"Of course, you don't need to ask." It surprised me to see him shut the door behind him. He sat opposite me at my desk and concern niggled at me. "What's wrong, Mackenzie?"

"I don't know. I feel a little bored with all I'm doing at the moment. There isn't a challenge and I'm not sure why I feel that way. It's all too easy."

I wasn't sure I knew him well enough to give the best advice, but he had opened up to me and I got the impression he didn't do that often.

"What challenges do you think you need?" I asked.

"I don't know." He laughed as he spoke and shook his head.

"How about a round of golf?" I asked, having no idea what to offer.

"Jesus, Alex, I've never played, and never really had any desire to, but the one time I was taken for a game, I can't remember where, it was excruciating." He went on to explain every lost ball, every attempt to hit the ball straight that failed, and that eventually, his partner had suggested they skip the last few holes, which, he admitted, was a huge relief. "All that nonsense about business being done on a golf course isn't for me. Anyway, this club that you took my best friend to, are we looking to replicate?" He was back to business, or so I thought.

"No, much better than that. The club in London is a nightclub with rooms, basically. Membership only, of course, and expensive, but the plans Veronica has are much more exclusive. It could be the challenge you're looking for," I said.

Mackenzie looked at me and frowned so I continued, "It's not your normal type of business. You've sunk your time and efforts into communications mostly. This is a place that's for relaxation and pleasure. Complete other end of the spectrum for you," I said.

'I hadn't thought about it that way."

"Maybe you need to leave me and Gabriella to manage things for a while and you concentrate on this club. It's a money maker, Mackenzie, I can assure you of that. I pay fifteen thousand pounds a year for my exclusive club membership and it isn't that high class."

"Why?" he asked.

"Why, what?"

"Why spend that kind of money if it isn't high class?" he asked.

I paused and looked at him. I viewed him as a friend, and it was only that reason that allowed me to confess. "Sometimes, I don't want high class. I want what *I* want in *my* way, and it's available to me there."

He nodded slowly. "Are they escorts?"

"Some, yes. They're the one thing about the place that is high class. They're very clean." I cringed as I spoke, I was doing the women a disservice, but they were the only words I knew to describe them.

"Do we need those women at our club?" he asked.

"I don't think so. I think we provide somewhere for couples, but I think we have a black book of telephone numbers Veronica can call upon if a client has a *particular* wish."

He laughed. "Yes, the club is the challenge I need, I think you're right. I'm bored of communications. Thanks, Alex, I appreciate our friendship." Mackenzie stood and smiled at me. "I might give Veronica a call."

"I know she'll be pleased to hear from you," I said. He nodded and left the office.

I thought on our conversation for ages after he'd left. I had lived a lonely adulthood and began to wonder if he had too. As he said, we were very alike. I had half a mind to invite him to my club. There was a VIP section where we could just get a drink and people watch, or hook up for sex with one of the many women available. The women in the VIP section weren't employed by the club, they weren't prostitutes but members that wanted sex with a stranger as part of their fantasy. Of course, their membership fee was a fraction of the men's because they brought in business, for sure.

I found it strange that prior to Gabriella, one thought of sex with a stranger would have seen my cock erect, but I had no desire for that at all. Nameless strangers, no matter how great the sex, or how experimental, weren't what I needed anymore.

My office telephone buzzed and at first I stared at it. It was the first time it had rung. I laughed as I answered it.

"Hey, I think you need to come rescue me. I'm being held hostage by some old woman," Mackenzie said. I could hear the *old woman* in the background demanding I attend immediately. The infamous Mary, the PA that had told Mackenzie she was only leaving in a coffin, I guessed.

"No, I'm scared of her. You're on your own, old chap," I lied, accentuating my accent.

"Get your arse up here, Alex," I heard Mary shout.

"Jesus, what does she want?" I asked.

"I don't know, but can you just do as she says, then we can all get out of here?" Mackenzie replied.

I laughed as I replaced the telephone. I shouted out to my new assistant that I was popping upstairs. She waved her hand in acknowledgement.

"Ah 'ere he is. Now, come on over 'ere," Mary said, as she sat with her pad and pen at the board table.

I took the seat indicated. "You never worked for my

family, did you? I'm sure I remember a school ma'am like you," I said.

"I'd 'ave tanned your arse, if I had. Now. I want to get my diary up to date. Holidays?" she asked and poised with her pen hovering over her pad.

"Erm, no, nothing booked," I said, shrugging my shoulders.

"You?" She pointed her pen at Mackenzie.

"Holidays? No, I don't think so. I have to fly home every so many weeks, though."

"Well? Dates?" she demanded.

"Can I email them to you?" he asked.

She sighed. "If you have to. Right, next on my list... chest and waist size?" I looked at Mackenzie who was looking at me. "You spill something down yourself just before a meeting, what you gonna do, huh? You're gonna send me out to buy a new shirt, aint you?"

I don't think I'd ever sent anyone out for a clean shirt, but I do remember having a meeting in the House of Lords with spaghetti down my tie. I rattled off my statistics thinking it a wonderful idea of Mary's.

"I want a bathroom fitted over there, with a wardrobe. I'll keep some things in it for you both," she said.

She went on, demanding birthdays, anniversaries, significant others' details. She raised her eyes when Mackenzie told her he was single, and I was sort of dating someone.

"Well, who?" she asked me in a very accusatory manner.

"Erm, Gabriella," I stuttered, having never been made to feel so *in front of the headmaster* before.

"Aw, she's a stunner that one. Bigger balls than you

two, I bet. I like her," she said. "That's it I think, you can go now."

For the second time Mackenzie and I just looked at each other. She tapped her pen on the table as if to gain our attention so I stood.

"I'll come with you," Mackenzie said.

We walked in silence to the lift and stood watching the numbers on the digital display. When the doors slid open, we bashed shoulders in our haste to get in. We both kept our gaze on the floor until the doors closed, then I slumped and so did Mackenzie.

"What the fuck…?" I said.

"I know, right?"

I laughed and he joined in as I pointed in the direction we'd just left. "Honestly, I had a school ma'am exactly like her, same age probably. Spanked my arse every day of the week with a bloody ruler. Which was rather arousing at the time."

Mackenzie laughed harder. "Don't tell me, that's why you like your club?"

"Probably, although I do the spanking now and I limit the upper age to just ten years older than me."

That was it, we both convulsed, missed my floor, and ended up in the lobby.

"I haven't got a fucking clue why I'm down here. I wanted to walk back to my own office, but I didn't want to pass her," Mackenzie said.

I checked my watch. "Well, I guess we could grab a glass of wine somewhere." It was pretty much the time I'd leave the office anyway.

"Lead the way," he said eagerly.

We spent a couple of hours drinking wine at a bar not

far from the offices. It was crowded, as it often was, but we'd managed to find a booth furthest from the bar.

"I can tell you something, your life is going to be so much easier with Mary," I said, chuckling at the memory.

"I think it will be. Or she'll murder me. I'm not used to having to tell someone what I'm doing," he said.

I nodded, understanding totally. "Lonely being in business sometimes, isn't it?"

"Sure is. Which is why I think we'll make a good team." I raised my glass to him, and he changed the subject. "I spoke to Gabriella today," he said. "She's coming home tomorrow."

I hadn't spoken to her and was delighted to hear that news. "I'm due to call her later. She said she wasn't overly happy with how the factory was operating."

"She has it tough there. I want to intervene, but I won't. They don't take too much notice of her sometimes and I've told her to start firing people. That will buck them up."

"How has she found it being in her position here overall?" I asked. In the money markets women rarely got on and it disappointed me greatly.

"It's been hard. She misses home but she won't leave me," he said, laughing. He then jumped in with, "You know we're just friends, yes?"

"Of course I know. I just wondered, that's all. I'd hate to think she finds it tough and I already want to step in but know I can't. Frustrating, isn't it?" I said.

When she had explained about the factory, I wanted to jump into my car and roar on down there to support her. I highly doubted she would have appreciated that, however.

We left the wine bar shortly after and went our separate ways. I caught a taxi back to my apartment. As much as I had a pool car with a driver at my disposal, I wasn't used to that luxury at that time. A good old-fashioned taxi kept me grounded. The cabby and I talked about the football and the weather, the upcoming elections, and what the rest of the world was doing. There was nothing better than a taxi driver for catching up with current affairs.

I walked into my apartment and made a call. "Mother, I'm just calling to see if there's any news?" I said, once she'd answered.

"No, nothing. I've spoken to the insurance company and they are being arses about it all. I think you might need to speak to them," she said.

"What have they said?" I asked, fully expecting a fight with them.

"They wanted to know what security I had, particularly around the painting, what locks, all those things."

"Okay, I'll call them. You need to forward me a copy of your insurance policy, I want to check the small print."

As she hadn't the facility to scan and email she agreed to pop it in the post. I asked after her health, hoping that this incident wouldn't cause her to slide into depression again. She seemed perky enough, enquiring after Gabriella and making me promise to bring her over for dinner next time. I then sat with a microwave meal, wincing with every bite at not just the heat, but the tastelessness of it. I cursed myself at having never learned to cook.

When I'd cleaned the dish and fork I'd used, I settled down to call Gabriella.

"Hey, you, I was just thinking about your mom. How is she?" she asked when she answered.

"I've just spoken to her and promised that I'd take you there for dinner soon."

"I'd like that. Tell me, how has your day been?" she asked. I could hear noise in the background.

"Interesting. I met Mary...rather, I was *interviewed* by Mary. So was Mackenzie. She wanted to know our inside leg measurements."

Gabriella laughed and that flip in my stomach occurred. "She's just a hoot, isn't she? I love her. I had to give my bra size in addition to my shirt size, so count yourselves lucky! Mackenzie so needs someone like her, managing him is a full-time job and one I can kick off my list now."

"Where are you? Am I disturbing you?" I asked.

"No, I'm walking back to the hotel, that's all. It's too nice to sit in a taxi, and I think I could...HEY!"

"Gabriella?" There was no reply. I shouted into my phone. "GABRIELLA?"

Still no reply and then the call was cut off. I redialled and got her voicemail. I did leave a message but then texted and called again. She didn't answer.

I called Mackenzie immediately. "Hey, can you give me the address of where Gabriella is staying? Something's happened." I said before he even greeted me.

"What's happened?" he said, his voice urgent.

"I don't know, I was talking to her, I heard her shout and then nothing. I've tried calling and she's not answering now."

"Which is quicker, me coming to you or the other way round?" he asked.

I was getting exasperated with the delay. "That depends where she is."

"Essex."

"Then you come here."

"Okay, ten minutes." He cut off the call and I tried Gabriella again.

I paced for that ten minutes and ran down the stairs to the main door as soon as I saw his Aston Martin pull up outside. I hadn't closed the door before he roared off.

"Remember, wrong side of the road," I said, as he swerved into the oncoming traffic.

"Shit, yes. Tell me again what happened?"

I recalled the conversation. I tried calling her again, that time her phone was off. "I bet someone has her phone," I mumbled out the thought as I held on to the handle when Mackenzie cornered so fast.

The tyres screeched as the car came to an abrupt halt outside the hotel doors. A doorman ran to the car as we exited, Mackenzie threw his keys to him and we ran in.

Sitting on one of the chairs with a receptionist kneeling in front of her was Gabriella. She stood when she saw us, and it was clear she had been crying.

"What happened?" I asked as I strode over.

It was a race between Mackenzie and me as to who got to her first. The confusion as to who she should respond to first, was evident in her eyes. I backed off. Their relationship had been longer established. Although Gabriella allowed Mackenzie to hug her, she reached on arm out to me. I took her hand.

"I was mugged. Did I scare you?" she asked.

"Yes. Now tell us what happened?" Mackenzie asked when he released her. She kept hold of my hand as we sat.

"I wanted to call a paramedic just to take a look at her head," the receptionist said.

I turned her to see blood and a small gash to the back of her skull.

"What the fuck...?" I said, anger boiling up inside me.

Her lip trembled as she relived the event. "He grabbed my bag and swung me around. I dropped my phone and a car ran it over, I think. But I fell when he pushed me off balance, and I hit my head."

"Who did this?" Mackenzie's voice was more like a rumble in his chest and I knew his anger not only matched mine, but was greater.

"We've reported it to the police and we have CCTV that we're going to look through," the receptionist said. She stood. "Let me fetch some tea or coffee for you."

I sat beside Gabriella and Mackenzie pulled up a chair to sit in front of her. I ran my thumb over her knuckles hoping to soothe her.

She was still a little teary. "Look at me blubbering, I'm sorry," she said, chuckling as she wiped her eyes.

"Don't apologise for being upset. You've just been mugged!" Mackenzie replied. "I think we should get your injury looked at."

Gabriella shook her head. "Honestly, heads bleed, you know that more than any of us." She chuckled. "I lost count, Alex, how often he would fight or fall and cut his head open. I'll have a shower and then we can see whether it needs attention or not."

The receptionist came back with a tray of coffee and a cup of tea for Gabriella. "Perhaps I can look at the CCTV?" Mackenzie said. She nodded.

I stayed with Gabriella who didn't seem to want to let go of my hand. "Will you stay with me tonight?" she asked gently.

"Of course I will. If you're done here, come home with me, let me take care of you."

She nodded and stood. "Shall we get my things? I'd really rather leave now, if that's okay?" She looked as if she wanted to cry again.

As we passed reception, I gave instructions to let Mackenzie know that we were packing her bags.

We took the lift to her floor in silence other than the occasional sniffle. I squeezed her hand whenever she did, I wanted to hold her but was unsure of any bruising.

"The first thing we're going to do when we get to my place, is put you in the bath and then bed," I said. I was sure, if there was any bruising, as soon as the adrenalin started to wear off, she'd be hurting.

"Bed sounds good, and I do mean to rest," she said, then chuckled. She also winced and I guessed her head hurt with that small facial movement.

I rushed around the room packing all her things, even though she tried to take her clothes from me to fold. We were back down at reception within fifteen minutes and Mackenzie was standing there waiting for us. He took her suit bag and holdall and we checked her out.

I squeezed myself in the back of the Aston Martin to allow her to sit in the front, despite her protests. My head was angled awkwardly, and my knees dug into my chest until I changed position to sit across the back seats. Mackenzie told us that there was an image of a man running carrying a handbag the same as Gabriella's. He wore a hoodie and dark tracksuit, stark white branded trainers, which suggested he wasn't necessarily homeless, but he couldn't see his face. The man clearly knew the area and kept his head down to avoid CCTV detection.

"What about the police?" Gabriella asked, remembering that the receptionist had said she'd called them.

Mackenzie replied, "I gave them my cell number. They'll call but I don't hold out much hope of a visit." He kept his gaze on the road.

"I have plenty of contacts, if they don't, I'm sure I can rustle up some interest," I said.

"What would I do without you both?" she said. "I do love you."

My heart froze at the statement. I saw Mackenzie glance in the rear-view mirror, but I was sure what she'd said was simply a *southern thing*, a term of endearment. It wasn't permanent, she might be leaving, I repeated in my mind.

"Can you take me to Alex's, please," Gabriella said, and I realised then that we hadn't told Mackenzie she wanted to stay with me.

"Of course." I thought his tone a little curt, and I hoped it was just that he was concerned for her.

As far as I knew, there hadn't been anyone significant in her life for years and I wondered how Mackenzie felt. I didn't think I was number one on her list, I was sure he was, but in that car when she was in need, there was a slight atmosphere, a shift in dynamic and I hated the thought of that festering.

"Unless you think she's safer at yours," I said, to appease.

Both looked at me, Gabriella with a frown and over her shoulder and Mackenzie via the mirror.

"Don't you want me to stay with you?" she asked.

"Absolutely, yes, I do. I want you safe," I said.

"From what? It was just a mugging," she replied.

"I know, I'm being silly," I said.

Mackenzie smiled and nodded very gently. I was sure at that point he understood what I was trying to do. "To Alex's then," he said.

While we drove, we peppered her with questions. Had she noticed she was being followed? Did she let go of her bag straight away? Had she made a note of the contents for the police?

"Boys, I highly doubt any woman knows the full contents of her handbag, moreso an oversized one. I had work documents in there, my purse with a small amount of cash. I cancelled my cards straight away. And no, I hadn't noticed him following me. I was talking to Alex when it happened. He took that opportunity to strike, I guess."

Unreasonable guilt slammed into my stomach.

"If I get my hands on him..." Mackenzie muttered.

I watched her place her hand on his arm. "It's done, I'm fine, please don't get angry," she said, as if she knew that would be the outcome.

He took a long breath in. "I hate seeing you hurt," he said.

"I know, but why be angry? It's a waste of emotion, isn't it, Alex?" she said, smiling over her shoulder at me. I got the impression that she was trying to calm and diffuse.

"I don't know, I think I'd like to get my hands on him too." I knew I hadn't helped so I tried to make light of it. "I'm well versed in the Queensbury Rules," I added.

Mackenzie chuckled. "Did you box much?" he asked.

"We had no choice, it was part of our school sports programme. I left that place unbeaten. I could have been a contender," I said, using my best *Rocky* impression.

"Why didn't you?" Gabriella said.

"A posh Eton boy, a Lord in the ring? I'd be eaten alive." I shuddered dramatically and received a tinkle of laughter, followed by a wince, from Gabriella.

"Well, I'm glad. Fighting is never the answer, is it Mackenzie?" she asked, pointedly.

He didn't respond but did laugh and the atmosphere changed from tense to a happier one.

Mackenzie pulled up outside the block and left the engine running while climbing out and pulling his seat forward for me to exit.

I creaked as I straightened up. "Fuck two door cars," I grumbled.

He grabbed her bags while I helped her from the car. "Are you coming in?" I asked him, wondering why the car was still running.

"No, I'll let you get settled. I'll call later, though." He hugged Gabriella and kissed her cheek so gently. He patted my shoulder and left.

"Are you okay to walk?" I asked.

Gabriella laughed. "I ache, I will confess, and I'm sure I have a large bruise on my hip, but I'm not completely incapacitated."

"Don't be sassy, I'm worried," I said.

"You love my sass, now open that door for me," she said. Again, my heart stopped at the L word.

I held her elbow and guided her across the lobby. The security guard jumped up from his chair and rushed over.

"Lord Duchoveny, is everything okay with your guest?"

She turned and smiled to him. "I was mugged, and I fell. I'm sure I'll be fine, but thank you for your concern."

Her southern charm nearly floored him, and I sighed.

He was like a lap dog with his tongue lolling and fussing around to press for the lift and hold the door open while we walked in.

"Does that happen all the time?" I asked, as the doors closed.

"Yes, get used to it. As I've already said, I love that little jealous streak of yours. I saw your stare, your face is very transparent, Alex."

By the time we entered the flat I could see she was in pain. I ordered her to sit on the end of the bed while I ran the bath. I poured in whatever I could find lying around to make bubbles and give a nice, soothing aroma. I then helped to pull her top over her head, guiding it away from the gash.

"Bollocks," I whispered.

"What?" she asked.

"I put bubbles in the bath, but you need to wash your hair," I said.

"Do you have a shower?"

"Yes."

"I'll wash my hair first and then soak in the tub."

She sat there, topless apart from her lacy bra while I slid off her shoes, and then she stood and removed her trousers. I could do nothing but stare at her.

"Alex," she said, bringing her attention back to her face.

I smirked and shrugged my shoulders. I walked her to the bathroom and left her to shower after making her promise that she'd call for help to get into the bath.

"Do you have pyjama's?" she asked.

"No."

"What do you sleep in?"

"Nothing, usually. Why?" I asked.

"I just wanted something clean to lounge in. You bundled all my clothes into a ball and I'm certain they're all creased."

"Oh, I'll see what I can find." Not for one minute understanding why crumpled clothes couldn't be worn.

I had a t-shirt and some shorts, although they'd be way too large.

She did call for me to help her and it was the first time I saw her completely naked in real time. She was exquisite, however, when she turned and I saw the bruising to her hip, anger washed over me.

"Don't, Alex, just help me into the bath." She had clearly seen the expression on my face.

I did as asked and offered to bring a glass of water and some pain relief. She settled back and closed her eyes sighing with contentment.

"I do think we need to take some photographs," I said. With her eyes still closed, she raised her eyebrows. So, I added, "For the police," for clarity.

"Mmm, yes, you're probably right."

I left her to soak hoping the heat would bring the bruising out quicker and soothe the aches. I laid a casual shirt and gym shorts on the bed with some toiletries from her bag.

For the second time only, I cursed the fact I had no idea how to cook. A lovely meal would have been ideal. Instead, I called up my favourite local Italian and asked for some food to be packaged up for delivery. I opened a bottle of red wine and left it to breathe.

Doing that for Gabriella felt quite normal. I'd never had anyone stay over in my flat. I couldn't remember the last time I'd had anyone in the flat *full stop*. The women that I fucked were generally at the club and I'd been at a previous apartment when I'd last dated anyone.

I paced around the living room, stopping by the windows to look out over London. It was turning into a dismal afternoon; rain clouds were rolling in and the temperature was dropping. I looked at my watch.

How long does a woman take in a bath? I wondered.

With that thought just done, Gabriella walked into the living room. She was barefoot and wearing my shirt, it was too long and covered the fact she did have shorts on. Her hair was piled in a loose wet bun on top of her head, and her face clear of any make-up. Her skin was flawless, and her eyes were bright.

"Hey, I was beginning to panic," I said. Smiling, I walked towards her and heard her sigh.

She let her head fall onto my chest and although her arms were limp by her side, she rested against me. I wrapped mine around her and I heard her gently cry.

"Shush, baby, it's over now," I whispered, holding her tighter.

"I was really scared. I was trying to let go of the bag, but it was caught on my coat button," she said.

She also went on to tell me that he had raised his fist to her, he'd swung at her willing to punch her clear in the face, but she fell instead. I had to clench my jaw tight for fear of shouting out in anger.

"He was shouting at me, he threatened to rape me, Alex." Gabriella then broke down.

I walked her to the sofa and helped her to sit. I sat beside her and held her, unable to speak at first. "Why didn't you say something earlier?" I said eventually, working hard to keep the tone of my voice even.

"Because Mackenzie would have insisted on trawling the streets, and if he'd seen anyone remotely like my attacker, he would have gotten into a fight. He's very hot-headed, Alex. He's been in trouble with the police so many times in the past and even once here in the UK. I'd hate for anything to happen to him."

I wasn't surprised to hear that about him at all. He had the physique of someone capable of looking after himself if necessary. It wasn't the best idea, however, to start fights on UK soil.

"Don't keep secrets from me, Gabriella, will you?" I asked, gently.

She shook her head. "It was the look in his eyes, Alex. It was as if he really hated me, but he didn't know me. His face was contorted in anger which I found strange considering he just wanted my bag."

"Are you sure you didn't recognise him?" I asked. It was odd for a bag snatcher to be so violent, I believed.

"I'll be honest, I kept my eyes closed a lot of the time because I thought he was going to hit me. He was a white guy and I'd say about my age."

The more she spoke, the more I was convinced it wasn't a chance bag snatch. Kids, teens stole bags, not grown men, unless there was a reason for it. I didn't voice that to her, of course, but I knew I'd be speaking with Mackenzie about it. He had to have enemies, and maybe Gabriella did without realising. It could have been a member of staff that had been let go when streamlining, it could have been someone slighted by either of them at some point. Although not able to speak from experience, obviously, if a bag snatcher, in the middle of the day, encountered a tough snatch, didn't they simply run away? To shout and threaten her with rape seemed something so far away from a chancer. I let her talk and told her how brave she'd been. She started to blame herself for walking and not paying attention to her surroundings. I allayed her fear, it was the middle of the day, she was walking in an affluent area, not some slum in the back of beyond. She wasn't to blame herself anymore.

"I called a restaurant to have some dinner delivered, is that okay? I'm really not a cook, not even beans on toast, I'm afraid," I said, handing her a tissue from a box on the sideboard.

"Surprisingly, I am hungry. I haven't eaten since breakfast and that was a quick pastry before I left this morning."

"Good. And can I say, you look so fucking hot sitting here in my shirt."

She looked up and smirked and by God if she didn't look even more beautiful with wet eyelashes and shiny eyes from crying. Her lips were plump and the tip of her nose slightly red.

She smiled, cocked her head to one side slightly and laughed. "I do adore you, Alex," she said. At least she hadn't said she loved me. I could do 'adore' easier than 'love.'

I kissed the tip of her nose and rose to pour us both a glass of wine. Rain lashed against the windows and the skyline was obliterated from view.

"How long have you lived here?" she asked.

"About three years, I think. I lived in the family home for a while and then we decided it needed to be sold to pay off death duty. Mother and I moved to a townhouse in a mews that she also owned. It needed a ton of work and she just wasn't up for London living anymore. She wanted to move on, so I kept the townhouse and she moved to the retirement village." I walked back to the sofa and handed her a glass of wine. "Then I sold that and for a short time I rented another apartment while this was being converted."

"Do you like it here?"

I pondered her question. "You know, I don't anymore. It's soulless and I hadn't seen that before."

"It could do with some colour, for sure," she said, looking around.

The apartment was very monochrome, boring in fact, with the basics and nothing homely. "Maybe I'll look for a house somewhere," I said before sipping from my glass.

We chatted about London life, anything other than what had happened. We talked about our families, and for the first time she mentioned an estranged brother. She mentioned Mackenzie's ex-wife very briefly; it appeared they had been a group of friends in their youth. She didn't say anything more about her brother.

The only *pause* was when she wanted to show me some photographs of her home and then remembered she no longer had her phone.

"I'll have to buy another, I'm sure I saved the images in the cloud," she said, hopefully.

A buzz indicated that our dinner had arrived. As I left the apartment to run down to the foyer, Gabriella promised to set the table. By the time I was back up, she'd found napkins, crockery and cutlery, and a candle in a silver stag horn holder. I was sure I'd seen the candleholder in the past but hadn't realised I had brought it with me to the apartment.

"Matches?" she asked, turning on the spot.

"No idea," I replied, laughing.

"Oh, well, it looks pretty anyway."

She took the box from me and we plated up our meals. She wafted her hand over the veal in lemon sauce and hummed. We sat to eat and one thing that I loved about her was, *she ate*! She didn't pick or push her food around. She leaned over her plate at times and sucked up spaghetti. She laughed as sauce splashed onto her cheek, and daintily dabbed it with her napkin. It was the most fun I'd had in my own apartment even though the circumstances that brought it about were tragic.

That evening Gabriella slept beside me. We didn't have sex as she was aching and sore. I just held her until she fell asleep. With her in my arms, I had the best night's sleep in ages.

CHAPTER EIGHT

I went to work the following day and Gabriella promised that she would do nothing but relax. I was dismayed to learn she had visited the local deli and stocked my fridge and cupboards.

"It will go to waste," I said, looking at packets of pasta and thanking the extremely long sell by date.

"I'm going to teach you to cook. I can't believe your momma didn't." She laughed when I told her we had a cook, and that Mother had never prepared a meal herself, either.

"At least you do your own cleaning," she said, looking around a spotless kitchen.

"Erm, you might meet Claire at some point," I said, chuckling as she threw a dishcloth at me.

"How was work today?" she asked, and it seemed the most natural thing in the world to sit with a coffee and tell her about my day.

"Uneventful really. We've moved everyone up now

and Mackenzie thinks he has a deal with another company. He also seems rather taken with Veronica."

"Really, Veronica?" Gabriella said, her brow creased with surprise. She sat with me leaving a tomato sauce bubbling away on the stove.

"Yeah, seems he's been visiting the club quite a lot lately. She wasn't gossiping but let it slip when I last spoke to her."

"Alex, I'm going to ask something rather rude. I know she's your cousin, but are they right for each other?"

"I know what you mean, and I highly doubt there will be a relationship. Von doesn't want one, never has. She's bisexual, and I don't think she knows what she wants other than the freedom to live the life she chooses. That isn't conducive to a relationship."

"Oh, I didn't know that. I do hope you don't think I was being catty?"

"You're looking out for him, I totally understand that," I said, smiling at her.

Veronica had never had a serious relationship but had many partners over the years. I told Gabriella about some and we ended up howling with laughter.

"So, she led him around like a dog?" she asked, wide-eyed.

"Yep. There was one time I visited her, and she answered the door dressed head to toe in black leather with the most awful metal studs all over. I was sure we'd had a coat of arms similar, anyway, in the background was a man on all fours with a saddle on his back and...get this...a butt plug that had a pony's tail attached. He had a bit in his mouth too!"

I thought Gabriella was going to fall from her chair.

Tears streamed down her cheeks as she laughed. She held her side. "Ouch, my bruises," she said, between gasps of breath.

When she had finally calmed enough to dish up the most tender pasta and tasty sauce, we sat at the table.

"Do you find it odd that you both have, you know, those kinds of kinks?" she asked.

I frowned. "I don't have anywhere near as many *kinks* as she has."

"But you know what I mean, don't you? You're not the average missionary position man, are you?"

I ran my hand over my mouth and chin, thinking before I spoke. "No, I'm not, you've seen the kind of things I like to do. Although I also enjoy the missionary position as you call it. As for why we both enjoy that lifestyle, although in different degrees? I hadn't really thought why."

She shook her head. "I'm sorry, I shouldn't have asked that."

"You can ask anything you want," I replied with a smile.

"I'd like to go back to your club; will you take me?"

I pushed my plate of food to one side. "What interested you the most?" Already my voice had lowered.

"I liked watching the couple," she replied. Her breath hitched a little.

"Specifically, what did you like to watch?"

Her cheeks coloured just a little. "I liked watching him." She rose from her seat and I slid my chair slightly back away from the table. She straddled my lap and I held her hips being sure to not hold too hard.

"I liked the way his cock so easily slid in and out of her.

How wet she was. I found that extremely arousing, Alex," she said, grinding herself gently.

"And what else do you like, Gabriella?" I asked staring at her intently.

"I'd like to be restrained. I like to be spanked. I'd like to be blindfolded so I have no idea what you're going to do next."

Certain words were the loudest in my mind. She had said she *liked to be spanked,* not that she *would like,* suggesting she'd already experienced that. The one that had my cock hard was, *you're.* She wanted that with me.

I ran my hands up her hips raising the shirt at the same time. She lifted her arms and I pulled it over her head. Her breasts were pert, her nipples erect, and her skin goose-bumped as I ran my fingers gently over them.

"You'd like me to spank you? With what?" I asked, quietly.

"Your hand, Alex. I want to feel skin on skin."

I cupped her breasts gently kneading them in my palms. I lowered my head and ran my tongue over one nipple, closing my lips around it and gently biting down. Gabriella placed her hands either side of my face, sliding them back to grip my hair and tightening her fingers each time I closed my teeth on her nipple.

I released her. "Do you like that?" I whispered, turning my attention to the other one.

"Yes," came her breathy reply.

"Do you like pain?" I asked. Again she replied with an even breathier yes.

My cock strained harder against my trousers. I ran my tongue over her chest up to her neck.

"Bedroom, now," I commanded. She slid from my lap

and walked ahead of me. The swing of her hips was deliberate and I wanted to fuck the arse she teased me with.

A noise rumbled from my throat and she looked over her shoulder at me. She smiled, knowingly. God, that woman knew exactly what she was doing to me. The shorts I had loaned her tightened across her buttocks as she walked. I reached forwards and grabbed the waistband causing her to stop just short of the end of the bed. I wriggled the shorts down her legs, and she kicked them off.

"Lean down, put your hands on the frame," I said. She complied and spread her legs a little for balance. She wasn't new to this and I was both excited and disappointed by that.

I ran my fingers down her bare back, leaning over to blow on her skin, and it pimpled in response. I continued to draw circles on her arse cheeks. I palmed the skin, squeezing and sliding my fingers between her thighs. Her pussy was wet and the fingers I swiped over her were slick. I slid my fingers back up, lubricating her.

"I like that," she whispered as I circled gently. I repeated the motion a couple of times before pushing two fingers into her arse, slowly.

She tensed, took in a deep breath, and blew it out. Her legs started to shake a little as I slid my fingers in and out. I used my other hand to reach around and massage her clitoris, coating my fingers for more lubricant. She gently moaned, stretching out, and forcing her arse towards me. Her breaths grew rapid and her moans frequent. I plunged two fingers in her pussy hooking them to find her g-spot. She cried out in pleasure.

When I thought she was about to come I removed myself from her, stepped back and spanked her, first on one butt cheek, then the other. I massaged in between. Her legs shook as her orgasm took over. Her pink flesh glowed with heat.

"More," she growled out, breathlessly.

I slid the belt from the loops of my trousers and wrapped both ends around my fist. I flicked it, gently, against her skin, careful to avoid her hip. The constant flicks against the back of her thighs made her moan again. She threw her head back and cried out my name. Her body shook and I wondered how long she'd hold on. A gentle flick to her pussy was the turning point. She stood and turned so quick her hair flew in different directions settling across her face. She grabbed the front of my shirt and in her haste to remove it, she tore it open. I fumbled with my trousers, eventually removing them, and she fell to her knees. She held my cock with both hands and lowered her head all the while gazing up at me. Just her expression made my legs tremble. She licked my cock, running her hands up and down at the same time. She teased, nipped, and gently sucked, her eyes challenging me. I grabbed her head and forced her lower. I heard her gag, she gripped hard, and then, once she had relaxed her throat, she sucked. Tears streamed down her face and it was divine. The way she looked up at me was pure wickedness and so erotic.

I wasn't sure how long I could hold on. I desperately wanted to come. I wanted to force my cock even further down her throat but knew I shouldn't. There was something about her that made me want to act out all my kink with her. When I was on the brink, I grabbed her hair and pulled hard. She didn't want to release and clamped her lips around me. I pulled more. She groaned at the pain she must have felt. I pulled her to her feet and without a word I turned her. Instead of leaning down and reaching for the bed frame, she leaned onto the mattress, spreading her legs. She used her own hand to pleasure herself, parting her lips, inviting me to join her. I ran the tip of my cock across her clitoris, over her pussy and then to her arse. I probed just a little, waiting for permission, she pushed back against me. It was the invitation I needed.

I fucked her arse while she fingered herself. She moaned, as did I. She was tight and accommodating, I was slow, and it was excruciating. It wasn't like we had a conversation about anal and I wasn't about to hurt her in any way. I held her hips, not even thinking about her bruises but she rocked against me, setting the pace.

When she began to bring herself to another orgasm, I couldn't hold back anymore. I pulled from her arse and I spurted my cum over it. While my milky fluid ran down her still pink skin, I spanked her again. She slumped to the bed and I, to the floor.

"Alex," she said, her voice hoarse.

She reached behind with her hand. I took it. Her fingers were sticky, and I threaded mine through hers. We stayed that way just for a few minutes while we got our breath back.

Gabriella started to laugh. "Oh my God, Alex," she said.

"Have I hurt you?" I asked.

She stood and then kneeled down in front of me. "Not enough," she replied with that sassy smirk she gave.

I grabbed her face and pulled her towards me for a kiss. A deep passionate, breath stealing kiss. I could feel myself hardening again. She reached down to cup my balls and gently squeezed. I broke the kiss.

"I need to clean up first," I said. She nodded.

I stood and held out my hand. I led her to my shower and turned it on. We stood while I washed my cock before sitting on the built-in bench. She straddled me and while water cascaded down, I fucked her, or she fucked me because whoever was in charge at one point, she was sure to make the switch. I bit down hard on her breasts, marking her skin as I came hard. My balls contracted and an ache rippled through my stomach. I cried out her name as she dug her nails into my skin, drawing blood. I wasn't stopping however, until she'd come again. I replaced my flaccid cock with fingers, two, then three.

"I want to fist you one day," I whispered. She didn't respond, but sank her teeth into my neck. There were so many things I wanted to do to her, and it wasn't because it was my *kink* as she called it, it was because I couldn't get enough. I wasn't deep enough, her screams weren't loud enough, my orgasm didn't hurt enough.

I just couldn't get enough of her.

We moved from the shower to the bed. I continued to pleasure her, and she did the same to me. The sheets were wet, tangled around us. Our legs were entwined, we rolled, we tussled for position and we fucked again. Sweat coated our bodies, cum was smeared over her thighs and the sheets. Our throats were sore and our voices husky, our eyelids hooded. We fell asleep at some point early hours of the morning.

I woke alone in bed just covered with a sheet. I could smell her scent in the room. I brought my arm up to see the face of my watch and then panicked. It was nearing on nine o'clock. I pushed the sheet back and called out.

"Gabriella?"

She walked into the bedroom dressed and holding a cup of coffee for me. "Ah, you're awake. I need to leave; I have a taxi waiting. Got to get back to work and I want to head home first."

I took the coffee and swung my legs over the bed. "Can you wait fifteen minutes and I'll drive you?" I asked.

She patted my cheek and then sat beside me. "Don't be silly. I have a taxi waiting. I wanted to see your smile before I left. I had an idea to wake you seductively, but I'll save that for another time."

"Seductively, huh?" I enquired taking a sip of my coffee.

"Anyway, my Lord, I need to get going."

"Gabriella, wait. I'm going to drive you. Just give me fifteen minutes to shower and dress." I placed down my coffee cup and stood.

As I did, she stood and raised herself on her tiptoes. "I had the most wonderful night, I'm sore in all the right places, and I'm big enough to get a taxi home. I'll call you later," she said, kissing me briefly on my lips.

"You are infuriating," I said. She smirked, raised her eyebrows, and nodded in agreement. I laughed as she left the apartment.

I took a shower, not wanting to wash her scent from my body but knowing I had to. I called the office to let them know I was on my way in and requested a car, and then dressed. I had a second cup of coffee and rinsed my mug, leaving it on the drainer beside hers. I stared at the two mugs for a moment. I couldn't recall the last time I saw two of anything in my flat.

Gabriella had obviously cleared the dishes from the abandoned dinner and at that thought, my stomach rumbled. I opened the fridge to see the pasta in small plastic containers. I grabbed one, along with a fork, and headed out. I sat in the back of the car eating the cold pasta, grateful for the carbohydrate refill.

While en route I checked through some emails on my phone and smiled when I saw a text pop up from Gabriella.

I'm home, showered, missing you already, my Lord ;) xxx

I chuckled at 'my Lord' and wondered why she chose to call me that. Perhaps she'd make a better submissive than she gave herself credit for. I laughed at the thought. She was the perfect sub in that she called the shots, for sure. She was demure when required, and a tigress when needed. If ever the perfect sexual partner was designed for me, it would come in the form of Gabriella.

I silently cursed myself for sounding shallow and crass. I didn't want to just view her as a sexual partner. I wanted more but knew I was the one holding back. It had been just a few months since we'd first met and that morning, having slept beside her for the whole night in my apartment, I felt bitter disappointment that she had to leave. I wouldn't ask her to move in with me, though. She was too independent for that, and the niggle that just wouldn't leave me kept telling me not to make it permanent, she could leave at any time.

By the time I arrived at the office, my earlier jolly mood

had soured a little. I needed to give myself a talking to in the lift on the way to my floor.

Mackenzie was waiting by my office door chatting to some members of staff. He straightened up and smiled when he saw me approach. "I'm hiding from Mary, she's on the rampage. Apparently, I forgot to mention a dinner at your old haunt tonight and, according to her, I don't have a clean dinner jacket."

I frowned. "Don't you have one at home?" Surely, he had more than one.

"Yeah, but I didn't give her an itinerary of what suits I had at home so now she's in a flap making sure I have a clean version in the 'wardrobe' just in case I work late and don't get time to change. As for this meeting, I think you should come."

"What's it about?" I asked as we entered my office.

"The current government wants me to be a business ambassador, or something, help ease UK and US relations. But there is the small matter of a very lucrative military contract that I don't want to lose. I think it wouldn't be prudent for me to be their ambassador. But you on the other hand... You're the Lord, after all."

"Mmm, not sure. Other than you, I don't really like many Americans," I said, and then chuckled.

"Only me?" he teased.

"Only you and one other, to be precise."

"I wondered why the pair of you were late in this morning." He winked and I shook my head.

"I have absolutely no idea what you could mean, and I won't be tricked into divulging what a fucking fabulous evening I had." I widened my eyes in mock innocence.

He laughed again. "Here's what I was thinking. Either

I do the ambassador thing and you be the front man for the military contract, that way, I'm separated from it. Or, I don't do the ambassador thing full stop."

"Is there a benefit to this role?" I asked.

"Dinners at the House of Lords," he replied, shrugging his shoulders.

"I can take you there any time," I said.

"Contacts, but then you can introduce those. I don't know. The meeting tonight will give me some more details, I guess."

"I'll come along, just for the crack," I said, also wondering what was on offer.

"Thanks. Two sets of ears and eyes, and all that. I'm just not sure why they chose me."

I nodded. It wasn't unusual to have prominent businessmen of other nationalities as ambassadors, but it seemed rather coincidental since he'd just taken over Trymast and they had one contract for military communications equipment.

"Shall I tell Mary that you need a suit as well?" he asked, as he backed out of the office.

I widened my eyes. "Err, no, thanks, I'm sure I can nip home at some point and grab one." Mary scared the shit out of me, I had no desire to anger her further.

I heard his laughter as he walked across the floor to the lifts. I shook my head and settled down to work.

It was a good couple of hours later that Gabriella called. "Hello, I was checking in. I'm on my new cell," she said, and then sighed. "The police called, absolutely nothing to identify my attacker but they started to ask some odd questions."

"Like what?" I asked.

"Well, about my work and Mackenzie and you. I thought it very strange."

"Where are you?" I asked.

"I'm just heading into a meeting. I'm fine, please don't worry. It was just odd. You and Mackenzie have your dinner tonight and that's important, but we'll catch up tomorrow and I can tell you all."

"I don't want you to wait until tomorrow, you might stew on it all night," I said.

"*Stew on it*, how funny," she said, and then laughed. "Honestly, I'm pooped, I had a rather exhausting evening so I'm all for curling up in bed with a hot chocolate and a good book."

"Right, but tomorrow we meet up, okay?" I made sure my voice was firm enough so she understood I wasn't messing.

"Understood, my Lord," she replied, quietly.

"Do you know what that does to me?" I asked, equally lowering my voice.

"Yes."

"You'll be the death of me," I said, and then chuckled. I disconnected the call and headed home to change.

CHAPTER NINE

It was a strange meeting, for sure. Two lower standing members of the government entertained us and spent most of the first hour just skirting around business talk. We thought the purpose of the meeting was to talk to Mackenzie about the ambassador role. Although not an ambassador in the traditional sense, it was a created position and they edged around wanting a professional, upstanding, and exemplary American businessman.

"I assume you can access any records you like, can't you? You've mentioned exemplary twice now. Are you asking me if I have a criminal record?" Mackenzie was getting bored, as was I.

"No, not really," one of the officials replied.

"Well, I don't, certainly not here in the UK," he said. The two looked at each other and I wanted to laugh.

I shook my head. "What exactly is this position? Maybe if we start there we might get somewhere. As much as this dinner is superb, I'm already a member of the

House of Lords, so I'm well versed in the traditions you've spent the past hours detailing. I think we need to get to the point."

There was a small amount of uncomfortable coughing. "We understand your ex-father-in-law had some troubles—"

Mackenzie cut in. "What on earth has he to do with me?"

"We understand that you and your ex-father-in-law have had some clashes resulting in takeovers of companies in perhaps a not so desirable way," came the clarification.

Before Mackenzie could speak the other official did. "All right, cards on the table. We want to have you on board, we think you're a great asset to the UK as it is. Your businesses are successful, you pay your taxes, and thanks for that, we do understand how easy it would be not to, but we don't want anything to blow up in our faces with regards to any dodgy deals."

Mackenzie sat back in his chair and shook his head, he laughed. "Why the fuck didn't you just ask that in the first place? And I'm guessing you've been sent to dig for the dirt, haven't you?"

"Yep, sorry."

"Since you asked, and that's all you've had to do, I can assure you nothing illegal was ever done with regards to the business dealings between my *ex*—as you rightly point out—father-in-law and me."

Mackenzie went on to tell them, and me, a little about his background. His father-in-law had bought his father's business when it hit financial troubles due to the recession. He then stripped it, put everyone out of work and caused his father to have a heart attack, so he believes. The problem was, he also backed Mackenzie initially and that had been used as the leash to tie him to a family he didn't want to be tied to. His father-in-law made it impossible for him to continue, so he walked away, leaving everything behind. He had then spent years, surreptitiously buying up stock in his father-in-law's companies. Nothing illegal about that at all, it was concluded. We left the meeting not having a clue what it was really all about and whether Mackenzie wanted the role or not.

"Gabriella said the police called and they asked her some odd questions. She said she's having an early night but will tell us tomorrow," I said as we stood outside waiting for taxis.

"What was odd about them?" Mackenzie asked.

"She was asked about her working relationship with us, both of us."

He frowned when he looked at me. "Both of us?"

"Yes, and I find that odd because I've only been on the scene a few months. I wonder if this attacker could be connected to a business deal, or a disgruntled ex-employee."

"Fuck, that's a good thought" he said.

"I don't believe it was as simple as a bag snatch." I didn't mention about the rape threat, I thought that best coming from Gabriella. She knew how to cool Mackenzie down if needed.

"I'm glad she called you, Alex," he said, and then waved his hand for a taxi. "We'll sit down in the morning and sort this out."

"You're okay with us dating?" I asked, as a second taxi pulled up.

"Of course, I'm pleased, Alex, honestly. She needs a

good man, and you're a good man. I'll see you tomorrow, we can also figure out what the fuck that was all about," he said, opening his taxi door and thumbing over his shoulder at the Palace of Westminster.

I didn't doubt Mackenzie had a past; no one got to his position in business without one. I'd done my research on him *and* the run-in with his ex-father-in-law, although I wasn't aware he was his father-in-law initially. The arguments were fairly well documented in the American business press. And Mackenzie wasn't the only one confused by the meeting we'd just attended. I wasn't sure either what it was really about. I decided that I'd call some friends and see if I could get to the bottom of it myself.

I settled into the back of the taxi and texted Gabriella.

I'm on my way home, I didn't want to call to disturb you. Sleep well, my darling, and I'll see you tomorrow. Alex.

I deleted the two Xs I'd typed because I thought they looked silly, then regretted it after I'd sent the message. Gabriella replied.

I appreciate your consideration, but I'd like to hear your voice. Gabriella xx

I chuckled and called her.

"Hi," she said, sounding sleepy and sexy as fuck.

"Were you sleeping?" I asked.

"Dozing, that's all. I like to hear from you. How was the meeting?"

"Meaningless and very odd." I chuckled. "Neither Mackenzie nor I have any idea what it was about. They eventually got around to asking about his business dealings with his ex-father-in-law and whether anything shady went on."

"Oh, how odd. What did Mackenzie say?"

"*Vagued* very successfully," I said, laughing and she joined in.

"Vagued, I like that," she said, still laughing.

"I just made it up, but it should be in the dictionary with a picture of two confused lower ranking members of our government and Mackenzie Miller."

"You do cheer me up, Alex," she said.

Concern rose in my chest. "Are you still feeling down?" I asked.

"A little, but I think I'm just tired. I'll be fine in the morning."

"Do you want me to come over for an hour?" I asked.

"Oh, don't worry, honestly. I'll grab a glass of water and turn off the lights."

I was disappointed at her answer, obviously, but accepted that she needed to get a good night's sleep and if we were together, that might not happen.

"Then I'll see you tomorrow."

We said goodnight and I disconnected the call as the taxi pulled up outside my apartment block. I waved to security as I crossed the foyer and took the lift to my floor.

As I undressed, I thought back on Gabriella's couple of days with me. It had felt so right to have her in my apartment although I didn't feel she was an *apartment* type of person. Perhaps I should look for a house. I chuckled at the thought. We hadn't had *that* chat yet; in all honesty, I had no idea what kind of a relationship we had and I was thinking about moving so she could live with me.

I slept through night, despite worrying when she didn't respond to a goodnight text. I dreamt of us living together, and then her leaving me because she wanted to go home.

Mackenzie, Gabriella, and I were sitting in his office. She had just arrived with take-out coffees even though Mary berated her for not asking her to go.

"What did the police actually say?" I asked.

While she removed the lid of her coffee and gently blew, she repeated what she'd told me about them having nothing to identify the attacker. Mackenzie looked at me and I frowned. The guy had his hood up but really? Absolutely nothing at all? I was leery of that.

"They asked what my relationship was to you," she said, looking at Mackenzie. "I told them we were friends and that we worked together. They then asked me about my relationship with Lord Duchoveny," she looked at me.

"What did you tell them?" I asked, and in my mind, I'd gone from what the police wanted to know, to what *I* wanted to know.

"I told them we're partners." She seemed surprised that I would ask. I smiled at her and gently nodded. She scowled. "I'm assuming that we are or should I have said we're just fuck buddies?" she said, abruptly.

I spat out the coffee that was in my mouth, just as Mary walked into the room. She tutted and walked back out, I looked around for something to dab at my shirt.

"Of course we are, partners I mean," I replied, stuttering.

Mary walked back in with a damp cloth, she first wiped the desk of the spilled coffee and then slammed the cloth into my chest for me to clean my shirt.

"Don't you be mean to her. She's had an ordeal," Mary

said then left. I sat open- mouthed while Gabriella smirked at me.

"Can we keep the domestic for later? What else was said?" Mackenzie asked, chuckling.

Gabriella stuck her nose in the air and turned to Mackenzie. "Obviously, I asked them why that was relevant. They didn't answer. I get the impression they don't think it was just a bag snatch."

"Why would they think that?" Mackenzie asked.

"Well, my attacker said something else... he threatened to rape me—"

Mackenzie slammed his palms on the desk. "He did what?" He growled out the words.

"It was just a threat to make me let go of the bag. I guess he didn't realise it was caught on my coat buttons," she replied.

"And they haven't got a clue who this is?" I asked, she gently shook her head. I sighed deeply. "You're staying with me for a while," I added.

"I'm fine, Alex. Honestly, my house is perfectly secure."

I looked to Mackenzie for help.

"I think you should stay with Alex. Just until we know more," Mackenzie said. I thanked him with a small smile.

Gabriella pouted as she crossed her arms. "I think you're both being silly."

"If you don't stay with me, then I'm staying with you and you sure aren't big enough to manhandle me out the door, Gabriella. Please, do as your told," I said.

She raised her eyebrows and before she could speak Mackenzie cut in. "You two are going to be fireworks, for sure," he said, laughing.

"I just wish she would do as she was told for once," I said, knowing it would rile her, I gave her a wink, just in case.

"We'll discuss this at home," she said, and I liked the way she said *at home* and not *at my house.*

"I think you should call the police and ask them why they wanted to know the connection," I said to Mackenzie and he nodded in agreement.

Gabriella handed over a business card that she had been left. She then rose. "I'm going to head home; I hope you don't mind. I have a headache. I guess, I'll see you later," she said to me before she left.

"Is she pissed?" Mackenzie asked.

"I don't know. You've known her longer than me, you must be able to tell."

"When she's pissed she's super quiet and refined. If she does that southern thing, straightening her back and raising her chin, you're in trouble, my friend." He laughed but I didn't think it funny.

"I guess I'm in trouble then," I said, as I watched her, chin raised, standing in front of the lift. "Something didn't add up for me, Mackenzie. I don't really want her on her own especially if she has her address in her bag."

"I agree. She needs to get the locks changed, I'll shoot an email to the agents and tell them, they'll need a new key. In the meantime, I'll give these guys a call." He picked up the business card.

"Okay, I have a couple of hours' work, hopefully she'll have cooled down by then," I said, chuckling.

"She's pretty fierce," Mackenzie replied.

"Yeah, I'm seeing that."

I left his office and blew a kiss to Mary who told me to, '*Feck off, you silly bugger,*' and I walked to the lift.

All the way to my desk I thought on what Gabriella had said. I hoped the police would be forthcoming with Mackenzie, if not, I was sure one of my contacts would help. It was a mighty good thing having connections in the police force sometimes. And that reminded me.

"Hello, Mother, just checking in. How are you?" I asked when she answered my call.

"I'm okay, darling. Still no answers on the elusive Duncan's whereabouts. How are you?" she asked.

I told her I'd call an old school friend, who just so happened to be Chief of Police. We chatted back and forth but something niggled at me and I ended the call rather sooner than I thought Mother would like.

I called that old chum of mine. "Harry, how are you?" I asked, when he answered.

"Very well, old boy. You?"

"I wanted to pick your brains. My mother was the victim of a con man, we think, now my partner has been the victim of a bag snatch but I'm not convinced it was simply a bag snatch. The attacker threatened to rape her. I'm not suggesting there is a connection but I'm wondering..." I tailed off.

"Which department is dealing with your partner?" he asked.

"I don't have the details. Mackenzie Miller is calling them to ask for some information, not that they'll give it to him, I don't think," I said.

"Yeah, data protection and all that crap. What's her, or his, name?"

"Her name is Gabriella Collingsworth." I gave him as

many details as I could, the date, a rough time. I also explained why I didn't think it simply a bag snatch.

"Did she have anything of worth in her bag?"

"Not that she can remember. There was some paperwork but nothing confidential. Her purse, obviously, but that's about it, I think."

"House keys?" he asked.

"No, she'd left them in her hotel, but I imagine there might have been something with her address on."

"Does she have adequate security?" Harry asked.

"I don't know, but I'm going to stay with her for a few days. Something niggles, Harry."

"Yes, I don't get a straight up mugging feeling here myself. I hope that it's just a coincidence, your mother and your girlfriend, but I'll have someone grab the files and run fresh eyes over both."

"Thank you, I appreciate that. Mother has resigned herself that she won't get the painting back and should the insurance company pay up, it will belong to them anyway."

We chatted about his wife, another old college friend, and promised to meet up for a beer, something we hadn't done in a few months.

"Before I go, can I ask a favour?" Harry asked.

"Of course," I replied, feeling obliged.

"Lord Stanton, what do you know about him?"

"Dodgy as fuck. Got a little consortium together to bail out some of the Lloyds 'names.' I'd suggest you check out a Russian that goes by the very Russian name of Jeremy Daughton."

"Laundering?" Harry enquired.

"I've no doubt. Stanton doesn't have anywhere near the wealth needed to do what he does."

"I appreciate the information. I'll be in touch," Harry said, and we finished our call.

I highly doubted my mother's theft was connected to the bag snatch, but I wasn't taking any chances, particularly after the police had asked the questions they had of Gabriella.

Eventually I got down to some work. I wanted to clear my desk, something that I rarely did but since Carolyn, my new PA, had taken over a lot of the crap I dealt with on a day-to-day basis, I was able to get on with the job of running the business and not worrying about bloody expense sheets.

However, I couldn't concentrate. I had sent a text message to Gabriella and she hadn't replied. It was simply to ask if she'd arrived home okay. I didn't want to crowd her but if she was *pissed* I, equally, didn't like the ignoring game. I was more annoyed when Mackenzie told me she was home and safe. She had the time to tell him but not me.

I don't like games, Gabriella. I'm leaving the office now. I'll collect some items from my apartment and then drive over.

I didn't sign it off, as petty as that was.

"Carolyn, you can get me on my mobile if I'm needed," I said, as I left the office in a huff.

I grumbled to myself in the car as I was dropped home. I was still moaning after I'd packed a couple of suits, some underwear and casual clothes, running shoes and work out gear, toiletries, and a book. I grabbed my car keys and stomped down the stairs to the car park.

My mood hadn't changed by the time I arrived at her house. I grabbed my bags from the boot and headed to the front door. Before I could knock, she answered smiling daintily.

"I've been texting you," I said, standing like an idiot on her doorstep.

She placed her hands on her hips. "I haven't seen a text from you. I thought you were being a shit."

"Am I invited in, or not?" I asked.

"Only if you leave the attitude with your car," she said, raising her eyebrows at me.

"Leave the...? Me? You're the one who's *pissed* as you Americans say." She was bloody infuriating. Without waiting for an invitation I stepped forward, dropping my bags in the hallway, and I pushed the door shut. She smirked.

I stood and faced her, and the smirk slipped. "I wasn't *pissed* as you put it. I was tired, I had a headache, and I was worried and scared and I didn't want to worry you or Mackenzie," she said, slowly.

I took a step towards her until she was backed to the wall. "Were you ignoring me?" I asked, quietly.

"No. I'm an adult, Alex, I don't appreciate being treated like a child," she chastised.

I took a deep breath in. "I'm sorry. I was worried about you," I said but didn't back off.

"I like that you're worried about me. I don't like that you have a childish attitude and you assume something before you discover the facts," she whispered as I lowered my face close to hers.

I shrugged. "I'm possessive, I'm a shit sometimes. I have no idea how to treat you the way you should be treated, because I've never met anyone like you. I want to protect you and when you don't let me, I don't cope well with that." I rattled off my sentence and then I kissed her.

She gripped the back of my hair and pulled me closer, taking control of my mouth, kissing me hard. She bit at my tongue and my lips and she moaned. I swallowed her moan and mine echoed back. I wrapped my arms around her, holding her tight. I didn't want to let her go but knew I had to. Our kiss slowed and eventually we leaned against each other and just breathed.

"We'll find our way, Alex, I know we will," she said. "I'm sure we'll battle until we do but if that's our apology to each other, I'm fine with that."

I felt her smile against my neck, and I chuckled. "So, you didn't receive my texts?" I asked.

She pulled away. "No, like I said. I'm too old for those games, Alex." I frowned and she continued. "Are you sure you were texting my new number? Did you delete the old one when you input the new one?"

I hadn't, I pulled my mobile from my pocket and showed her the number I had. She rattled off her new one and I changed it. "Jesus, I've been acting like a schoolboy," I said.

"Yes, you have. Now, would you like to come on in?" She smiled and held out her arm. "You can leave your bags there; we'll take them up later."

Gabriella and I sat in her kitchen and sipped on red wine. She wanted to cook dinner for me, and I was more than happy for her to do so. It felt peaceful and, dare I believe it, normal. It was the same feeling I'd had in my apartment. It wasn't the location, I'd determined, but the fact it was her.

"I'm thinking of selling my apartment and buying a house," I said.

"I thought you liked your apartment," she replied, as she laid out ingredients for our meal.

"I don't think I do. It's simply somewhere to shower and sleep, I guess."

"I love my house. It would be wonderful if you could find something that makes you love it too."

I didn't answer immediately but wondered if that was her way of warning me off from asking her to move in with me.

"Maybe. Do you want me to help?" I asked.

"No, I've got this. Relax, there's more wine here. Go and change if you want to. I'm sure you'll find the master bedroom easily enough, it's the only one with a bed in it." She laughed.

I left her in the kitchen while I took my bags upstairs. She was right, of the five bedrooms, only one had a super king-sized bed in it. One had wardrobes, an endless run of wood, all of which were empty. One had a desk; another was set out as a snug with a couple of chairs and throws facing a large window looking out over the back garden. The last bedroom was just simply empty. I returned to the master room and unpacked my clothes. There was a small dressing room and I was thankful there was space to hang my clothes. Off the bedroom was a large bathroom and I placed my toiletries in the cupboard above the sink, next to hers. I smiled to myself, running my hand over my chin wondering if I should shave.

I stripped off my suit and showered then threw on a pair of jeans and a t-shirt before heading back downstairs. My hair was wet, and I was sure I'd be able to tie it back; I hadn't had it cut for a while. Gabriella had her back to me; she was humming as she cooked. I wrapped my arms around her and snuggled into her neck.

"Mmm, that feels nice," she said.

"Do you want any help?" I asked, looking over her shoulder. She was frying off some strips of steak for fajitas.

"No, all done. Sit yourself down and I'll plate up."

I loved messy food, dishes that could be eaten with my hands. It wasn't something I'd had much of growing up. Every evening meal had been an event back then, correctly dressed attire and three courses as a minimum. I remember getting my first burger at a fast food restaurant and asking where the cutlery was. I told Gabriella that story as I wrapped and ate. Salsa dripped through my fingers and I licked them clean. Gabriella did the same, except, what she did was way more delicate.

I ate much faster than she did and I learned that next time I must slow down. When I sat back and pushed my plate away, she did the same although only half finished.

"Carry on," I said, indicating to her plate.

"No, I'm done, and it's rude to continue to eat alone," she said, chuckling.

"Well, with all the manners instilled in me, that's a first. Let me clear these dishes." I stood and gathered the plates, then stood and looked around the kitchen not knowing where to put them.

"Under the sink, to the left," she said.

I followed instructions and opened a cupboard to find a dishwasher.

I piled everything in and heard her sigh. "Have you ever stacked a dishwasher before?" she asked.

I looked at her and laughed. "No."

"No?"

"No."

"Well, let me teach you because *I'm* sure not doing it every time we eat," she said and proceeded to show me how to stack the dishwasher properly...or at least to her exacting standards.

"Not rocket science," I said, watching where to put the cleaner and which programme to select.

"Would you like another glass of wine?" she asked. I nodded. She grabbed the bottle and I took the two glasses from the counter. I followed her to a living room.

"This feels strange," I said, sitting on the sofa.

"I know, but it's a nice strange, isn't it?" she answered.

"Have you lived with anyone before? Not that we're living together, but you know what I mean?" I stumbled through my question.

"No, not really. You?"

"No, never. I like my own space sometimes," I said, and yet again wanted to curse myself at her crestfallen face. "That was, until now," I added.

"Do you want to watch the television?" she asked.

There was awkwardness that we hadn't experienced in my apartment. "No, do you?" I responded.

She shook her head. "Good Lord listen to us. You'd think we were teenagers on a first date." Her gentle laughter caused my heart to miss a beat.

"Tell me something about you that no one knows," I asked.

She frowned, thought for a moment, and then sighed. "I think Mackenzie knows pretty much everything about me. Let me think," she said. She pursed her lips and looked to the ceiling. "I know! When I was little, I found a dead frog and I thought if I kissed it, it would come back to life. Not necessarily turn into a prince, just come alive again as if I was the princess." Her smile was broad at the memory.

"Did it?"

"No, but I had a nasty infection on my face. I was left with scarring which, luckily, has faded over time. Can you see?" She shuffled closer and pointed to some very faint lighter skin above her upper lip.

I ran my finger over the scar, and she kissed my fingertip. "Now you," she said, settling back next to me.

"When I was a child, I had an imaginary friend. I was homeschooled by a tutor and I was an only child. I hated every minute of it. I was terribly lonely. Anyway, my imaginary friend, Eric, used to do really naughty stuff."

She giggled. "Eric? And what naughty stuff?" she asked.

I wrapped my arm around her shoulder. "Well, one day he hid a dead fish in his tutor's curtains. For days her rooms stank, and no one could find out why. My father was convinced that she was up to no good, although I have no idea why, and he fired her. I felt awful, *really* bad, but I was too scared to confess by then. Eventually, the cook found the fish, she didn't tell my dad, but she slapped my head with it!"

"Urgh, how yukky," Gabriella said, laughing.

"Yeah, it was pretty decomposed by then, it splattered in my hair. I voluntarily bathed that day."

"So, I kissed a dead frog and you got slapped by a dead fish. How bizarre that we both chose cold-blooded, dead creatures," she said, still laughing.

"I guess we're more alike than we care to admit," I said.

She looked up at me and smiled. "You make me feel secure," she whispered.

"I'm glad that I do."

We sat in silence for a few minutes, sipping on our wine and watching the sun set through the windows. When the room darkened significantly, she rose and placed both our glasses on a sideboard.

She returned, straddled my lap and ran her fingers through my hair. "I like you with longer hair," she whispered. "You're the *anti-Lord* when you look like this," she said.

I laughed. "Anti-Lord?"

She gently gyrated on my lap. "You look like you want to eat me. You look rugged. Your pupils have dilated."

"And my cock is hard, Gabriella."

She smiled. "Maybe I need to attend to that first." She gently stood and parted my legs. She lowered to her knees while I unfastened my jeans and raised my hips so she could pull them down a little. My cock sprang free.

"I love the taste of you," she murmured as she closed her mouth on it.

I rested my head back, and my arms on the back of the sofa while she licked, sucked, massaged, and let me fuck her mouth. I moaned at the warmth of her tongue against the head of my cock, of the wetness of her mouth and the strength of her suck. When I thought I was about to come, I pulled her head. She wasn't letting go.

"I'm going to come, Gabriella," I said, breathlessly. She sucked harder.

She swallowed as quickly as she could. A little of my cum seeped from her lips rolling back down my cock. When I was done, she licked me clean.

"Jesus," I said. My heart hammered in my chest and she continued to stroke my balls while I regulated my breathing.

"Fuck me, Alex," she whispered.

I didn't need to be asked twice. I stood abruptly and she fell back on her heels. I stripped while she looked up at me and then I held out my hands. She took them and I pulled her to her feet. I unbuttoned her shirt, sliding it from her shoulders then unzipped her trousers letting them fall to her feet. She stood in a white lace bra and matching panties. I reached around and unclasped the bra. Before she could reach the waistband of her panties to lower them, I grabbed the material at the front and ripped a hole. I stuck two fingers into her pussy while she still stood.

I grabbed her thigh and she placed her foot on the sofa, I angled my body slightly sideways so I could finger her hard. She was so wet and slick, and I could smell her arousal. I removed my fingers and wiped them over her nipples, then lowered my head and sucked, biting down and holding the sensitive nub between my teeth. She gripped my hair, pulling and scratching at my skin.

She moaned when I released her. "Alex," she whispered.

I turned her away from me and then I sat. With her back to my chest, I lowered her. She felt underneath herself and grabbed my cock, before positioning it at her entrance, stroking herself with it. I kissed her back, nipping at her skin until she lowered, and I was inside her. At first we were both still. Her legs were astride mine and she placed her palms on my thighs. Then she moved, rising and lowering herself slowly, too slowly for me. She gripped my knees and leaned forwards. My cock gently stroked her walls. The next time she rose, I mirrored her actions and when she began to lower herself I slammed into her. She gasped and I rose and fell in time with her.

Skin slapped on skin, gasps and moans could be heard from us both. I called out her name, twisting her hair in my hands and forcing her head up. I gripped her hip, mindful still of her bruising, and dug my fingers into her skin. It just wasn't enough.

"Stand up, Gabriella," I said, forcefully. She stilled for a moment, her breathing erratic. She moved from my lap and I watched my wet cock slide from her pussy, strands of her arousal connecting us still.

"I need to see your face," I said. I took her hand and led her upstairs to the bedroom.

I gently pushed her to the bed, and I climbed on, crawling up her body.

"You want vanilla, my Lord?" she said, licking her lips.

"For now," I replied.

Without another word, I pushed into her. She wrapped her legs around mine and I held myself above her. She didn't close her eyes at all. She looked at me all the while I looked at her. She sighed and moaned, she writhed with pleasure. She parted her lips and I lowered my face to kiss her.

I did something I hadn't done, ever. I made love to her.

After that, I fucked her twice more.

CHAPTER TEN

I woke and looked at Gabriella. She was lying naked next to me, her hair fanned around her face. She looked serene. She slept with a gentle smile on her lips and I hoped whatever happy dreams she was having, they featured me.

I slid from the bed in need of a cold drink and walked naked down to the kitchen. I retrieved my phone and our clothes from the living room and left them on the kitchen floor. I was sure I'd find the laundry somewhere.

I opened the fridge and retrieved a bottle of water. The cool air caused my skin to pimple. I took two long swigs of the cold liquid before taking a breath. I shut the fridge door and waited for my eyes to adjust to the darkness again.

I thought about what I'd done. I highly doubted Gabriella understood the significance but I'd never made love to someone before. I loved her, I knew that, but I wasn't about to accept it. I pushed the thought and feelings down. She mentioned how fine she was in her home, how much she loved it and how nice it was to have her own space, or was that me reading between the lines? We danced around subjects, but then the relationship, whatever it was, was still new. Perhaps I was expecting too much.

I took another swig of water and then carried the bottle back to the bedroom.

She mumbled as I climbed in and I gently kissed her lips.

"Cold," she said without opening her eyes.

"Just had a drink of water," I replied.

She opened her eyes slowly to look at me. "Do you have any left?"

I took the bottle from where I'd placed it and handed it to her. She sat up slightly and took a sip.

She smiled at me. "Will you hold me?" she whispered.

When we lay back down, I wrapped her in my arms, and she drifted back to sleep. I stayed awake long enough to see the sun rise and to get my fill of the sunlight bouncing off her delicate features.

I didn't hear anything from Harry for a couple of days and Mackenzie had no joy in getting an answer from the detectives that interviewed Gabriella, either. I went about my day, and Mackenzie and Gabriella about theirs. Each night I spent with Gabriella a dread set in that I was going to have to go home at some point. It was three days later then the subject came up.

"I'm guessing you're going to need to head home at some point, aren't you?" Gabriella asked. I had just left the en suite and she was sitting on the bed.

"I guess so. I'm certainly out of some toiletries," I replied, wondering if that was her asking me to go home. "Perhaps I should do that tomorrow."

She nodded slowly and I felt deflated. Our relationship hadn't taken a normal route, I thought. We'd had sex before we really knew each other, I had her stay with me, then I stayed with her. We hadn't been out on a date for a few days because we were both tired from work. We were like a married couple that had skipped the courting.

"How about I take you for dinner?" I asked.

"Now?"

"Why not?"

She smiled and leapt from the bed. "I'll be ready in fifteen minutes."

The one thing I liked about Gabriella was that she was true to her word. Whether she wore jeans with her hair piled on her head and no make-up, or a ball gown with a full face, it didn't take her long. I guessed her natural beauty aided that.

I called my cousin. "I know it's opening night, but are you fully booked?"

Much to our surprise, Veronica had completed a lot of the internal renovations at the club faster than expected. She had sourced a top-ranking chef and opened the restaurant. Five of the ten speciality bedrooms were complete, and planning was underway for the cottages.

"I'll make space for you. Or you could dine with Mackenzie and me, we have a table."

"You do?"

"We've been...*seeing* a lot of each other lately," she said. Mackenzie hadn't mentioned anything and knowing my cousin, it wouldn't be for dating. She didn't do that.

"I've been teaching him my *likes* and although a reluctant student, he's taken to it like a swan to a lake." She chuckled at the analogy, and I wasn't sure I wanted to know. I ignored it.

"I don't want to gate crash your party, a table for two on our own would be lovely."

"Eight o'clock?"

I confirmed and disconnected the call. I had been invited, as had Gabriella, to the opening of the restaurant and I'd originally declined. I had thought that perhaps Gabriella might like a few nights at home for comfort and safety, I was wrong. I think she had grown restless, maybe even bored. We had great sex, we talked for hours, she slept in my arms, but I wasn't sure it was enough.

That was the driving reason most of my relationships failed—I was never sure I was enough.

"Dress code?" Gabriella shouted from the bathroom.

"Smart," I replied, slipping on a shirt and selecting a tie. I really did have limited clothes at her place, I decided, as I threw a tie to the floor that sported a food stain.

"Wonderful, I have a lovely new red dress to wear," she called back.

I was downstairs when she joined me. I had a glass of cold white wine poured for her and as she walked towards me, my stomach curled in on itself. I stood from the stool I perched on and smiled. She returned the smile and curtseyed, then turned slowly.

"You look divine. I'm going to be all over the place tonight. I'm sure all the men will be watching you," I said.

She patted my cheek and picked up her wine. "There will only be one man taking me home, though, won't there?"

I just didn't know what she wanted; she was full of mixed messages. Half an hour ago I was being encouraged to go home, then I was being told I was taking her home. I parked the thought to one side.

"Where are we going?" she asked.

"It's a surprise. Finish your wine," I said, checking my watch. We had plenty of time but I wanted to show her around before we dined.

A little later, I drove and we chatted. It was silly things, like asking for a reminder to add shampoo to the shopping list, or *did I lock the back door*? *Couply* things.

"Have you spoken to Mackenzie much lately?" I asked.

"No, he's been super busy. Why?" she asked.

"No reason, I just realised we hadn't seen much of him lately."

"I think he might have a lady friend," she said, laughing.

I chuckled, knowing that he did but not necessarily in the dating sense.

She checked her mobile and mentioned a text message from her mother had arrived. She replied and we continued our journey in a comfortable silence.

We had to wait at the gate for it to be opened and the drive to the house was as magnificent as I remember.

"Wow, this is wonderful," she said.

I parked and a valet walked towards us. I announced myself.

"May I take your mobile phones, please?" he said. Gabriella frowned, I handed mine over. "We don't allow any recording devices inside, I'm sorry," he explained as he took her phone. "They'll be safely left with your vehicle."

"How odd," she said as we walked to the main door. It was immediately opened by my cousin in her usual attire.

She held out both hands. "Darling, I'm so thrilled to meet you, finally," Veronica said, ignoring me and taking hold of Gabriella's hands. "I've heard a lot." They air kissed even though it was obvious Gabriella had no clue who she was air kissing.

I laughed. "Gabriella, meet my cousin, Veronica."

"Oh my, why didn't you say? I'm sorry, Veronica, and I'm thrilled to meet you, too. I hope all you've heard is good!"

"I can assure you it is. Now, come on through to the bar. Mackenzie is there. Have a drink before you sit."

Confusion crossed Gabriella's face. I leaned down and whispered in her ear. "I think Veronica is the reason Mackenzie has been a little preoccupied of late."

She turned to smile at me. "Well, they would be a perfect match." She chuckled as she waved at Mackenzie.

He was sitting at the bar, one foot on the stool rung and one on the floor. He nursed a glass of whisky with ice. The room was pretty packed with people. Some stood, some sat in the clusters of seats. All were impeccably dressed. I caught the eye of some that I knew and nodded in greeting. I received some nods in return, and one or two lowering of heads in embarrassment. I laughed.

"Hello, you two. Veronica said you'd be here," Mackenzie said, he extended his arm to me and we shook hands, he kissed Gabriella on the cheek.

"I didn't know about you and Veronica, you naughty pair," she said.

"This is a magnificent building. Show me around?" she said, looking at me.

"What do you want to drink?" Mackenzie asked, she replied with wine and I opted just for sparkling water.

"Be back in a minute," I said, and he nodded.

"Follow me," I said. We met Veronica in the hallway. "I'm just going to show Gabriella around."

She smiled and nodded. "All rooms are vacant until after dinner," she said. "You'll need this master key." She handed me a brass key with a red satin material tassel.

"I'm intrigued," Gabriella said as I guided her to the stairs.

"Downstairs, there is a restaurant, obviously, a library, the bar, Veronica's office, security, and a couple of meeting rooms. Upstairs are playrooms."

She smirked. "Lead the way, my Lord."

I closed in on her. "We are going to use every single one of these rooms over time, do you understand that?"

"I was hoping you'd say that."

I patted her arse and encouraged her to walk ahead of me. I liked the view very much. The first room we came to, I fumbled with the key.

"What's inside?" she whispered.

"I don't know. I haven't been here since before they started to refurb it," I replied.

As the door swung open, we were faced with a room of instruments and my cock twitched. There was a rack with paddles and whips, belts and restraints. One wall had various hooks and pulleys that clanked as she ran her hands over them. There was a bench in the middle of the room, padded with black leather, each of its legs had hooks.

"Oh, this looks fun," Gabriella said, turning to me. She did the stance, the bent knee with her hand on her hip, shoulders slightly turned, and head cocked to one side. It was her challenge stance.

"I think we could have a lot of fun in here," I said, reaching for a paddle and gently slapping it against my hand. "Sadly, not tonight. I didn't book a room."

She pouted theatrically. "Damn," she said. I laughed and replaced the paddle.

The next room was the wet playroom. Although there was a bed to one side with satin sheets, the flooring and halfway up the walls were covered in a waterproof material. To the other side was what resembled an above ground swimming pool although shallow.

Gabriella walked to it. "Don't tell me, mud play," she said, and I laughed.

"Could be. Or food, or...whatever."

"Mmm, not sure about this room. Feels like a birthing pool in a maternity ward."

"Urgh, yeah, let's move on."

"Have you ever thought about children, Alex?" she asked as I locked that room and moved to the next.

"No. Now, are you ready for this one? I think I know what this is," I said, distracted by the thought of the interior and not concentrating on her question.

"Oh, I certainly like this one," she said.

We had walked into a suite set up for voyeurism. There was a one-way glass wall and we could see into the neighbouring room. The one in which we stood had a large bed and two wingback chairs facing the glass. The one through the glass had a large bed, a bench, a cupboard that I knew would store toys and lubricants—every room had that—and a St. Andrews Cross.

Gabriella walked closer to the glass and stared. "Will you show me that one day?" she asked quietly.

"Show or..." I tailed off.

She took a deep breath. "Tie me to it."

I stepped close behind her, placing my hands on the glass at either side of her head. "I'll show you everything. I want to *do* everything with you." I breathed out the words. She leaned back against me.

She didn't reply but we left the upstairs. I had an uncomfortable walk back, my hard cock rubbing against my trousers.

"I recognise a few people in here." Gabriella subtly glanced around.

"We've been building up a new clientele," Mackenzie said, sliding our drinks towards us.

Veronica, who stood beside Mackenzie and placed her hand on his shoulder, soon joined us in a toast. He didn't offer her his stool, which I thought rather ungentlemanly, until I realised; just looking at her body language suggested she'd moved into a submissive role with him. I chuckled into my glass as I took a sip of water and Mackenzie gave me a knowing look.

We were called through to dinner at our set time and although we went our separate ways, our tables weren't that far apart. I pulled out Gabriella's chair for her and she sat.

"Veronica has done a wonderful job here, I know I keep saying that, but this is going to make bank, Alex, for sure." She flicked open her napkin and placed it on her lap.

"At thirty grand a year membership, I'm sure it will," I replied, giving her a wink.

"No way?"

"Keeps the riff-raff out," I said.

A bottle of champagne was cooling beside the table and I poured us both a glass opting not to wait for someone else to do it. The restaurant, although it had waiting staff, obviously, was also about intimacy. Plants and objects such as statues and a fountain were strategically placed to give privacy to the clients. There was no table for more than two occupants. Veronica had said it was to keep the noise level to a minimum.

"I'm so glad you decided on this," Gabriella said. "I was going a little stir-crazy indoors."

"In what way?" I asked.

"I know this might seem silly but knowing the attacker might have my address has somewhat soured the house for me."

I wasn't sure I'd feel the same way but nodded anyway. "You are more than welcome to stay with me," I offered.

She placed her hand over mine. "I know I'm welcome anytime but in spite of what I just said I feel I need to stay in my home alone, just to get over this silliness."

I breathed a sigh of relief at that point. She wasn't asking me to leave because she didn't want me there, but so she could re-establish herself in the house and shrug the fear from her shoulders.

"I can totally get that. I just want you to do whatever it is that you want and to feel safe doing it."

"That's why I—" She was interrupted by a waiter with menus.

She never finished her sentence, instead we discussed the food options, marvelling at some of the choices. I had no doubts the restaurant would achieve Michelin stars at some point, if one could be given to a *club* of its type.

We placed our orders and our chat moved to our families. Gabriella was keen to revisit my mother and showed concern when I'd said the police didn't seem to have much to go on where the deception was concerned. We continued to chat through three courses of mouth-watering food.

We drank the champagne and moved on to a nice red. I kept my intake to a minimum knowing I had to drive. At some point we noticed the restaurant start to empty. We also saw how, when the bill was presented in a black leather folder, so was a key with a coloured tassel. Couples headed off to their respective rooms.

"Lucky people," Gabriella said, laughing gently.

I signed our cheque and, reluctantly, led Gabriella to the hallway. "We didn't say goodbye to Mackenzie," she said.

"He seemed to have snuck off, didn't you notice his empty table?" I laughed.

She shook her head, then took my hand. My car was ready, the engine running and on each seat were our phones.

The valet stood beside the passenger door. "Thank you for visiting, Ms. Collingsworth, Lord Duchoveny," he said.

I slipped him a tip while he helped Gabriella into her seat then walked around the car to mine.

She sighed as she settled back and reached over to place her hand on my thigh. "I've had a lovely evening, thank you, Alex," she said.

"There is no need to thank me. Although you keep rubbing your fingers in that exact spot if you want," I said.

As she'd slid her hand to my thigh, her fingers just brushed my stiffening cock.

She chuckled and cupped the bulge, squeezing gently. "You keep your eyes on the road, my Lord," she said, reaching over to undo my trousers. She freed my cock and wrapped one hand around it.

I took in a deep breath as she slid her hand up and down while I drove. The faster she moved, the harder it was to concentrate, moreso when she lowered her head and took me in her mouth.

"Jesus, Gabriella," I hissed out.

I raised my hips causing my foot to lower slightly on the accelerator. Thankfully, we were on a rather empty motorway and I laughed as a camera flashed, wondering what image would be sent through with my speeding fine.

She released my cock from her mouth and whispered, "Find somewhere to pull over."

I immediately indicated and pulled into the left-hand lane. Whatever the next junction was, I was taking it.

It took another five minutes to pull off the motorway, and then find a country lane with an entrance to a field that offered enough shielding. I put the car in park as she unclipped both our seat belts and straddled me. I pushed my seat back as far as I could. She pulled her panties to one side and without any words, guided my cock inside her.

"I've never fucked in a Bentley before," she said, moaning at the same time.

"There's a first time for everything."

She rose and fell. I met her halfway. She sunk her teeth into the side of my neck and gripped my hair with her hands. I held her hips guiding the pace, moaning along with her. The scent of sex and arousal filled the car and that hardened me more.

"Oh, my God, Alex." Gabriella moaned out the words

as she came. I felt her muscles contract and I let go too. I'd been trying so desperately to hold back, wanting her to orgasm first.

She leaned her head on my shoulder and kissed my neck. "That's the first car sex I've ever had. Can you believe that?"

"Well, my Lady, it's a first for me too," I replied.

Getting back into her seat wasn't as easy or as gracious as it had been when she'd managed to leave it. She laughed and her cheeks reddened particularly when I handed her a tissue from the side pocket to wipe the seat with.

"Although I don't care if you leave your mark on my calf leather seat, this is going in for a service tomorrow."

"You make me sound like a tomcat," she said, laughing some more.

I reversed the car from the farm track, and we managed to find our way back to the motorway. I gently nudged Gabriella awake when we pulled up outside her house.

Sleepily, Gabriella climbed the stair to the bedroom while I headed to the kitchen for a cup of coffee. I was still buzzing and although the caffeine was most certainly not needed, it was welcome. It was then I noticed a missed call and a text message from Harry.

Think I might need a meeting with you and Mackenzie Miller. Can you arrange somewhere discrete?

Despite the time, I texted back.

I can. I'll message details tomorrow.

I puzzled on what it could be that he wanted to meet about and assumed it had something to do with Gabriella's mugging. She hadn't been invited to the meeting, so I wondered if he wanted to discuss the reasons for the detective's questions. I sipped my drink as unease washed over me. The coffee gave me heart palpations; at least I was blaming the caffeine.

I headed up to the bedroom to find Gabriella asleep and curled up on her side. I undressed and quickly showered, then joined her. She snuggled into me, pushing one of her legs between mine.

I didn't sleep well at all. I tossed and turned which disturbed Gabriella, so I decided to get up and dressed. I packed all my things and took them downstairs ready to send to the dry cleaners. Having found a pad and pen in a utility drawer, I left Gabriella a note.

Good morning, my beautiful.

I've left early for a meeting and taken my things for cleaning. Call me when you wake up. And, Gabriella, thank you. It's been wonderful to stay with you, but I know you need a little space to get yourself back in love with your home. Last night's car sex – I'm assuming you don't have a cleaner who likes to read notes, if you do, hi - was mind blowing.

Speak soon, Alex.

It wasn't quite dawn when I backed my car from her drive.

CHAPTER ELEVEN

"Morning, so where is this meeting being held?" Mackenzie asked, as he took a seat. I had been waiting for him in a coffee shop not far from the offices.

"Sandler and Sons. No one is going to bother us there," I added.

Sandler and Sons was a wine producer in London. I had taken Gabriella there and it was where I stored my investment wines. I'd called to see if I could book a tasting room, without the tasting, for a private meeting. It had been agreed. Coffee would be provided at an exorbitant cost, but it was always paid. If ever there was a need for a private venue they could offer it. They had a back door and tight, reliable security.

Harry was a fan, and clearly a member since he was there before us. He rose from a chair and walked, holding out his hand. Mackenzie shook it first, then I.

"Chaps, we've had a rather interesting development. I've kept this quiet for the moment, otherwise we're going to have all sorts of agencies over us. What do you know about this Jeremy Daughton you told me about?" he asked, addressing me.

"Not a thing. Stanton thought I might want to take him on as a client. I declined, obviously," I replied. Mackenzie looked at me and I couldn't remember if I'd told him, so I recalled my meeting with Stanton at the club.

"Have you heard of the name?" Harry asked Mackenzie. He shook his head.

"How about André Kuznetsov?"

I looked at Mackenzie who was glancing at me. "I know that name, never met him, though. He was a 'name' at Lloyds until the government got involved with investigating Russian Mafia money," I said.

"He also owned shares in Trymast before I bought him out," Mackenzie added.

"Daughton and Kuznetsov are one and the same. Can I ask, was the buyout a friendly one?" Harry asked Mackenzie.

"Not initially. I bought up shares until I was the majority shareholder then went for the others. I believe his stock was minimal and he had a broker deal with me. He didn't put up much of a fight, to be honest."

"So, you took Trymast from him, and you lost him money at Lloyds," Harry said, looking between us.

"*I* didn't technically lose *him* money. Everyone lost money," I said, hoping we'd moved past the *who brought down the largest insurance financial institution in the city* thing.

"What has this to do with Gabriella, or the stolen painting?" Mackenzie asked.

Harry pursed his lips briefly. "I'm not entirely sure

other than, word on the street is that he's pissed off with both of you, and he does collect art."

"Would he have gone to all that trouble to have a man move into an apartment to befriend my mother, and then steal her painting? Or have someone mug Gabriella in the street?" I wasn't sure that the fact we both knew the same individual could be the connecting factor to the crimes.

"It could be if the last sighting of Kuznetsov was in Dominican Republic, which just so happened to be the last sighting of Duncan Wilson," Harry said.

I frowned, still not convinced on the connection.

"Where does that leave us, Harry?" Mackenzie asked.

"There appears to be a rather secret investigation into Kuznetsov's investments and business dealings in the UK right now. Someone, and it was probably Stanton, has let word out that you both know André. The Russians and a military contract don't mix well in the upper echelons," he said, and then laughed.

"Oh, I don't know, Harry. I'm sure there are a lot of Russians controlling the upper echelons whether they want that or not. My biggest question, why Gabriella as a target?" I asked.

He shook his head. "That, I haven't gotten to the bottom of. I wonder if it's a little scare tactic, perhaps. You turned down his offer to invest for him. Your mother had a lovely piece of art valued at what, a million? How much did he lose at Lloyds?"

"A million," I said, slowly.

"This is multi-faceted then?" Mackenzie asked.

Harry shrugged. "It could be connected, it might not. All I do know is, you had a meeting, a fact-finding meeting, and facts weren't found so questions are being asked to discover if you both know André more than you're letting on." He looked at his watch and then stood. "Enough surreptitious meetings, I have a real job to do." He gave me a nod and shook Mackenzie's hand. "Don't worry, I'll get to the bottom of it. I owe Alex this."

Once Harry had left the room Mackenzie asked, "How straight is he?"

"As an arrow, but willing to bend the curve to get where he wants to be," I replied.

Mackenzie nodded. "Do we think Gabriella is in any danger?"

"I don't know. If she was I'm certain it wouldn't have just been a bag they snatched."

Mackenzie and I finished our coffee and walked out into the street. "Did you ever meet this Russian guy before Stanton introduced you to him?" Mackenzie asked.

"No, there were thousands of Lloyds names. Everyone lost their money and it was a few years ago now. I can't see it as a strong enough connection. It has to be coincidence. First, why wait this long? Second, how on earth would he know my mother had a Van Gogh and then go to all the trouble of having someone move in to befriend her and then steal it? Doesn't make sense to me, to be honest."

"And if he was adamant about keeping his Trymast shares, he would have fought for them."

"There's more to this than we know, for sure," I said.

We headed back to the office and I took a call from Gabriella. "Good morning, have you just got up?" I asked, and then checked my watch.

"I've been up a little while. I laughed at your note and no, I don't have help. I missed you when I woke," she said, quietly.

"Same. Mackenzie and I are just heading into the office," I said, giving an excuse not to be *mushy* over the phone. "What are your plans today?" I asked.

She told me she had a series of meetings that would keep her out of the office all day, but she was using a pool car to get around. I asked her to check in with me every couple of hours.

She laughed and agreed. "You really are my knight in shining armour, aren't you?"

"Please, just do it, otherwise I'll have to come looking for you. And that won't be pleasant," I lowered my voice, trying to whisper. Mackenzie sniggered beside me.

"Is he with you now? Did you just say that in front of him? Oh my God, Alex," she said, giggling.

"Just call me, okay? I don't do worry very well."

She promised she would, and we disconnected the call.

"How's that going?" Mackenzie asked.

"What part?" I sighed in response.

"The, *getting her to do what you want* part. Or the, *are we in a relationship* part?"

I laughed. "You know her so well, you tell me. I don't know, she's so independent that I struggle with that. I've never met anyone like her before. As for *are we in a relationship*, I don't know, Mackenzie, I can't tell." I stopped to face him.

"She thinks you are, so if you're not, you ought to tell her that," he said. His voice was kind but firm, and I appreciated that.

"What happens when she leaves?" I asked, not looking at him, but over his shoulder.

"Leaves for where?"

"Home. What happens when she leaves for home and I've fallen for her?"

He frowned and there was a look of incredulity in his eyes. "She won't. Or you go with her. Are you holding back because you think she's going to leave?"

"Does she think I'm holding back?"

He shook his head, his exasperation showing. "I don't know. Jesus, Alex, you Brits sure are complicated. Just go with the flow *Old Chum* and see what happens. She certainly hasn't mentioned any plans to return home anytime soon."

Although I was pleased with that knowledge, I still had the thought stuck inside my mind and I knew it both held me back and would be to my detriment.

"You've been together a few months now, maybe it's time to sit and have a chat about where you're going," he said. He checked his watch and then raised his hand for a taxi. "In the meantime, I have a session with your cousin." He grinned and stepped out into the traffic whistling as if he was on Broadway.

I rolled my eyes and shook my head. "Catch up later," I said, and walked off. I knew there was a taxi rank just around the corner, which is why all the drivers were ignoring Mackenzie. I would make a point to wave to him as I drove past.

We were busy for the next few days; contracts needed to be renewed for not just employment, but Mackenzie and I were off to the Ministry of Defence for numerous meetings. It was arduous being surrounded by *pompous shits*, as

Mackenzie called them, but that was when my title could be used. I knew people, bosses of bosses and colleagues. It always paid to ask after people when meetings were not necessarily going my way. After a tiresome week, we walked away not only with the existing contract, but a new one for communications equipment for battle ships.

"I haven't seen you in days," Gabriella said when I answered her call. She drew out the word, *days*.

"I know. It's been one of those weeks so far. How are you doing at home?" I asked. I wasn't sure how long she wanted her time alone to reconnect with her house.

"All fine here," she replied. She then asked how our meetings went and squealed when I told her we had a contract renewal.

The military contract wasn't just a lucrative one, but it opened doors to sell the same equipment to other countries, and that was where we wanted to head.

"What are you doing now?" I asked.

"Weeding the garden so don't be starting your naughty chat," she said, and then laughed.

"Sounds dirty, and I like dirty," I replied. "I missed you this week."

She quietened. "You can come on over for dinner if you like."

"I'd like that. Shall I bring dessert?" I asked.

"Yourself, you're my dessert and I feel like feasting," she replied and I could hear the lick of her lips.

"Now who's piling on the dirty talk?"

She chuckled and I heard her wince a little. "Are you okay?" I asked.

"Just trying to stand after kneeling for so long. I need more practice," she replied. I began to speak but she stopped me. "Before you say it, Lord Duchoveny, I have many ways of practicing being on my knees, you've only seen one. I'll see you after work."

She cut off the call before I could comment again, and I laughed all the way back to my office.

I heard a familiar voice say, "Someone's happy." And I turned to see Mary.

"I sure am, Mary. It's a fine day, work is great, and you're here to make me smile," I said, bowing to her.

"Get away with ya. Where's Mackenzie? I've been trying to call him," she said as she dumped some files on my desk.

"Has a meeting with a new company he wants to buy," I said, wondering why he hadn't just told her that. Not doing so could cause him endless hours of grief. I felt for her husband, should she have one.

"Bloody bitch of an ex-wife of his been on the phone," she said.

By then, we had all encountered Addison and her demands to speak to Mackenzie. They had been divorced for years but every now and again, she made a trip to the UK, I had no idea why. She wasn't welcomed by him, but he did seem to entertain her when necessary. It reminded me that I wanted to ask him why.

"What did she want?" I asked.

Mary shrugged her shoulders. "Didn't ask, I just told her to phone his *cell*. She asked for his number and I said I didn't have it." She cackled rather than laughed and it reminded me of a character from a Shakespeare play, the title of which we must never mention.

"These are for me?" I asked, picking up the files.

"I don't make a habit of just chucking files all over the place, eejit," she said, and then walked off.

"Did she see me?" I turned to see Mackenzie hiding behind a divider between desks.

I tilted my head. "What the fuck are you doing?"

"Hiding," he said, and then laughed.

"Why?"

"Because it annoys her. What did she say about Addison?"

"Only that your *bloody bitch of an ex-wife* wanted to speak to you. Now, if you have nothing to do, you can tell me why I have these files. If not, I'm busy," I said, moving behind my desk and sitting down.

He smiled as he walked into my office. "Those are a brief overview of all my businesses, mostly the ones in the States."

"Interesting, thank you. I'll take them home for reading, although not tonight. Tonight, I'm going to spend time with Gabriella."

"I won't expect you in early tomorrow, then," he said with a wave over his shoulder, he left.

"Don't piss Mary off," I shouted after him. He laughed, as did Carolyn.

"Carolyn," I called out, she bustled into my office with her pad and pen. "I don't usually ask for this kind of thing, but I could do with a really nice bouquet of flowers."

"Leave it to me. Credit card?" she said, holding out her hand.

I fished in my wallet and told her the code. I had absolutely no doubt it wouldn't be abused; in the short time she was working for me, Carolyn had become invaluable.

Later, when I drove up to Gabriella's house, she was at

the door. She smiled as I exited the car with the flowers and gently kissed my lips when I handed them over.

"They're gorgeous. I really ought to give you a key," she said, as she walked back towards the kitchen.

"That would make us grown-ups wouldn't it?" I asked in a light-hearted tone as I followed.

"No, it would mean I could continue to stir this risotto without having to worry it's burned." She placed the flowers on the counter and continued to stir the rice. She added more wine, then handed me the bottle. "Could you pour?"

I found two glasses, handed her a filled one, and then sat at the kitchen table. "How was your day?" I asked.

While she bustled around making a salad and fresh garlic bread, she told me about her day. She seemed excited by the new company Mackenzie was looking into; although she hadn't met any of the staff yet, she had met the owner, Pamela, so she told me.

"Initially, Mackenzie was going to buy shares, but I convinced him to buy the company. It might make a nice fit within Trymast," she said.

"Okay, and I'll get to know about this, when?" I teased.

"I'm telling you now. I thought I'd share my thoughts with you over dinner and see what you think?" She waved a wooden spoon at me and I ducked as a piece of risotto flew my way.

As daft as it was, I still found it a little *daunting* that she was, technically, my boss even though she had very little to do with Trymast. I also believed her choice to stay out of Trymast was because we had a relationship going on.

"Can you take these?" she said, and I left the table to collect dishes.

"This smells wonderful, thank you," I said, laying them on the table.

She sat beside me and we ate, chatting about our days before she talked about this company she had mentioned.

"Would it be terrible to tell you that I found a female CEO strange?

"Why is that strange?"

"I guess I don't see that so often in the UK."

I had to think of all the companies I'd had dealings with and whether there were any females at the top of the ladder, and then I agreed with her. There weren't many, and that was a shame.

"So, you think it might blend in well with Trymast?" I asked.

She then proceeded to give her analysis and overview. She set her fork down after her explanation and finishing her meal then sat back in her chair and smiled at me.

"You have a great business head," I said.

"It's nice to be able to share discussions like this with you."

"Can't you do that with Mackenzie?" I asked.

Her smile slipped a little. "I don't seem to get much time with him nowadays. One day we were inseparable, but now we're ships passing in the night." Sadness laced her voice.

"Call him, invite him out for a meal. Go to the theatre or see a movie," I said.

"I should do," she replied.

"But?"

"I don't know. We get enough bad press without me

being seen on your arm one evening then his the next," she said.

I sat back and eyed her with awe. "Gabriella, you surprise me. Why on earth do you care what someone else thinks? We know the facts. He's your best friend, call him, make a date."

She chuckled. "I'll text. I don't know what nasty he's up to right now." She slid from her chair and cleared the dishes.

I didn't stay that night as I had no clean clothes. Instead, we sat on her terrace with her wrapped in a blanket as we drank coffee and chatted. It was nice, relaxing, but equally, it was frustrating.

"I best be heading home," I said, checking my watch.

She smiled sadly. "Let's spend the weekend together, please?"

"Absolutely. I look forward to that."

As I walked to the front door, she asked me to wait. She rifled around in a drawer in her kitchen and presented me with a key. Although a small gesture, it felt significant.

She stood in the doorway and I faced her. She had her arms wrapped around her body to ward off the chill. I wrapped mine around her and held her close.

"We fit so well, don't we?" she said.

She raised her face and I kissed her goodnight. I twisted the key in my hand as I walked to my car and I thought about her the whole journey home.

I had pulled into my car park when my mobile rang. I frowned at the unknown caller displayed and noted the time was just gone midnight. "Hello?"

"Alex, can you hear me? The line is cracking up." I didn't recognise the voice at all.

"I can hear you. Who is this?"

"Duncan. Please, don't put the phone down. I need to speak to you."

"You need to tell me what the fuck you've done with my mother's painting!" I shouted down the phone as I felt my face flush with rage.

"Her painting is with Sotheby's," he said, and it was clear there was confusion in his voice. "They were meant to contact her."

"You stole her painting," I said, although even I could hear the sentence was said without conviction.

"No, I didn't. Is that what you think?"

"What the fuck are you calling me for then?" I demanded.

"Sure, I've done some stupid things in my life, but stealing your mother's painting isn't one of them. I am genuinely fond of her and I was ringing because I wanted the opportunity to explain."

"First, how did you get this number? Second, explain what? You took her painting; she didn't see you again."

"She gave me your card, that's how I got your number. I took her painting on her insistence of having it re-valued for insurance purposes, and I happened to be going to London that day. She rang Sotheby's and made the arrangements. She isn't answering her phone to me."

"Explain where you went, then," I said, not trusting him but also, not trusting that my mother hadn't done that, either.

"America, she knew I was leaving but I did say when I returned, I'd make contact and I've returned." A crackling noise obscured the rest of his sentence and the line went dead.

"What the fuck are you on about, Duncan?" I whispered as I entered the lift.

I called Mackenzie. "I've had the strangest conversation. The art thief rang me, he might not be a theft after all."

"You up for a late-night drink?" he asked.

"Sure, swing on by. You can stay here if it gets too late," I said. I disconnected the call and walked into my apartment.

Mackenzie was buzzing at the front door of my building within a half hour of our call. I let him in and set the coffee machine to pour. I also grabbed a decanter of whisky and two cut glass tumblers. By the time I'd placed those on the coffee table, he was at the apartment door.

"Evening," he said, as I let him in. "Did you have a good one?"

"Lovely, you?"

"Entertaining," he said, and then laughed. "What did the art thief say?"

I repeated what Duncan had said, and as I did, I scrolled through my phone to see if his number had recorded. Annoyingly, it hadn't.

"What does your gut tell you?" Mackenzie asked.

I paused for a moment, sighed, and ran my hand over my day-old stubble. "He's telling the truth. He genuinely seemed confused when I talked about him stealing the painting and then disappearing."

I was actually reluctant to admit that thought to myself, but something was telling me he was being straight up. I poured the whisky before I spoke again.

"Did you call Sotheby's?" he asked, and I shook my head. I'd call them first thing. All I hoped was that the insurance company hadn't processed the theft. I didn't want them owning the painting.

We sipped our drinks and I poured more.

"So we're left with the government thinking we have a connection to a Russian mafia chap who wants to launder money with me and is pissed off that you won't let him have shares in a company that has a secret government contract," I said.

He raised his glass to me. "I think that about sums it up."

We both laughed and got drunk.

Mackenzie was long gone by the time I finally woke. He'd left a text message to thank me for the overnight stay and that he'd call later that morning. Before I left for the office, I remembered the call to my mother.

"Hi, Mother, just a quick question if I may? Have Sotheby's contacted you at all?"

"No, why?"

"Because that is where Duncan said he took the painting."

"You've spoken to him?"

"Yes, he's been trying to contact you. Do you remember a conversation where you might have suggested a re-valuation?"

"Oh, darling, I can't remember. I've accused him of theft, called the police! What if I've got it all wrong?"

"Leave it with me, let me see what I can find out."

I said goodbye and then googled Sotheby's for a telephone number. After being given the runaround for ten minutes and demanding to speak to the CEO, it was finally confirmed that, yes, the painting was indeed in their care.

"I want it returned immediately," I said.

I got the expected, *need to prove ownership*, and all that, even though they had it in my mother's name. I became frustrated and promised a visit. I also texted my mother and asked her to call them, explain that she had asked her son to deal with the painting on her behalf. Whether she had taken in everything I said, was another matter. She was just super pleased to know the painting wasn't stolen and her friend, as she referred to him again, wasn't a con man.

I had just about sat at my desk when two detectives showed up at reception. A call came through to my office to let me know they wanted to chat to me. Not knowing why, I decided to invite them to the boardroom upstairs. I took the stairs up and they were shown to the lift.

I met them on the upper floor. "Gentlemen, how may I be of help?" I asked as they walked from the lift.

"Is there somewhere we can talk?" one asked, looking around.

"Right here," I said, and walked to the centre of the room. I indicated to one of the many chairs around a highly polished walnut table.

"I wondered if we'd be able to speak in private," the other said, looking at Mary. She was staring at her monitor and appeared to be humming.

"Mary, do you have your headphones in?" I asked. She ignored me. I smiled at the detectives. "Now before we start, shall we exchange names and badge numbers?" I was dutifully given business cards and also shown ID after requesting it. "Please, take a seat." I had purposely not suggested refreshments.

Detective Burrows started. "Can I ask where you were between the hours of two and three this morning?"

"Why?"

"We need to know your whereabouts, Lord Duchoveny, if you please," he replied. He was trying to be polite, for sure.

"In bed. Now what is this concerning?"

"Do you have anyone that could collaborate that?"

"Mackenzie Miller, we spent the night—" Before I could finish, Mary spluttered. We all looked over. She was still staring at her monitor but held a bottle of water in her hand.

"We spent the night talking and drinking, he stayed in my spare room. Now, I'll ask one more time before I have you removed. What is this about?"

"Harry Denmark was found drowned last night. We are trying to trace his movements prior to his death," Detective Millward added.

"He's what?"

"Dead. His body was found in the Thames."

"Jesus," I said, genuinely stunned. I slumped against the table. "What happened to him?" I asked.

"We're awaiting reports, obviously, but at the moment we are treating it as suspicious."

"And that's why you wanted to know where I was last night?" I asked, starting to get angry. "Why would I be connected to the death of Harry Denmark?"

"We know that you met him recently, and we also know that you may have been working with him in an operation that he was not authorised to undertake. What is your connection with Jeremy Daughton?"

"I don't have a connection with Jeremy Daughton and right now you are going to leave my office and return when I have a legal presence."

"You met him the other night," I was told. The only person that could have told them was Stanton.

"You think you need a lawyer for an informal chat?" Burrows asked.

"I think I need a lawyer for an accusation, however informal, that I may be involved with the death of the Chief of Police."

They looked at each other. I stood and buttoned up my jacket. I wasn't about to speak one more word to them. After a minute or two, they walked to the lift. I watched them leave.

"Get that?" I asked.

"Every word. Who you been bumping off then?" Mary asked. She held up a Dictaphone that she'd recorded the conversation with.

"I haven't *bumped off* anyone."

"Shame, getting a bit boring around here at the moment. I'm all on my own up here and I've caught up on all my soaps." She pointed to the screen paused during an episode of Coronation Street.

"I'll be back later," I said. "And thanks, Mary, you're a gem."

"I better get a bonus for this. I might be implicated in something. You know Jack the Ripper was a Lord, don't ya?" she shouted across the room as I walked away.

"I know. I believe my grandfather warned his father not to take the murder thing too far, but he wouldn't listen." Her laughter followed me. I wasn't laughing, though; I was worried.

I met Mackenzie at his house half an hour later. I recalled the meeting and we sat nursing a coffee.

"So, they think someone killed Harry? But why ask us, or rather, you?" he said.

"They must think it has something to do with André stroke Jeremy. *Someone* told them I'd met with him, and that someone could only be Veronica or Stanton. I'd trust Veronica with my life. That means Stanton."

I knew a lot about Stanton, everyone in our 'circle' did. It wouldn't have surprised me in the least to discover he was a snitch, he'd been on the edge of criminality for years and got away with it.

"Let's think. What has Harry stumbled on that could have gotten him killed?" Mackenzie asked.

"He knew whatsit and whatsit were the same person. He knew he was connected to laundering, but then that wouldn't take a genius to work out. He knew he had shares in Trymast and that now he doesn't. He also knew that our names had come up in an investigation way above his pay grade..." I paused. "Either he had found something else out or *they* think he has."

"Must be highly embarrassing for the government to learn that the Russian mafia had access to their military contracts. Not that I can really see what information they could gain from them that would give an advantage," Mackenzie said.

"Would to your competitors, though, wouldn't it? Who else was pitching for that contract?"

"I don't know. We never get told that kind of information. Maybe that's what Harry stumbled on."

We were interrupted by a phone call. I glanced at my mobile. "It's Gabriella," I said, whispering as if she could hear us.

"Hello, how are you?" I asked when I answered. She went on to explain about her morning and that she was tired and heading home. She wanted me to know in case I was trying to contact her. A thought popped into my head. "Can you remember what work documents you had in your bag when it was snatched?"

"That's rather random, Alex. Is everything okay?"

"Yes, it really has just popped into my head."

"A boring Health and Safety policy for the factory floor. I wanted it updated. Honestly, Alex, I can't tell you what a sweatshop that place was. I keep meaning to talk to Mackenzie about it, get rid of it. I don't think it's a company we want on board anymore."

"Okay, how about I call you a little later?" We said goodbye and left it at that. I turned to Mackenzie. "That factory has nothing to do with Trymast, does it?"

"It's where they manufacturer some of the components for antennas, why?" Mackenzie answered.

"What if someone snatched her bag assuming they'd find some interesting documents in there?"

"Wouldn't they just break into the office? Why assume a woman walking up the street would have classified information in her handbag?" he said.

"Not just any old woman, *our* woman leaving a company tied to Trymast."

Mackenzie laughed. "You have been watching way too much television. Let's just concentrate on why Harry was floating in the Thames and why the police think we might be connected to it for now. In the meantime, maybe use your *old boy* network to ask some more questions."

"I know we're having a chuckle about this, but I am worried. I'd like to be able to call Ellenor, Harry's wife, but I don't have her number."

"Let's just see how it pans out. They haven't contacted me yet, and let's see what we can find out about Stanton. We know we can discredit him in any way we need to. If this blows up more, we'll just leak some photographs. Have you seen them?" he asked.

"No, maybe we should take a trip over and look," I suggested. Mackenzie nodded his head slowly. I added, "Also, take my girlfriend out on a date, she's missing you."

He nodded as if it was the most normal statement to make but if anyone heard us, I'm sure we would have received strange looks.

"Holy shit," I said, as Veronica laid photographs on the table.

Spread across the polished wooden desk were images of a woman that had been beaten black and blue. Both eyes were virtually closed, she had hand marks around her neck, blood ran from her nose and from a busted lip.

There was a handwritten statement with a typed version signed by the woman and Veronica. In addition, there was a videotape, copies of which had been made, of Stanton beating her during sex and until security rushed into the room and pulled him off her. There were also images of Stanton and Daughton in compromising positions with many other women.

"Did she press charges?" I asked.

Veronica nodded. "She tried, surprisingly. I thought she might balk at the idea. Of course, it wasn't investigated properly, and he wasn't charged with anything. He said that it was consensual violent sex!"

"Consensual?" I asked, astounded.

She nodded and then gently shook her head. "He scarred her for life, Alex. As much as I hated using her, and she gave me permission to ruin him when possible, those items have been invaluable."

"Why is he allowed here?" Mackenzie asked. The anger in his voice was electric, his jaw was rigid, and his eyes had darkened.

"He isn't now. But I don't know. I liked having that little bit of control over him, I guess. He's ruined so many lives, Mackenzie, caused so much pain to both Alex's family and mine. Keeping him close was a reminder that I had something on him."

"And could have gotten you floating on the Thames too," he said, practically growling the words. She recoiled and her face paled as she nodded slowly. Mackenzie held out his hand. "Give them to me, Veronica. I don't want them here where you can be harmed. I'll make sure it's known that I have them."

She gathered up all the documents, replaced them in the ziplock folder and handed it over. "I'm not stupid. Those items aren't left lying around. I think it highly likely anyone could steal them from me," she said, quietly. She *peeked* up at him.

I frowned at her. Where were her balls? And then it dawned on me. The *visits* I knew were sexual, of course, but she was his sub and she was trying to challenge him.

"In the meantime, you get tortured. We'll take them," I said.

Mackenzie and I left; he hadn't said a word to her although I had kissed her goodbye.

"Can we keep the sex out of it next time?" I asked as I sat behind the steering wheel.

Mackenzie turned sharply towards me. "Huh?"

"The game, can we keep that out of this situation. She's my cousin, you're my friend, we're being accused of murder, potentially, and we have evidence to bury Stanton who may, or may not, be the one that set us up. I don't think we need to add a Dom and sub scene in as well."

"I..." He had the grace to look a little embarrassed.

"You have no shame, do you?" I said, driving away from the house, and laughing.

"Sorry," he said, shrugging his shoulders. "Although I think our *relationship* is coming to an end. I don't think I'm up for her next level of play. There's someone else better suited. I've told her that. It was fun while it lasted, I want you to know, I very much respect her, and we've never actually had penetrative sex, just—"

I held up my hand, not wanting the details. I fully understood what he meant, of course "Shall we make a call?" I asked, and he nodded.

"Hello, old boy," I said brightly when Stanton answered his phone. He stammered through a greeting and I continued, "I'm pleased to receive your notification that my father's debt has been paid in full. Maybe we need to chat about the other people you've strangled over the years."

"Business is business, old chap. I didn't put a noose around their necks, did I?"

"Ah, yes, talking of necks. I have some rather unflattering photographs in my possession. They're not at the club anymore. They're rather compromising, Stanton."

"You bastard. How much do you want for them?" If we had been face to face I could imagine being covered in spittle such was the force of his words.

"Nothing. In fact, I've handed them to a friend. I'm not sure you've met Mackenzie Miller, have you?"

There was a long pause where Stanton didn't speak. "What do you both want?" he asked eventually. "I assume he is there with you?"

Mackenzie answered him, "I am. *We* want nothing, but you're going to close your loan shark operation down, write off all debt and keep your mouth shut from now on." Stanton cut off the call without answering.

"How bloody rude," I said, focussing on the road ahead.

CHAPTER TWELVE

When we arrived back in London it looked like a posse had been formed.

"Where have you been?" Gabriella asked. "We've been trying to contact you for over an hour."

I checked my phone to see that I had it on silent and there were three missed calls, two voicemails and two text messages.

Mary stood with her arms folded and Carolyn was smiling as if she had nothing to do with anything.

"Jesus," Mackenzie said.

"Don't you bring the Lord's name into this," Mary said, and I tried hard not to laugh. I highly doubted she was religious at all.

Mackenzie pulled at his collar. "We've been at a meeting, what's so urgent?" he asked.

"The police are here, been waiting for bloody ages and I can't get rid of the buggers," Mary said.

"Alex, what's going on?" Gabriella asked. Her brow was furrowed with worry.

"A misunderstanding," I replied. I looked at Mackenzie. "Shall we?"

Carolyn walked back to her desk and the four of us made our way upstairs. As the lift doors opened, we could see the two policeman—the same two that had visited before—lounging against the large desk. One was looking at his phone and the other was just staring out the window.

"Can I help you?" Mackenzie said, striding across the room.

"Ah, Mr. Miller, Lord Duchoveny, we've been waiting for you."

"You should have called. Made arrangements to meet instead of just turning up to a business establishment demanding to see us, again. Now, unless this is official, in which case I want to see your warrants, make it quick," I said, aggressively.

Burrows had the good grace to look embarrassed. "Is there somewhere we can speak that's private?" he asked.

"This is it," Mackenzie said holding out his arms to the room.

Burrows looked at Gabriella as she passed and continued to look at her while she entered her office. Mary coughed and he turned his attention back to us.

"Well?" Mackenzie asked.

"Erm, Harry Denmark was found to have a large amount of barbiturates in his system. Did he take any recreational drugs?"

I scowled at the ridiculous question. "How would we know?" I said.

"You visited him, both of you."

"As Lord Duchoveny said, how would we know? Unless you're implying we were all sitting around a table taking drugs. I'm pretty sure he didn't share his private life with me or you, did he?" Mackenzie turned his attention to me.

I shook my head. "Do you believe we had anything to do with his death?" I asked.

"No. I do believe that he stumbled upon some information while asking questions about you two. I wish I could be more forthcoming than I am, all this bullshit just ties us up in circles," Millward said. "May we?" He indicated to the chair he was leaning against. I nodded and we all sat.

"Unless you're going to be *forthcoming* we're done here," Mackenzie said.

Millward nodded. "Harry Denmark stumbled into an investigation of a peer of the realm and the Russian mafia. An investigation that I'm part of. What complicated things was another name was thrown into the mix, Duncan Wilson. I need to know what your relationship to any of these people is to rule you out, but the fucking annoying thing is, I can't divulge why."

"I can tell you our involvement," I said.

I still held the Ziploc bag with Stanton's incriminating photos and had placed it face down on the desk. I turned it over and slid it slightly towards the middle of the desk. Millward's eyes grew wide but when he reached for it, I pulled it back.

"Let me tell you what I know. Lord Stanton, and that's the person you're talking about isn't it?" I didn't wait for an answer. "Stanton has a *friend* Jeremy Daughton, you recognised him in those photos, didn't you?" Again, I didn't wait for an answer.

I reached for the water that sat on the table and poured myself a glass. "Stanton and Daughton have a loan business, totally illegal I should imagine, initially set up to bail out Lloyds Names. They charge extortionate interest rates and, I suspect, it's a perfect way to launder money. Stanton introduced me as a possible candidate to assist in some investment in the UK. I declined. I passed him on to a very straight old chum who will be knocking on your door the minute he smells anything fishy.

"Here's the funny part. Stanton has a penchant for beating up women, as you just saw in those photographs." I tapped the documents. "Mackenzie and I have managed to acquire the evidence, enough for us to present to Stanton and have him shut down his loan business. Thus, saving the tax payer a vast amount of money in investigations and a failed prosecution. Let's be honest here. Your frustration comes from the *old boys' network* that is protecting him, isn't it?"

"And at least it releases your family from his clutches, doesn't it?" Burrows asked not answering my question. I ignored him believing it to be an assumption. They would have known my role in bringing down the firm.

"Duncan Wilson moved into my mother's complex. She believed he stole a piece of art from her. I fear she is losing her marbles since it transpired, she had asked him to take it to London for valuation. He didn't call himself Wilson, though. Why is he connected?"

Millward shook his head. "I can't tell you that, I'm sorry. It's vital that we learn whether he's connected to Stanton and Daughton or not."

"Wilson, or whatever his name is, works for the government in some form, doesn't he?" Mackenzie asked. There was no answer. "When Harry started to ask about Daughton, and we know his real name, and then added Wilson into the mix, you panicked, I'm guessing. Harry is murdered, possibly, and you're assuming that it's because he uncovered something he shouldn't have." Mackenzie leaned forward and reached for the water while silence ensued.

"Throw in that Gabriella Collingsworth had her bag stolen in rather strange circumstances after leaving a company connected with Trymast, a company that holds several military contracts, did you, then, assume we were involved with them as well?" I asked. It seems we had nailed it. Burrows simply sighed.

"The man who snatched her bag works for Stanton. I don't think it's connected other than retaliation in some way when you pissed him off," Millward said. "Other than that, I can't comment."

It was all the answer that we needed. "I'll have a copy of these sent over to you, Detective Millward. I have the originals, and there is one other copy in a very secure location. Harry Denmark was an old school friend, one, however, I hadn't seen in a long while much to my shame. I feel somewhat responsible for his demise, not in the way you expected, of course. I don't have his home telephone number, but I wondered if you'd be able to pass on my condolences to his family? I'm sure you've spoken to them about us and I would hate for my name to be slurred any more than it currently is."

Millward nodded. He looked at Burrows and both rose. "I can't apologise for wasting your time because we have learned some valuable information. I also can't promise this will be our last visit. Unfortunately, I'm sure you know how this shit works, someone has to take the blame."

I raised my eyebrows at him. "Even if that party is innocent?" I asked.

"I'm not suggesting you'll take the blame. I'm suggesting that someone upstairs who wants to protect Stanton is hankering after putting the blame on Wilson, and I *don't* believe in convicting innocent men. Be a shame if those images got into public domain. That kind of thing tends to have the *old boys* network distancing themselves, leaving their *friend* wide open with no protection," Millward said. He nodded at us both and then walked away.

We sat in silence until he was gone. Mary waved her Dictaphone as soon as the lift doors closed behind them and Gabriella left her office to join us.

"Oh my God, boys, what on earth was all that?" she asked. Mackenzie and I filled her in on the past few days.

"And I'm a culprit, they made me record it," Mary shouted over.

I frowned. "You're complicit, not a culprit, Mary," I replied.

"Whatever. My grandson works for The City. Nasty newspaper, should just be used as arse wipe, I bet they'd love that kind of scandal."

"Mary, I think I love you," Mackenzie said. He snatched the envelope from the desk and gave it to her to copy all the documents but kept hold of the tapes.

When it was copied, she placed all the documents in a brown envelope and called her grandson. She then admitted he was a mailroom worker but that it was a perfect location for him to be able to deliver the envelope to the right person without it falling into anyone else's hands. She threatened to slap me upside my head—I pondered on that location, *upside* my head and wondering where the *downside* was likely to be—when I asked if he was both reliable and not likely to run off with the documents thinking he can make a quick financial return on them.

"He's the only one of my lot that's bloody sensible. Wants to be a journalist, he does. Loves the trees and environment. Scuba dives as well," she said, puffing up with pride.

Gabriella placed her hand on Mary's arm. "He sounds wonderful, Mary. And I'm also sure a little financial reward from these two actually should be expected," she said, raising her eyebrows at us.

Faced with the two of them, there was no argument. Mackenzie pulled out his wallet and when Mary saw the colour of the note being pulled, she coughed, he grabbed a couple more. She took the money and the envelope, slung her bag over her shoulder and left the office.

"Is that going to be the end of it?" Gabriella asked.

I sighed and shrugged my shoulders. "I don't know. I do have the advantage of knowing how the system works and who's who when it comes to this *network*. I might spread the word in other areas and see what we can do."

"I think your mom will be pleased to know that Duncan, even though that might not be his name, isn't the baddie she thought," Gabriella said.

I couldn't have agreed more. "It would be a shame if she returned to her depressed state, I must admit."

"Why don't we take her out to dinner, all of us?" she asked.

"There is a rather lovely restaurant not far from where she lives," Mackenzie said, I saw the smirk form on his lips.

I widened my eyes in his direction. "Jesus, Mackenzie. Take my mother to a sex club? Honestly, back in the sixties I'm sure she visited loads but... It actually might be nice for her to meet up with Veronica, but let's choose a pub somewhere." I chuckled at the thought.

"What are you doing this evening?" Gabriella asked.

"I shall be catching up on some paperwork, reading a book, and having an early night, probably," I said.

That evening Mackenzie was taking Gabriella to dinner. "I feel odd going out and leaving you at home," she said.

"You can always come over when you've eaten," I replied.

"Sounds good. Now, I have some work to do before I head home to get ready." She leaned up and gave me a brief kiss before walking back into her office.

We'd wasted a good half a day at the club, then the rest of it with the police. By the time I got back to my office, it was mostly empty. I gathered what I needed and called down for a car myself.

I must have dozed off, as I jolted awake at the sound of the buzzer.

"Hello?" I asked into the intercom.

"It's me, is it too late?" Gabriella said.

I pressed the button to release the door. I waited by the apartment door and smiled when she exited the lift. "It's never too late for you," I said.

"I wasn't sure. Mackenzie was late to pick me up, as usual. The service was terribly slow and the restaurant super noisy. We couldn't really chat, to be honest. Still, it was nice to spend some time with him. I think I'm a very lucky girl to have you both in my life," she said.

I stepped to one side and allowed her to walk into the apartment before me and I admired the view, as always. She stopped in the middle of the lounge and turned to look at me. I didn't speak for a while, just visually drank in her curves, mentally caressing every one.

She raised her eyebrows and smirked. She placed her bag on the sofa and then slowly unbuttoned her shirt, letting it slide from her shoulders to reveal a white lace bra. Then she reached around to undo the zip of her pencil skirt, it too slipped to the floor and she stepped out of it.

She stood there in her underwear, hold-ups and fuck me high heels. I watched in awe as she reached up to pull out the pins holding her hair in a messy bun. It cascaded over her shoulders and she used her fingers to ruffle the curls.

I strode towards her and, grabbing each side of her face and holding her head, I kissed her. It was a brutal, lip bruising kiss. As stupid as it was, I was reclaiming her. I wanted her to taste me, to feel the hardness of my cock as she stepped closer. I wanted her to smell me. She fisted my shirt in her hands as she moaned into my mouth. I took her breath and held her tight.

When I stepped away her eyes were hooded with desire, her lips plumped, and her hair tangled. I held out my hand and, still in silence, I led her to the bedroom.

While she stood, I kneeled. I ran my hands up her legs, circling my fingers behind her knees. I licked her skin, tasting the body moisturiser she used, inhaling her scent. When my hands reached her hips, I gently slipped my fingers under the band of her panties and very slowly lowered them. I licked and nipped at her inner thighs close to where I wanted to be but teasing.

Gabriella grabbed handfuls of my hair and she parted her legs, lowering her pussy closer to my face. I ran my nose over her opening, her clitoris, smelling her. I wanted all my senses filled by her. I flicked my tongue over her clitoris, and she gripped harder. I ran my hands up her backside, digging my fingers into her flesh and forcing her closer as I lapped and gently took her clitoris between my teeth. She moaned out as I did. I flicked the end of my tongue over the sensitive flesh and felt her legs shake gently. She thrust her pelvis closer, pulled on my hair, demanding more.

I stood, denying her what she wanted, and she grabbed my face, kissed my lips, licked her juices from my chin, and I pulled back. Denying was one of my favourite things.

"Alex, please," she whispered.

I didn't speak but I did circle her. I trailed a finger over her collarbone, her shoulder, and across her back to her spine. I slid my finger down, pushing between her arse cheeks until I found her opening. I swiped my finger over and back up. Her breath hitched in her throat.

I continued to walk until I faced her again. Her eyes were closed so I clicked my fingers to gain her attention.

Her eyelids sprang open. "Alex," she whispered, again.

"What do you want me to do to you, Gabriella?" I asked, my voice low and husky.

"I want you inside me."

I pursed my lips as if in thought. Just fucking her

wasn't ever enough. I had an idea. I walked to my wardrobe and retrieved a tie. I twirled my fingers until she understood I wanted her to turn away from me. I grabbed one wrist and secured it to the other behind her back. I grabbed her hair, pulling her head back so I could look down on her.

"Okay?" I whispered. She nodded.

I walked her to the bed and pushed her body until she bent at the waist. I kicked at her ankles until she parted her legs more. I pulled my shirt over my head and peeled off my jeans then stood behind her. I ran my fingers down her back, watching goosebumps appear on her skin. I held her tied wrists and I spanked her arse with my palm. She gasped with surprise and followed that with a moan. Her flesh pinked and I gently massaged it. I crouched down and licked. My tongue circled her skin and cooled the heat. I nipped, leaving marks, and sucked. When her arse cheeks had had enough attention from me, I stood upright. I held my cock and I slowly slid my hand up and down the shaft, holding the head at her entrance. I rubbed over her clitoris.

She turned her head to one side, her hair fanned out, and in just her bra, stockings, and high heels, bent double over my bed, she was a sight to behold. I wanted to capture the image in a photograph for nights without her, but my memory would have to be good enough.

When I thrust my cock inside her, she wasn't expecting it. She slid over the bed. I held her wrists and one hip and I fucked her hard. I fucked her fast, then slow, rotating and adding a finger or two. I fingered her arse while forcing my cock to go as deep as I could. She cried out in pleasure and demanded more. I reached around her, teased her clitoris at the same time and then she came.

She forced her body back onto me as she cried out. Tendrils of hair had stuck to her damp forehead as she tried to look over her shoulder.

"I want more, Alex," she said, her voice hoarse.

"My lady will get what she wants, always," I replied, grunting out the words as I moved in and out of her still.

Sweat dripped from my forehead, blurring my vision and stinging my eyes. It ran down my chest and between my shoulder blades. I pulled out of her, flipped her over so her back was on the bed and her legs dangled off. I fell to my knees and while I pleasured myself, I lapped up her cum. I sucked on her hard. I bit the skin around her opening, loving the swelling that followed.

I grabbed her thighs and raised them, placing them around my waist and she tightened her grip. I pushed into her again. She cried out, that time in discomfort, I thought. I stilled.

"It's okay," she said.

She would be sore after my *feasting* and it was the friction that I wanted her to feel. The warmth would drive her mad, I hoped. I was correct. As I pumped into her, she arched her body. She threw her head back and screamed out, still she demanded more. I don't think I'd ever fucked someone so hard and fast before. My legs shook, my arms did the same. My abs ached, and my heart pumped so fast I feared it might arrest. I gulped down air and held back my orgasm until she'd done so a second time. When I could hold back no more, I let go. My body went rigid as I spurted my cum inside her. It filled her, running back out and down to her arse. I slowed, until I eventually pulled out.

It was all I could do to make it to the bed where I

collapsed beside her. I pulled her to face me, using one hand to untie her and she wrapped her arms around me. She wrapped her leg over mine and we lay facing each other without speaking, just trying to regulate our breathing. We fell asleep in that position, across the bed, on top of the duvet, coated in sweat and cum.

An hour or so later I woke. Gabriella still slept in my arms. Her make-up was smudged, lipstick stained her cheek and mascara had rubbed onto the skin under her eyes. Her hair had tangles, and to me, she looked just as sexy as she did when she first stripped for me. I untangled myself from her arms and walked to the bathroom. I turned the taps and ran the bath, picking up a band that Gabriella had left on the sink when she'd visited before.

I returned to the bedroom and I removed her shoes and stockings. Gabriella stirred. She stretched, winced, and smiled, still partly asleep. I unclipped her bra and she held her hands up as I slid it off. I then scooped her up in my arms and she wrapped hers around my neck, resting her head on my chest.

"Is it morning?" she asked, sleepily.

"No, but it is clean up time," I said, chuckling.

I let her down and she stood, a little unsteadily at first. I gathered up her hair and tied a ponytail on the top of her head, impressed as it was the first time I'd ever done one. I turned off the taps and then climbed into the bath. I held out a hand and she climbed in, sitting between my legs. She rested back against me and I kissed the top of her head.

We sat and allowed the hot water to soothe us, initially. I gently cupped water and let it fall through my fingers over her chest. She hummed with pleasure. I reached for the gel and squirted some, rubbing my palms together to create a foam. I started at her throat, gently running my hands over her skin, moving down her chest and to her breasts. I massaged slowly, letting my fingertips circle her nipples that had puckered under my touch.

A small moan escaped her lips and she covered my hand with one of her own, squeezing.

"Fuck yourself for me," I whispered.

I watched as she slid her hand down her stomach. She placed her feet outside my legs, parting her own. I shuffled up a little so I could watch. I palmed one of her nipples, rubbing in time with her. She wasn't embarrassed as she pleasured herself; she fell into her zone, inserting two fingers into herself. Water gently sloshed from side to side, becoming more rapid as her desire grew. I cupped both breasts and kneaded, rolling the flesh between my hands. She raised her hips, forced her head back into my chest, and parted her lips. Her breath was rapid, and her cheeks flushed as she made herself come.

She rested back down in the water and chuckled. "What are you doing to me, Alex?" she asked, quietly.

"I think I should be asking you the same question," I replied.

She took a deep breath in and released it slowly. "We're both holding back a little, aren't we?" she said. I nodded, not that she would have known that. She added, "Why?"

"I don't know. This relationship is different for me, Gabriella. It's...real, I guess. I want to hold on to you so tightly, but I'm aware I might suffocate you at the same time."

She tilted her head back enough so she could kiss my

chin. "I think I've fallen in love with you, Alex," she whispered.

My heart raced at her words. "You think, or you know?" I asked.

"I know."

I didn't repeat the words. I wanted to; but they were stuck in the back of my throat. I was desperate for them to spring free, but something blocked them. Something blocked me.

As if she read my mind she whispered, "It's okay, Alex. The words will come when you're ready, or they won't."

I wrapped my arms around her and held on. I wanted to shed tears. I wanted to open up to her, to love her, and tell her that. I knew I would, one day, I just hoped I wouldn't say the words too late.

CHAPTER THIRTEEN

I awoke before Gabriella. I slid from the bed and headed to the kitchen to make coffee. I'd slept well; it was comfortable having Gabriella in my arms all night. It felt totally normal. I made two cups and took them back to the bedroom. I placed one beside her and took mine into the bathroom. I showered, and then stood in front of the sink to shave.

Gabriella walked, naked, into the bathroom and sat on the loo to pee. Then she smiled as she passed me to step into the shower. Humming a tune, she washed her hair, then her body while I watched her reflection in the mirror. I was so distracted that I nicked my skin. She laughed as she wrapped a towel around herself and pulled a tissue from a box. She licked a corner, tore it off, and stuck it to my face.

There was no awkwardness. We both walked around naked, finding clothes, and dressing for work. I was leaving earlier than Gabriella. I kissed her cheek and before I left, I handed her a pair of keys. One for the apartment door and one for the main building. The fact she took them confirmed she was serious about what she'd said.

I smiled all the way into work.

"Why are you so happy?" Mackenzie asked, walking into my office.

"I wasn't aware there was a non-happy policy in this building," I replied, smirking.

He laughed. "Did you have a chance to look through those businesses yet?"

"I haven't, sorry. I intend to use this evening to catch up."

"That's okay. I'm thinking of consolidating, I want your opinion on that."

"Consolidating?" I was under the impression that he loved to travel back and forth but maybe not.

"Yeah. I'm thinking of not travelling so much."

"Have you decided where you'd like to stay?" I asked.

"Here, I think."

"I can't imagine anyone choosing London over the States," I replied.

I'd travelled a lot for work, and I always enjoyed coming home, of course, but if I'd had the choice, I think I might have enjoyed a stint abroad. That was before Gabriella, though.

Mackenzie left and I watched him walk to the lift. He didn't seem his normal self and I wondered why. I should have asked. We were friends enough to do so, I believed, but he didn't appear *open* that morning. Maybe I'd have a chat with Gabriella. She might have picked up on something from their evening out. I got my head down to work.

A sandwich and coffee were placed on my desk. I was

so engrossed I hadn't heard anyone come in. I looked up to see a smiling Gabriella.

"Hello, I didn't realise the time," I said, taking the coffee. "Sit, have your lunch with me."

I waited until she did and then asked her if she thought Mackenzie was okay.

"You know, I was going to ask you the same thing. I do know that Addison is planning to visit the UK. I have no idea why, she sent me a text message and I don't know how she got my number, it's new."

"From your family?" I asked.

"I doubt it. My mother dislikes her as much as the rest of us. Although my brother... Mmm, I haven't given him my number, but he could have easily gotten it, I think."

She didn't often mention her brother and it seemed he was a no-go for discussion. I pushed a little, though. "I take it you don't get on with him?" I took a bite of my salt beef and mustard sandwich.

"No. I can't stand the man. He and Addison had an affair. The shock though, Alex, isn't that they just had an affair, but she is my cousin! How redneck is that?"

My mouth stayed open mid-chew and I quickly closed it for fear of losing the bite of sandwich I'd taken. "No way?" I asked.

She nodded and sipped on her coffee. "I'm sure Mackenzie will tell you, it's not a secret. She came home pregnant while she was married to Mackenzie."

"And it couldn't have been his...Mackenzie's I mean?"

"No, he can't have children due to a car accident," she said. Her voice tailed off and I did wonder then if she felt she'd said too much.

"Jesus, that's tough." I really did feel for the guy then.

"I can't imagine creating a dynasty without anyone to leave it to," she said. "Have you ever wanted children?" she asked.

I paused, not knowing the correct answer. The truth was I had no clue if I wanted children or not—it wasn't something I'd thought much about—or what she wanted to hear bearing in mind our developing relationship and ages.

"I haven't really thought about it, is the honest answer," I said, deciding on the truth. "I've never been in a relationship that was strong enough, or that I thought was going to last—"

I was about to say 'until now' when Mackenzie walked into the office and interrupted us. Although she blinked a few times, her expression didn't change.

"Fucking Addison," he said in an exasperated voice.

"What has she done now?" I asked, distracted from my conversation with Gabriella.

She stood. "I think I'll leave you two to chat. I have things to do," she said, gathering up the debris from lunch. She didn't look at me.

"Wait, I need to tell you something," I said, trying not to be further distracted by Mackenzie pacing.

"I'm sure it can wait," she gave me a small smile and then left.

I sighed. "What's the sigh for?" Mackenzie asked.

"You interrupted the end of my sentence, which means she's left thinking something that isn't correct." He frowned at me but I waved a dismissive hand. "Never mind, I'll sort it later. What's happened?" I asked.

"She's demanding I take her to dinner; says she has important things to talk about."

"Does she?"

He scoffed. "No, she has nothing to say that I want to talk to her about."

"Why do you entertain her then?" It seemed to me that if he didn't want anything to do with her, he should just tell her so.

"Because I get information from her about her father. She's very loose lipped after a couple of glasses of wine. She wants us to get back together, which will never happen."

Mackenzie had told me previously that her father had ruined him, and he, in return, was doing the same. It seemed the vendetta had been going on for years and, to me, was completely unnecessary.

"Why are you wasting your time, Mackenzie? What can you possibly gain now? You're successful, you beat him already. Unless you like the fight, still?" I raised my eyebrows in question.

He chuckled. "Okay, I do love to fuck with them occasionally."

"And that stops you moving forwards."

His smile slipped a little. "Maybe," he said, shrugging his shoulders.

"Do you want to settle down with someone?" I asked.

"Sure, I just haven't found the right one. I mean, we're not easy men to love, are we?"

There was no doubt we were very similar. "What about a family?" I asked, although I remembered what Gabriella had said, he could still meet someone with children, or adopt.

"Not sure. You?"

"Not sure," I replied, and then laughed.

I heard a noise outside and looked up to see Gabriella

walking away. I wasn't aware how much of our conversation she'd heard and why I hadn't seen her at the doorway, unless she hadn't been fully visible.

"Everything okay there?" Mackenzie asked.

"No idea. She told me she loved me. I couldn't say it back and it wasn't because I don't... something holds me back and I don't know what it is." I decided to be honest in case she'd said something to him.

"She knows you're holding back. She thinks it's because you believe she'll leave to head back home. There's nothing stopping you following her, Alex, if that was ever the case."

I didn't answer, but simply nodded. If I could understand, truly, what was holding me back, I'd be fine. I thought, originally, it was because she was American and could leave, but I wasn't sure anymore.

My heart told me that I loved her; I just couldn't get my brain to stop coming up with excuses.

Mackenzie left and I called her but the call went to her voicemail. "Hi, can you call me when you have a minute?" I asked.

I placed my phone back on down. I was too distracted to work and I looked at the pile of folders on the desk. All of Mackenzie's businesses in the States were in there. If Gabriella ever wanted to go home, I had a job, I knew that. If I sold my flat and liquidated other assets, I'd never have to work again. Of course, there was Mother's paintings and her apartment that would eventually come to me. But I needed to work. I was used to getting up at the crack of dawn to check the money markets, working through the night and then catching a few hours' sleep during the day. I loved the hustle of working, of negotiations, even just having something to do during the day. My golfing buddies, Len and Pete had retired young. They spent their days on courses all around the world. That wasn't for me. I'd be bored shitless.

I called Gabriella again and left another voicemail. "I'm heading home to work, it's a little too distracting here. I'd love to chat, and if you're free, maybe dinner. I'll call again soon."

I gathered up the files and headed for the car park. The journey home was long even though my apartment block wasn't that far from Canary Wharf. The traffic was appalling. According to my driver, there had been yet another terrorist attack and London was on lockdown again. I stared out the window at endless lines of people going about their day not knowing if it might be their last. I sighed and wondered what on earth was becoming of the world that running over, stabbing, and blowing up people was becoming so normal we weren't necessarily affected by it anymore.

Would I want to bring a child into a world like that? I thought. I couldn't honestly answer.

I had poured myself a glass of red wine and was halfway through the pile of folders. I hadn't taken any notice of the time, but the sun was dipping over the horizon. Mackenzie sure liked to dabble in many different types of businesses. He had bars and hotels, fine, that went in the entertainment pile. He had a car restoration company and I guessed that might have been to help out a friend. He invested a lot in manufacturing, that could all be grouped together. I didn't think, for one minute, he'd be able to consolidate the lot and bring it under one umbrella, it was too diverse. I couldn't imagine one CEO that would have the knowledge to manage the lot.

I heard a click and it startled me. Then I chuckled as Gabriella walked through the front door. She placed some delicious smelling bags on the kitchen table as she walked towards me.

She leaned over the back of the sofa and kissed my neck. "I bought dinner as an apology," she said.

"An apology for what?"

"Not replying to your messages. I wasn't ignoring you, time just flew today," she replied with a smile.

"Well, thank you. And no apology needed. I've been going through Mackenzie's folders," I said, indicating with my arm the various piles.

"Makes for an interesting read, doesn't it?" she said. "I've got Thai, is that okay?"

"Thai is perfect, and yes, it does. He said he wants to consolidate, I'm not sure that's entirely possible but I do have some interesting thoughts to share."

I stood and raised my glass. "Can I pour you one?" She nodded as she removed her coat and walked into the bedroom to hang it up.

I loved that she felt so comfortable that she would just move around the apartment as if she lived there.

"You know, I think I'm getting old. I can't wear these heels for too long anymore." I heard her sigh as she kicked off her shoes, one bounced across the wooden floor and she laughed.

"If you check in the closet, I'm sure you'll find a brand

new pair of slippers that my mother bought me for Christmas one time."

I heard the doors opening. "You have! How lovely of her, Alex," she called.

I frowned and smiled as I poured her wine, and then peeked into the bags. I grabbed a couple of plates, some chopsticks and emptied the paper bag of its little plastic dishes. When Gabriella returned, I had to laugh. She wore one of my t-shirts, a pair of my shorts rolled over at the top and the blue *granddad* slippers.

"You look sexy until I get to your feet," I said, chuckling.

"Comfort today, my darling."

"You should leave some clothes here," I offered, not really thinking of the enormity of that statement.

"That's just one step under moving in, Alex, are you sure? I mean, I'd hate to rush you," she teased, winking at me. I gave her a fake laugh in response. Then genuinely laughed.

"I'll make some space, it seems silly you staying over then having to rush home to change," I said.

We sat and ate, and I thought on what I'd said. Small steps, that's what I needed. Just small steps to allow my head to catch up with my heart.

When we were done eating, we sat on the sofa and watched a movie, something I confessed to not having done for many years. It was nice just having her wrapped in my arms even though she fidgeted way too much.

"Will you keep still?" I said, sighing out the words in exasperation.

"I'm trying, your sofa isn't very comfortable," she moaned.

I admitted to not having sat on it much. If I did sit in the living room, it was on one of the chairs.

"Who decorated your apartment?" she asked, shuffling to a sitting position and looking around.

"I moved into it like this. The furniture came with it, it was the show apartment I guess."

"Ah, so that will be the reason it's so...sterile. You don't even have photographs of your family."

I looked around and, for the first time, I got what she meant. The walls were a light grey, the wooden floor was highly polished. Grey and black furniture was placed very strategically, and I don't think I'd even moved anything to see if it suited a better position.

"I bet they didn't have a woman to design the interior," she mumbled, and then looked at me. "Am I being terribly rude?"

"Not really. I can see your point. I never thought about it. I wasn't home enough to worry about pictures on the wall or coloured rugs." I laughed as I spoke. "Maybe we can go furniture shopping together."

She sat up. "Whoa there, Mister. That's another half step toward a *proper* relationship. First you want me to leave some clothes, now you want me to help you pick out a new couch?" She reached forward to place her hand on my forehead. "Alex, are you well? Or has someone kidnapped *my* Alex and replaced him with one who isn't relationship phobic?" She laughed and I joined in, until I had an idea.

I grabbed her wrist and pulled her forwards. She fell onto my lap. I grabbed her arse and hauled her up the sofa, so she was fully over my knees. She wriggled and laughed as I lowered the shorts. She had no panties on, and that pleased me. I spanked her arse and her wriggling and laughing stopped. She stretched out her arms and held on to the edge of the sofa. I ran my fingers over her pinked flesh, circling, and teasing.

"Is this the Alex that you like?" I whispered and spanked her again.

"Yes," she replied, breathily. She parted her legs as far as the pushed down shorts would allow.

"Am I relationship phobic?" I asked, it was a question that I genuinely wanted her to answer.

"Yes," she said.

I watched her hands grip the edge of the sofa. My palm glanced off her arse cheek and she moaned.

Was I? I asked myself silently.

I didn't come up with an answer. Instead, I ran my fingers over her opening, feeling her wetness and heat. I dragged that wetness up, coating her arsehole, a place I liked to visit, and one I was sure she enjoyed as well. She tensed a little and I heard her take in a breath. She nodded. As I pushed my finger in, she let out that breath slowly, moaning at the same time. My rigid cock strained against my jeans and became painful. I reached down to undo the button and zip, giving myself some relief from the pressure. Gabriella raised her arse in the air, and I freed my cock from its confines. When she rested back down, her skin against my cock gave the same effect as her hand. She wriggled slowly back and forth, and it was as if her body was pleasuring me. I removed my finger and using my other hand, I teased her clitoris. I probed and stroked, feeling her wetness and tightness.

"Turn over," I whispered. She rolled on my lap until she was lying on her back.

I had the pleasure of seeing her pussy up close and watching the slickness coat my finger as I rotated and pushing in and out of her. The t-shirt had ridden up and her toned stomach muscles tightened and rippled as her orgasm built. She arched her body as she came.

She gently chuckled as she settled her body back down into my lap. "Mmm, that was nice, my Lord," she whispered. "Is there a round two?"

"Why do you call me that?" I asked, running my fingers up and down her stomach.

"Because I like to think that you're mine and you like it."

She swung her legs to the floor and stood, holding out her hands, she took mine and helped me to my feet. The shorts fell to her ankles and she stepped out of them then pulled the t-shirt over her head and stood naked in front of me.

She turned slowly. "Do you like what you see?" she asked.

"Very much so."

"Do you like that my ass cheeks are pink and hot from your spank?" Her voice had lowered.

"Very much so," I repeated.

"I love the sting, it turns me on," she said, coming to face me again. "But I want more now."

"How much more?" I asked, my breath came in gasps as I spoke.

"I want you to do whatever you want."

"Get dressed. Choose some clothes, any clothes, it doesn't matter." She frowned so I added, "Just trust me, please?" She smirked and then nodded.

She was gone no more than a minute when she

returned in another t-shirt and some joggers. She had bare feet and I found some flip-flops, way too big but they would do for what I wanted. I grabbed my keys and took her hand. We left the flat and I didn't speak again until we were in the car.

"At any time you want to stop, you say so, okay?"

"Okay." She drew the word out as if she was a little unsure.

I opened the car door for her, and she slid in. I drove, probably way too fast and sent a text as well. It was totally illegal, but I had something in mind.

Gabriella smiled further when she recognised the gates we drove through, and the valet that took our car, and my cousin who stood in the doorway just holding a key. Without a word, I took the key and didn't break pace. Gabriella air kissed Veronica as we passed and both women laughed.

I pulled Gabriella up the stairs and then paused outside a room. "Sure?" I asked.

"Err, yeah. Alex, my pussy is dripping. Now open the goddamn door," she said, and her vulgarity turned me on more.

I grabbed her and forced her back against the wall. I held her by her throat and I kissed her hard.

She bit down hard on my lip, drawing blood. "Open. The. Door," she hissed into my mouth.

The room I'd texted Veronica about was one that had racks of implements along one wall, a cupboard of lubricants and massage oils. There was a large bed in the middle of the room with rings on each corner post.

"Naked, now," I said, striding to the racks. I ran my hand over the wooden paddles causing them to clack against each other. When I came to the end, I selected wrist cuffs and ankle cuffs.

I held them while I walked towards her. She stood, as expected, naked and I could see the wetness shining on her inner thighs. I was desperate for her. I fell to my knees and grabbed her hips. I licked and sucked, needing to taste and smell her want for me. I bit gently, harder when she moaned out loud. I dug my fingers into her skin, and I growled with frustration that I couldn't get my tongue deep enough inside her. I stood and picked her up without another word. I threw her to the bed; she bounced and then shuffled up. She smirked at me, raised one eyebrow as if laying down a challenge. I grabbed one wrist and cuffed it to the corner post, doing the same with the other.

I then climbed on the bed and kneeled between her legs. I slid my hands under her arse, and I lifted. I brought her pussy to my face and I held her there, folding her body at the waist slightly so I could get my tongue as far inside her as possible. She cried out, she moaned, she screamed out my name and that was a sound I loved more than anything.

"Say my name again," I shouted, she did. As I licked and sucked every last drop of her previous orgasm, and the one that was heading my way like a freight train, she kept saying my name.

She came so violently she squirted, and I drank it all in. She twisted, surprised by what had happened. I held her steady not releasing her. I knew what was happening to her, of course. Her orgasm was so strong her stomach would be aching. I was holding her in a position that did not allow her relief. I licked her thighs and only when I was done, did I allow her to lower her legs and stretch out her stomach.

"Oh my God, Alex," she whispered. Sweat had beaded on her forehead, on her upper lip.

I crawled up her body and I licked the sweat from her skin. "Taste," I said, holding my face just above hers. She gently licked my lips.

I moved from the bed and picked up the two remaining restraints. I clasped them around her ankles and secured each to the last two corner posts. I walked around the room, admiring her from different angles. She followed me, turning her head, and licking her lips. I remained fully clothed but I, once again, unfastened my jeans and stood beside the bed and wanked. I slid my hand up and down, pumping furiously. I needed a quick release; my balls had been hurting since the apartment. I came and white milky fluid spurted in ribbons over her body. The contrast against her tanned skin aroused me. Although I'd come, my cock was still hard, painfully so. I growled out in frustration.

I walked to the racks and picked up a flogger. Its leather clad handle gave way to strips of the same black leather. I slapped it gently against my leg. Gabriella's eyes widened and she licked her lips.

"Are you thirsty, my Lady?" I whispered. She gently nodded.

I placed the flogger on the bed and grabbed a bottle of cold water from an ice bucket on the top of the sideboard. I unscrewed the cap and took a sip myself before holding her head and pouring it into her mouth. She swallowed although some ran down the sides of her cheeks. She gasped when I tipped the bottle further and drizzled ice-cold water over her chest, her nipples, down her stomach and then between her legs. The water washed my cum from her skin.

I trailed the flogger from an ankle, up her leg, over her hip and across her stomach. I let the leather tails circle her nipple then moved down again. I drew the flogger across her pussy watching the leather soak up some of her juices. She screamed out when I flicked it against her. She raised her hips and the cuffs strained as she pulled on them.

"You say when you want to stop," I whispered and she nodded, understanding.

I flicked again, and again. Her nipples puckered hard and I couldn't wait to hold them between my teeth. I was having too much fun tormenting her to stop. When the strands of leather were slick, I trailed it up her body and commanded her to open her mouth. I slipped the ends into her mouth and she sucked on them.

Before she could relax again, I flicked the strands against her nipples. She cried out in pain and I paused.

"It's fine," she said, her voice ragged.

I flicked again, gentler that time. I imagined her skin was hypersensitive from such an intense orgasm, that's what I was hoping for, anyway. I wanted her body hot, then cold, and then hot again. I wanted sensations to zap in her brain, confusing themselves, until she was just one mass of feeling. Only then would I fuck her.

When her skin pinked from the flogger, I cooled it with the water. I picked up ice in my hands and placed the cubes in the hollow of her neck, in her navel, and I pushed an ice cube inside her. Flicking against her clitoris with the flogger while the ice melted and had the desired effect. Gabriella screamed out writhed, rattled her restraints. She *demanded* that I fuck her. I wasn't done teasing, though.

I unfastenend the cuffs and made her turn over. At first I thought she was going to leap at me. She got to all fours and smirked. She licked her lips as if about to devour me. That was until I slapped the flogger over her back. She lay down then, punished.

Her arse was crying out for attention. I swapped the flogger for a paddle, a large wooden instrument with a flattened end. It made a satisfying sound as it connected with her skin. She gripped the bedding, dragging it to her. She parted her legs as far as she could, and her arousal was clear to see. I slapped her again, and then doused the fire with yet more iced water.

When I was done, when I thought she was ready, I stripped off my clothes and climbed on the bed. I grabbed at her hips, raising them. She moved to all fours and I fucked her from behind. I pumped in and out so hard and so fast I had to hold on to her. She cried out my name over and over and fell to her elbows when her arms shook too much to hold her up, biting the bedding to quieten her screams.

It was I that screamed out loud. It was I that shed tears when I finally came. My release was overwhelming and painful. My balls tightened so hard and my cock pumped cum into her over and over. My muscles cramped in my thighs and my stomach. I threw my head back and bit down so hard on my lower lip I drew blood for the second time. The metallic tang was powerful.

I released her gently and she slid to the bed. I moved down and lay on top of her. I dragged in air through my nose trying hard to regulate my heart rate. I rolled to one side and lay on my back then threw one arm above my head, stretching my stomach muscles, and closed my eyes.

I felt her hand on my chest, her fingers circling my skin, and then the bed moved. I opened my eyes to watch her straddle my knees. She lowered her head and took my flaccid cock in her mouth. She was so gentle, licking and sucking, bringing me slowly back to life.

When I was rigid again, she rode me. Slowly at first, she rose and fell, rotating her hips. I could feel myself buried deep inside her. I sat up. I wrapped my arms around her body and together we came again. She cried into my neck. Hot salty tears ran down my chest as she told me she loved me. I took hold of her head and raised her face and I kissed her. I kissed her like I loved her back. I couldn't say the words, but I could convey the feeling. I lowered pulling her with me. She lay on me wrapped tightly in my arms. For half an hour or so we didn't speak. We were just being, just feeling, and just connecting.

I dropped Gabriella back at her house even though her bag, shoes, and clothes were still at mine. I made a promise to bring them over in the morning. It had been her decision to return home and I understood why. What had happened between us had been powerful, an exchange of absolute trust and pleasure, of mutual pain and desire. We needed separation to process that.

I showered, regretting losing her scent, and climbed into bed. I picked up my phone from the bedside cabinet to see a text message.

I love you. Thank you for this evening. Gabriella xx

I replied.

Likewise. Alex xx

I slept the sleep of the dead that night. When I woke an hour later than I would normally, I ached. My cock was sore, my balls still tight, and my muscles felt like I'd run a 10k then jumped into a boxing ring. Neither of which I'd done since school. I chuckled as I rolled from the bed. I walked into the living room and startled.

"Good morning. I'm sorry but I needed my bag and you were sleeping so soundly, I didn't want to disturb you," Gabriella said.

I strode over and wrapped my arms around her, she snuggled into me. "I adore seeing your smile in the morning," I said.

"Careful, Alex, that's another millimetre towards living together."

"How far have I got? We exchanged keys, I offered you closet space, you wore my slippers—that must mean we are practically married—you're choosing a sofa with me, and now I said I adore seeing you in the morning. There must still be a few centimetres, an inch or two to go, mustn't there?" I teased.

It was stupid, I knew I'd live with her in a heartbeat and I wanted to punch my own lights out for being hesitant.

"Small steps," she said, cupping my face for a kiss.

She waited until I'd dressed, we grabbed a coffee, and travelled into work together.

CHAPTER FOURTEEN

For the next couple of days Gabriella either stayed with me, or I with her. We moved clothes and toiletries and then found the nuisance of this.

"Do you know where my aftershave is?" I asked, as we were getting ready for a night out with my mother.

"In the cupboard, there," she said, pointing to one above the sink.

"No, not that one. I don't like the smell of that."

She shrugged her shoulders. "Maybe you have the one you want at your house?"

"Maybe. I thought it was here."

We had both started to duplicate items. She had recently waved around a gadget that straightened her hair, informing me that she had to buy a second one as she needed it in both properties.

"This is ridiculous," I said. I started to walk from the bathroom. "We should just live in one house." The words were out of my mouth before my brain engaged. I turned to look and she stared at me with raised eyebrows. "Right. Yes. Fine. Okay. This is madness, where do you want to live?"

"Oh, what a wonderful way to invite me to live with you," she said, and then laughed to assure me she was teasing.

I winced and then smiled, rubbing my hand over my chin as if it would give me the courage to speak the words I wanted to.

"Gabriella, my Lady, would you do me the honour of moving in with me? Or I move in with you, or whatever we do." I stuttered towards the end of my sentence.

Despite still cleaning her teeth and having toothpaste on her lips, she walked over and kissed me. "I'd be delighted to. You're becoming *so* grown up, Alex, your mother is going to be delighted."

I slapped her arse as she walked back to the sink. "We'll, err, sort the details later," I said. I left the room to the sound of her laughing.

"God, I'm such a jerk sometimes," I said to myself as I sat on the bed to tie my shoelaces.

"Ah, but you're my jerk," came the reply.

I hadn't seen Mother for a couple of weeks, she'd been busy, or I had, and it was with trepidation that I knocked on her front door. I wondered, with Duncan gone, if she might have slipped back into her dark mood. However, the bright smile that greeted us, assured me otherwise.

"Come in, my darlings. Let's have champagne before

we leave, shall we?" she asked, before linking arms with Gabriella and leading her to the living room.

"I'll just follow on, shall I?" I grumbled and followed them.

"He's as crusty as his father was sometimes," Mother said and Gabriella laughed.

"Mother, Gabriella and I are going to live together," I said once I'd sat and raised my champagne glass.

"A toast then," she replied. "Although I'll keep the best stuff for when you propose to this gorgeous girl."

I nearly spat the champagne from my mouth. Worst was to come. Mother and Gabriella then chatted about where we were going to live. They had conversations I expected Gabriella and I to have although, I had to admit, it would be reluctantly on my part. I didn't care for wall coverings or what paintings of Mother's we should have.

"I mean, they will all come to Alex at some point, you might as well have them now," she'd said.

"Mother, please. We're way off this yet. There's a lot to discuss, let's leave the paintings where they should be, and that's in the safe. I'm assuming you've had the Van Gogh back?"

"Yes, and we're having fun, aren't we, darling?" she said, patting Gabriella's hand. "The insurance might need adjusting since the valuation has increased."

I promised I'd get on that the following day. "Shall we get going before we lose our table?"

Mother and Gabriella didn't stop talking the whole journey, through a three-course dinner, and then in the car on the way home. Occasionally, I was invited to participate but, to be honest, I was thrilled. I was so happy they got along so well; it was as if my mother had yet another lease on life. Gabriella had promised to collect Mother for a girls shopping trip in a couple of weeks, too.

Gabriella and I walked Mother into her apartment. She offered us more wine, but I had an early start and was driving anyway, therefore we declined.

"Another time, Henry," Gabriella said, yet again I was thrilled to hear her call my mother by the shortened version of her name, and one only reserved for family, normally.

"I love your mom," Gabriella said on the journey home.

"I can see. And I believe she feels the same," I replied, smiling.

"You can't say the word even when it isn't related to us, can you?" she asked, quietly.

"Huh?" I tried to keep my concentration on the road but was genuinely baffled.

"You can't just say, my mother *loves* you, too, can you?"

I glanced over at her. "You've lost me. I'm sorry."

"I text you that I love you and you reply with *likewise.* I tell you that I love you and you show me that you do but you don't use the words. I tell you that I love your mom, and you say that she feels the same. Why, Alex?" she asked, gently. She placed her hand on my thigh.

"Are you sure that you're not overthinking this? Do I need to say the word?" I was deflecting, I knew I was, and I was aware I was also pushing a boundary that might cause our first row.

"No. It would be nice one time, though," she replied, removing her hand and settling back in her seat. She didn't speak for the rest of the journey.

That night, although we shared a bed, we might as well

not have. We slept with our backs to each other, facing opposite ends of the room. In fact, Gabriella was *asleep* before I even left the bathroom. I'd climbed into bed and spooned into her, but she'd shuffled, grumbling that she was too hot.

The following morning, although smiling and *polite,* she was distant.

"Have I offended you?" I asked on the journey into work.

She turned on her seat to face me. "Have you considered counselling?" she asked. I glanced at the driver who glanced back at me in the rear-view mirror.

"Sorry? Have I...No. Whatever would I want counselling for?" I knew my manner was brusque, and I'd probably reverted to a very formal Lord Alexander kind of voice.

"Might help you remove that stick from up your ass," she mumbled clearly enough for both the driver and me to hear.

My mouth fell open. She turned to look out the window and I could see her smirk in the reflection of the glass. She didn't speak for the rest of the journey, neither did I.

"Fucking infuriating," I mumbled as I pulled my chair away from my desk.

"Who?" Mackenzie asked as he walked into my office.

"Your best friend. Honestly, she makes me behave like a bloody teenager," I said, slamming papers down.

"Yep, although she says the same about you."

"What did she say?" I demanded.

"Nothing today, I haven't seen her yet. Can I sit or are

you going to throw the contents of your desk all over the floor?"

I stopped my slamming and aggressive piling of already piled papers and slumped into my chair. I waved my hand at the chair opposite.

Carolyn stood at my doorway. "Coffee?" she said.

Both Mackenzie and I answered simultaneously.

"Yes," I said.

"Definitely," he replied. "Wanna talk?"

I scowled. "No. Yes. I don't know. Not here. Now, I need to take my mind elsewhere. This consolidation. It's doable for sure, but I think you've got one or two businesses that might need to be cut loose now. There's no reason not to take the money and run." I then gave a list of the companies I thought would be better off sold.

"Great, that's what I was thinking as well. How about we shoot out to the US and get that underway?"

"Sure, when?" I asked and then smiled at Carolyn as two coffees were placed on the desk.

"I don't know, tomorrow?"

I stared at him. "I can't just hop on a plane tomorrow," I said.

"Why?"

"I don't know *why*, other than us Brits just don't work that way. We ponder, research the best method of travel and then book the first one we looked at. We...we deliberate, procrastinate, and other '...ates' I'm sure I'm missing," I said, stroppily, and then laughed. "Gabriella thinks I should have counselling to get the stick out of my *ass*. Maybe I do need to hop on a plane to America tomorrow to prove I don't have one up there!"

Mackenzie raised his hands in mock surrender. "I don't want to get into the middle of a domestic here."

"No, you're not. You've just given me an opportunity to show my spontaneous side. You want Mary to book the flights?"

He reached over to my desk phone and called upstairs. "Hello, my wonderful PA and all-round lovely Mary. How are you this fine morning?" he said. I chuckled.

I heard her shout her reply. "Feck off, eejit. What do you want?" I covered my mouth and laughed.

Mackenzie explained he'd like two first class seats on a mid-morning flight. He'd also like her to secure a pool car for the journey.

"Anything else? Iron your underpants, maybe?" she enquired.

"Mary, if you caught sight of my *underpants* you wouldn't be able to contain yourself next time you saw me," he said, to which she cut off the call.

"That is so childish, so juvenile," I said, laughing with him.

"Listen, she loves me, I know it."

I quietened then and my smile slipped. I blinked a couple of times.

"Oh, the fight wasn't over the L word, was it?" he asked, leaning forwards a little.

"Sort of. I'm not talking about it here. We'll talk tomorrow. Now please go away because I do have a business to run here, believe it or not," I said, waving him out of my office. He laughed as he left. I shook my head, not for one minute regretting taking up the offer to work with him.

I hope your morning has been good. I'm off to America tomorrow with Mackenzie. I'm

sure he'll tell you. Well, I wanted to tell you. I'll call later. Alex

I cursed myself after I'd sent the text message. Even my texts were anal!

Oh, yes, I need the stick removed. I'm not sure on the counselling element of it, though. Alex xx

I added two kisses, two!

Hello, my darling. Little steps, I know. I love you and you'll have a blast. Please, please meet up with my mother, otherwise she'll never forgive me, you, or Mackenzie. XXX Three kisses, Gabriella

She inserted a winky face too.

I had no intention of meeting her mother without her. That would be extremely rude as far as I was concerned.

Come with us? I texted back.

Not sure I can. How long will you be gone?

I called her. "I'm sorry, I can't have a conversation by text, it takes me forever to type. I think we'll only be there a few days. I've advised Mackenzie to sell a couple of businesses as part of his consolidation plan."

"You go with him. You'll have fun. Don't worry about meeting Mom unless you have a spare minute. I won't mention that you're out there. And we'll make a plan to return in a couple of weeks or so. How's that?" she asked.

"Perfect. I don't deserve you, Gabriella, I know that," I whispered.

"Let's chat later."

I said goodbye and continued with my work although my mind was very clearly not on the communications industry but Gabriella. I liked the thought of meeting her family, even the treasonous brother if I had to. Her mother sounded a classy lady; *Southern Royalty* Mackenzie had called her. I chuckled as I thought of her mother and mine sitting at the same table.

An image flashed through my mind of us at our wedding. It caught me off guard and I swallowed hard. I felt a pang in my chest, a want or a need, I wasn't sure. Maybe counselling was an option. I had no idea where my hesitancy came from. I was no longer worried that Gabriella would move back home, that feeling had passed. If she did, I'd go with her. It wasn't because my parents had a terrible marriage. They had an 'upper class' marriage and I know my father had a mistress that my mother knew about, but that was par for the course in our circles. I wasn't afraid of committing to something; I stuck out jobs way longer than I should have. I just didn't know. Gabriella was the perfect woman for me and if I didn't get my act together, I ran the risk of losing her. I was sure her patience would wear thin at some point. In addition, I was sure she wanted children and there was a time limit on that.

Mackenzie and I were settled into our seats ready for the flight to the States.

"How was Gabriella last night?" he asked.

"I didn't see her. An old *out of town* friend called and invited her to dinner. I said she should go."

"I wonder who that was?" he mused.

"No idea, I didn't catch her, or his, name."

A steward fussed around ensuring we were comfortable and that we had everything we needed. We fell silent while we took off and all the while the plane ascended.

"Any further on with the *moving in* together?" he asked, as he unclipped his seat belt.

"Jesus. I don't know why it has to be so complicated, to be honest. I own an apartment, she rents. Either we live in mine, or I sell, and we buy somewhere together. I don't want to live in a rented house but she loves her house."

"Buy her house then," Mackenzie said, as if it was the easiest thing to do.

"Landlord won't sell, we asked."

Gabriella had contacted the landlord's agency a while ago with a view to purchasing the house, only to be told he wasn't willing to sell. I guess, like I would, he wanted the security of knowing he owned a home should he return to the UK from Dubai. I didn't want to live in a rented house for fear of losing it should the owner want it back or sell it.

"It's odd because she's not like that, normally," he said, opening his newspaper.

"Like what?"

"So indecisive. She's a *had a thought, gonna do it now* type of person. I know she likes that house, but God knows why she wants to hang on to it when she could buy any of them in that neighbourhood."

"My apartment isn't as large but it's certainly big enough for us and, as I said to her, *give up your house, move in with me, until we find a more suitable property*," I said.

"Mmm, odd. Maybe I'll have a chat and see what fears she has," he said.

I opened my laptop and finished up some reports that I'd been meaning to do. I also started to think that maybe Gabriella was having second thoughts about living with me, although it had only been a couple of days since she'd been chatting with my mother about décor. Maybe my inability to tell her how I feel was causing her to back off, just in case. I mean, I'd be hesitant at moving in with someone if I didn't know whether they loved me or not. I turned to discuss the matter with Mackenzie to find him asleep. The man slept from the minute we crossed Europe until the time we landed!

"How do you do it?" I joked when he finally woke as the seat belt sign was turned off and we were being encouraged to leave.

"Practice," he replied, grabbing his flight bag and suit carrier from the steward.

We had nothing other than cabin luggage so sped through arrivals. Of course, we had to separate at customs but met the other side. Once outside, a car was idling in a no park zone waiting to collect us. Mackenzie thanked the driver and we set off for his house.

Mackenzie's home was a house that would be my retirement dream, should he ever sell it, which I knew he wouldn't. It had been his parents' house and sat on the beach. It was a wooden house with a wraparound porch and that evening, after grilling steaks, we sat on wooden chairs and drank beer. The sound of the ocean was hypnotic and whether it was the time difference or a sense of absolute peace, I felt myself drifting off.

"Head on up to bed, Alex, if you want."

"I think I shall. Thanks for the food and beer, and for the hundredth time, this house is bloody amazing! If one comes up for sale nearby, be sure to let me know."

I'd texted Gabriella to let her know that we had arrived and how much I adored the house. I also told her that I was totally exhausted and heading to bed. She wished me pleasant dreams, of her, she added, and promised to call the following day.

I don't recall my head hitting the pillow before I was asleep.

The following morning, we were off. First stop was the car restoration company that Mackenzie had invested in. An old school friend welcomed him with a handshake and a pat on the back. We looked over accounts, seeing a flourishing business but one that didn't have the cash flow to buy Mackenzie out.

"Jake, I really want to offload some of my businesses. I want to consolidate, keep things closer together. There isn't the cash flow here to buy me out so I'm just going to transfer my shares to you, okay? Call it an early Christmas gift," he said.

I had the feeling that Jake was assuming the worst when the meeting started and his face when it ended was the opposite. A broad grin showed off straight teeth that had a permanent toothpick wedged between them. He chewed on it, flicking it from side to side. When he spoke, it was through those gritted teeth and I wondered if he actually had his jaw wired shut at one point. However, he gave a yelp of surprise, the toothpick fell to the floor. Only then did I notice quite a few dotted around. I laughed; his surprise was infectious. He pumped my hand and thanked me over and over, not that it was my decision for Mackenzie to just give him the business.

"Well, that was a surprise," I said when we left.

Mackenzie shrugged his shoulders. "Not much more I could do, to be honest. My shares aren't worth that much and he's about to be a father again soon. I can't say I'll do that the next stop though. Be ready for some...*interesting* people and a not so friendly welcome," he winked and laughed.

He was right. We entered a factory and were, initially, ignored or sneered at. Mackenzie strode around, greeting workers warmly. One or two returned that, but sheepishly as if they'd be caught and punished. Some just gave a brief nod. The factory manufactured universal car parts, bolts and wheel nuts, that kind of thing. I knew that it had initially belonged to his father and was *stolen* from him by his father-in-law. That was until Mackenzie ended up with the majority of shares.

We climbed a metal staircase and walked along a corridor that held a series of offices. At the end it opened up.

"Well, hello, there," a female voice said. I looked over to see another blonde, although a stunner, nowhere near as beautiful as Gabriella.

"Addison, meet my partner, Alex." Mackenzie had never referred to me as his partner before and I wasn't, but I knew who Addison was.

She slid from the desk she had been perching on and walked over with her hand out. I took it and shook. "It's a real pleasure to meet you, Alex. I've heard a lot about you," she said.

"The pleasure is all mine. And I've heard a lot about you, too," I replied, bowing my head.

"I hope it was all good," she answered with a giggle. I didn't reply.

"Where is he?" Mackenzie asked, looking around at empty desks.

"Flying. He has a new plane to try out," she replied.

She walked over to Mackenzie and placed her hands on his lapels, she stroked one as if removing a piece of lint.

He held her wrists and slowly removed them. "He knew we were meeting today," Mackenzie said, anger laced his voice.

She shrugged. "I guess he had better things to do," she said, smiling. She made my skin itch.

"Not a problem, we'll just get on. We'd like two coffees," he said, and then turned his back on her. He beckoned to me to follow and I tried not to laugh. Her mouth had fallen open and her eyes were wide with outrage.

We walked into an office that could have been taken off the set of Dallas. Wood panelled walls held the stuffed heads of deer and bears. Red carpet lined the floor and there was a large, dark oak sideboard with crystal cut decanters. Even I, not having any interior design skills, would have put this back into the eighties.

"Shall we?" Mackenzie said, waving at a sofa. We were soon joined by some of the accounts team.

Secretaries gathered files and coffee was offered. Addison had disappeared. When we had all that we needed, I compared the figures we had to the ones we were shown. Since our meeting appeared to be a surprise to the accounts team, the documents didn't match. An interrogation ensued. I asked the head of accounts to explain why the figures we were being sent were lower than the ones printed off. The company was doing far better than we were being made aware of.

It was also discovered that Addison was an employee paid an extortionate salary.

"What does she do here?" I asked.

"Erm, I'm not sure," came the answer. "Fire her," Mackenzie said.

Four men looked between themselves, not one was sure on what to say or do.

"Or keep her, I don't care, actually," he added. "What we're here for is to let you know that I'm removing myself from this business. I intend to sell my shares on the open market."

Again, the four men looked between themselves.

"I think we're done here?" he said, looking at me. I asked for some photocopies of accounts, and a secretary rushed off. I then nodded.

Half an hour later we were back in the car. "I knew he wouldn't be there," Mackenzie said.

"Who, exactly?"

"Her father. He's the one who runs that business."

"I thought you hated each other?"

"We do, and it's a shame he wasn't there. You would have gotten to see the very *unwelcome* welcome." He laughed and we headed back to his house.

That evening we sat with two lawyers and went through what was needed for Mackenzie to offload the two businesses. Paperwork was drawn up and it was left to them to finalise. Mackenzie received a call from his ex-father-in-law and without it being on speaker, I could hear the shouting and swearing. It appeared that he couldn't afford to buy Mackenzie's shares and he didn't want anyone else in the business.

"I imagine that you're feeling very much like my father did when you took that factory from him. I don't care if you can afford to buy my shares or not. They're for sale, and whoever buys them, you'll have to work *for*."

He disconnected the call. He had mentioned to his lawyers a couple of businessmen he wanted them to approach, with a view to selling to them. He ran through the details with me. It seemed a very poor decision, and would not net Mackenzie anywhere near the worth of his shares, but there was no convincing him. This was a pure revenge deal and it worried me a little.

"Why, Mackenzie?" I asked when we were alone.

"He nearly killed my father and he didn't care, Alex. He made my life hell for years, making me beholden to him. He's as illegal as it comes where business is concerned, so don't feel sorry for him."

"I don't. I worry about you. Getting rid of these shares means letting go of that vendetta once and for all," I said.

He smiled. "I know. I'm finally ready to. On that business, anyway." He smirked leaving me with the impression the ex-father-in-law had other businesses that Mackenzie 'owned.'

I wasn't aware of all the details surrounding his relationship with his ex-wife and her family, only what Gabriella had said, and the small things he had shared, but it did seem to be a vendetta that had been going on for years.

It was nice to spend a couple of days with Mackenzie on our own and although still *at work* we had plenty of time to chat. We drove to various places so he could show me where he went to school, where he lived in the past. We visited his father and it was very clear there was a fractious relationship there that both seemed desperate to repair but didn't know how. Finally, we had a fleeting visit with Mrs. Collingsworth.

Gabriella was stunning, and it was so easy to see where she got those genes.

"Let me introduce Alex. He and Gabriella are an item, as such," Mackenzie said as we were greeted at the front door. I wasn't sure *I* would have liked to hear it in that way and by the raised eyebrows, neither had Mrs. Collingsworth.

"Well, if you are an item *as such,* you ought to come on in and explain yourself," she said. I caught the twinkle in her eye and the slight wink to Mackenzie.

I'd never met a more wonderful woman, other than her daughter, of course. She was gracious, regal, welcoming, and so very *proper*. She loved that I was a Lord and peppered me with questions about who I knew and whether I was related to royalty or not. We drank iced tea, something that wasn't quite to my taste, and we ate dainty sandwiches. Save for the cold drink, it could have been a traditional British afternoon tea.

When it was time to leave, she insisted on speaking with Gabriella on the telephone. I had offered to Face-Time, but she wasn't having any of that. She assured Gabriella that she hadn't frightened me off, she didn't believe, and that I was a charming English gentleman, the likes of which she wished her daughter had met a long time ago. Gabriella's sighs were loud, and I laughed.

"Now, Alex. I don't like *as such* or even *sort of* relationships," she said.

I took her hand and raised it to my lips. I bowed and kissed her hand, clicking my feet together. "I can assure you, Mrs. Collingsworth. I am very much in a relationship with your daughter."

She blushed, waved her hand in front of her face and

swooned. Her housekeeper rolled her eyes and Mackenzie laughed. We left the house.

"Does that work all the time?" he asked.

"Yep."

The drive back to the house to collect our things before leaving for the airport filled me with sadness. "I don't know how you can leave this place, honestly, I don't," I said, looking out at the ocean as we drove past.

"It's not easy but, for the minute, London is where I want to be."

"Because of...?"

He shook his head and sighed. "I love my home, well, technically still my father's house, but I still get that pang of hurt that I was forced to leave it. I hate LA and my apartment is up for sale now. If I was to come back it would be to the beach house but only once I've got someone to share it with."

"Maybe we need to trade places for a little while. You do London and I do here," I said, waving my arm at the ocean and laughing.

"That might not be a bad idea one day," he replied.

CHAPTER FIFTEEN

I slept for a straight nineteen hours, so Gabriella told me. I woke stiff and uncomfortable, hot, and with a fuzzy head. Gabriella was bustling in the kitchen and I smelled coffee. I rose from the bed and walked, naked, to wrap my arms around her from behind.

"Back in the land of the living, are you?" she asked, laughing.

"God, I hate jet lag. I feel awful, and we've only been away a couple of days."

I didn't recall suffering so much before but on occasions past, I'd spend a week away, so I guess I was able to adjust over a slower time frame. This time around we had landed and then spent two days running without stopping.

"I have to head on home in a minute. I've left you coffee," she said.

I sighed. "Wait, let me at least drive you."

"My driver is on his way." She turned in my arms and

smiled. "I'll be back later, of course, so keep that erection saved for me, won't you?"

My cock pressed into her stomach. "I might not be able to wait all that time," I said, teasing.

She patted my cheek. "Then you better pleasure yourself now so you're ready for me in a couple of hours." She smirked as she walked away.

I laughed and shook my head. She was something, for sure. I showered and dressed, and then headed into the office.

"Alex, can you spare me a minute?" Mackenzie said when I answered the phone.

"Sure. I'll come on up."

"I'll come down, I think I need some air," he said. I frowned as I replaced the handset.

He was in my office in a couple of minutes. "Want to go get a coffee?" I asked. He nodded. As we left the building I asked, "Are you okay?"

"I'm not sure."

We crossed the road to a small coffee shop, one that Mackenzie owned, and grabbed two take-out Americanos. We found a bench and sat silently for a moment or two just sipping on the piping hot, but delicious drinks.

"This is going to sound odd, but I look at you and Gabriella and I want that for myself. I want a *proper* relationship but I'm not sure I'm capable."

"Okay?" I replied, a little confused by his confession.

He must have caught my expression as he explained further, "Sometimes, I think I'm too like my father. It's all work and I love it, and I resent any time I'm taken away from the business. On the other hand, I'm bored by a lot of what I do. I'm forty soon and the urge to settle down is tugging at me.

"It just sounds to me, Mackenzie, that you're in a rut. Perhaps you need a new challenge, we've said this before."

He nodded and then laughed. "Look at us, two grown men, adults, who should know fucking better than this." He shook his head.

"Slow down a little. Take some time to really understand what you want from life right now. That would be my advice." I wasn't sure it was the best advice, but it was all I had on offer. "Which is what I think Gabriella is doing," I added.

"She hasn't said anything to me," he replied.

"It's just a feeling. One minute she's all over this living together, the next, coolness and no discussion."

"Were we like this as teenagers? Or young adults?" he asked, and then laughed.

"I honestly don't think so. But then, were we ever really this serious about life back then? I feel, Mackenzie, we are late bloomers, as my mother would say." I smiled as I spoke.

Both Mackenzie and I had spent the best part of our younger adult lives working all the hours. Of course, we'd dated, fucked, and he had married, but we'd never really settled down.

"There's one other thing, Alex. This might be a lot to ask considering, but would you consider taking over my US businesses for a while? I know while we were there you said you'd swap but I wasn't sure how serious you were. I don't want to keep flying back and forth for the moment and I know you and Gabriella together would make an amazing team."

I paused for a moment. A little in shock. "Oh, I wasn't expecting that. I'm not sure. I mean, I'd jump at the chance, but would Gabriella? Would we put her in a position where she has to choose between us?" I asked.

"She'd choose you over me any day," he said, a frown of confusion crossed his forehead.

"I'm not so sure," I replied.

"Can we at least talk about this another time? I don't want you to dismiss this out of hand. Once the consolidation is done, we can bring everything back in-house here," he said.

"So, it's not a long-term move?" I asked.

"Not unless you want it to be."

"I think it could be quite an exciting project at least until the consolidation is complete. After that, we'd have to see."

"You're the only one I can trust, Alex, and I hope I'm not imposing on you too much."

We sat for another few moments in silence as we thought on what each had said and finished our coffee.

"This adulting lark is quite the pain in the arse, isn't it?" I said, chuckling to myself mostly.

We threw our coffee cups into the recycling bin and took a slow walk back to the office.

I decided not to mention to Gabriella what Mackenzie and I had spoken about. I didn't want the possible move to the US discussed until I knew what was holding her back from moving in with me. I sure didn't want to get all the way to the US and then find she was cooling over our relationship.

"Hi, I was looking for you two?" Gabriella said, as we crossed the reception to the lifts.

"Just went for a coffee," Mackenzie replied.

"A boy chat, huh?" She smiled at us both.

"Something like that," he replied, giving her a wink.

"Are we still on for dinner this evening?" she asked.

We had decided the three of us would have dinner. We hadn't done that in a while.

"We are," Mackenzie said. He patted me on the back. "Meet here?" I nodded in response and he walked to the lifts.

Gabriella linked her arm through mine. "I've missed you today," she said.

"You only saw me this morning," I replied. "Where are you off to?"

"A little shopping. A girl can't have too many shoes and my usual store have called to say they have some new stock they think I'd like. I want to get in before everyone else does," she laughed.

"If we do buy a house, we're going to need an annexe simply for your shoes," I replied.

She rose on tiptoes and planted a kiss on my lips. "I do demand a walk-in closet of my own, at the very least," she said, and it was the first reference she'd made about *our* home in ages.

"I'm sure that can be arranged, my Lady."

She smiled and promised to be back in an hour to meet for dinner. I shook my head as I walked to the lift.

"Lord Duchoveny?" At the sound of my name I turned to see a young man walk into reception. A security guard stood waiting to see if I needed him.

"How can I help?" Since he had addressed me by title, he clearly knew who I was. He held a large white envelope.

"You might be interested in this," he said.

He reached out with the envelope, but I didn't take it. Instead, the security guard did. He ran it through an X-ray machine before handing it over to me.

"Why would I be interested in this?" I asked.

"My grandmother works here," he said, and then smiled.

Realising he was referring to Mary, I said, "Then I shall be delighted to accept whatever you have here."

"If I can be of service again, please feel free to reach out." He felt inside his suit pocket for a business card. I was slightly taken aback by him; he was poles apart from Mary. Well spoken, for a start.

I looked at the card and then back to him. "Sebastian, thank you. I'm sure we'll chat again."

He nodded and turned to leave. I watched him walk away and through the glass, I saw him wave for a taxi. He held an air of confidence about him, more than I would expect for someone who worked in the postal room of a newspaper. Something didn't add up, for sure. Maybe Mary had simply got it wrong.

I was back in my office with the envelope on my desk in no time. I rang upstairs to speak to Mackenzie and left a message when Mary said he was on the phone.

"I met Sebastian today," I said.

"Aw, he said he was popping in. I wonder why he didn't come and see me, the little git. Probably because he owes me a tenner. I bet he didn't give it to you to pass on, did he?" she asked.

"No, sorry. Are you sure he works in the postal department at the newspaper? He looked terribly smart, dressed in a suit," I said.

"Well, he did when he first started. I can't imagine he's the boss now, didn't pass any exams, the lazy sod. His muvva is a bit posh. She left my Trevor years ago, we said he was her bit of rough!"

"Perhaps he's worked his way up in the newspaper," I said, making a note to investigate and ignoring the Trevor comment. I was sure I'd heard he was in jail but I wouldn't ask for fear Mary's wrath if I was wrong.

"Anyway, I'll get the boss man to call you when he gets off the phone. He's obviously talking dirty to someone; he has his blinds closed."

I had no idea how to answer that, I didn't want to know if he was talking dirty to anyone, but I knew I ought to mention to Mackenzie that's what Mary *thought* he was doing when his blinds were closed.

"Thank you, Mary," I said, then replaced the handset before she could divulge more of Mackenzie's secrets.

I opened the envelope and tomorrow's newspaper slid out. Front page was Stanton's face, in his House of Lords robes, and then next to that, him on a bed with a woman tied up and Daughton watching from the sidelines. His genitals and her face were blacked out, of course, but it was absolutely clear what was going on. The headlines screamed out:

Lord of the Realm in threesome with Russian agent and prostitute – Do we have another Profumo Affair?

He wasn't a Lord of the Realm, but I guessed that wasn't the point. "Fucking hell," I said to myself.

"What's up?" Mackenzie asked as he walked in. I slid the newspaper to him.

"Fucking hell," he echoed.

We read the article, which was a huge embellishment on the facts but did, thankfully, leave out all reference to the woman's name. There was a further photograph of her bruised body, again, her face was blacked out, but mention was made of her split lip and swollen eyes.

The article went on to say that the woman had reported the assault but the police had dismissed her case. Plenty of women's rights and #MeToo activists were taking up the case on her behalf, it said. A lawyer had come forward to offer his service pro-bono.

"Wow, that's blown up," Mackenzie said.

"Yeah. I worry for Veronica, though. He knows she gave us the photographs."

"Mmm, hadn't thought about that."

"I'll call her in a minute, make sure she has enough security around," I said.

The story went on to feature on the inside front cover and the next page as well. What pleased me was seeing so much support for the woman, questions as to why the police hadn't acted and calls for the *establishment* to be held accountable for crimes. The journalist had reached out to Stanton for a statement, he'd obviously declined to answer; all questions were to be directed to his lawyer.

The purpose of the article was to break up the *loan shark* business he had on the side and that seemed to be working. The journalist, and I needed to check the name, had delved deeply into Stanton's business arrangements, found a link to his *let's bail out the Lloyds 'names'* business and started to ask questions about them. Add in Daughton and the journalist had made a presumed link, or maybe not, to mafia money being laundered in the UK. It was a story that would run and run, I had no doubt about that.

My mobile phone rang.

"Darling, have you seen the papers?" Veronica asked.

"I have a copy of one here right now. I was going to call you. I didn't expect the connection with Daughton to be so prominent and I'm worried about you," I said.

"Don't be, Alex. I have enough security here around the clock, I'm sure I'll be fine. I think that the emphasis will soon change. More women are going to come forward, bring the story back to Stanton."

"How do you know?" I asked.

"Because he didn't just start his nasty activities here. He was a member of other clubs and I believe one threw him out. Mark my words, there'll be other women coming forward."

I breathed a sigh of relief. For a moment I thought she had first-hand knowledge, other women at *her* establishment that had been beaten by him. I'd have to rethink my opinion of my cousin if I thought she'd *allowed* that to continue.

"Okay, but I want you to check in with me regularly, please?" I asked.

"I will. It's all so terribly exciting, isn't it?" she said.

"No, exciting isn't a word choice I'd have used but effective, for sure. Seems his business partners are all distancing themselves from him."

We said our goodbyes and I returned to the paper. I went back to the start of the story. Sebastian Dye. I pulled the card from my pocket and matched up the name.

"Who is it?" Mackenzie asked.

"Seems Mary's grandson isn't just a postal boy," I said, showing him the card and laughing.

"Very useful to know."

Having insiders in the media had always been an asset to large businesses and corporations. A heads-up on a news story about one's company or a competitor always goes down well and certainly ensures a very nice bottle of whisky at Christmas.

Mackenzie's mobile phone buzzed to alert he had an incoming message. He looked at it and then smiled.

"Stanton is being re-arrested for the assault. The Serious Crime Squad are involved, as are the Financial Action Task Force," he said, chuckling.

The FATF was a multi-country task force to combat not only money laundering but the financing of terrorist activity. If they were involved, Stanton really was in the shit.

"I wonder what they'll get him on first. No doubt he'll settle on the assault charges if he gives up all his contacts," I said.

Personally, I didn't care about the laundering aspect. I cared about the people he had hurt with his loan business, and I mostly cared about the women he had abused. People like him needed to be taken off the streets.

I looked at my watch. "Shit, look at the time."

We were meant to be meeting Gabriella for dinner. I dialled her mobile and received her voicemail.

"Hello, I assume you're still shopping. Do you want to meet at the restaurant?"

"Where did she go?" Mackenzie asked.

I shrugged my shoulders. "Her favourite shoe shop, she said."

"We'll go and collect her. She could be hours," Mackenzie replied, laughing.

I often wondered what people thought when they saw

the three of us together, especially when she had her arms linked with both of us. Although a fairly jealous guy by nature, her friendship with Mackenzie didn't bother me at all. I wasn't of the *school* that necessarily believed a man could have a female best friend without there being just a little sexual tension, but that certainly wasn't the case with those two. They were more siblings than friends.

A car was idling outside the office and we'd left instructions that should Gabriella return, she was to wait for us.

"What on earth...?" I said as we pulled up outside a darkened windowed store with no name.

Mackenzie grinned. "Your cousin introduced me to this store, and I mentioned it to Gabriella. She hasn't left it since!"

We pushed a button and waited for access. The door opened automatically. The store was sectioned nicely. One side displayed all the shoes that I knew Gabriella loved, the high heels that seemed impossible to walk in and that created an endless length of leg. There were beautiful dresses to another side, and then it changed a little...or a lot.

We walked through and into another room that held all the implements needed for the club, plus items I'd never seen. Everything the discerning BDSM enthusiast required was for sale. Latex and leather outfits, holes cut out everywhere, lace and string adorned mannequins with mind baffling examples of how to wear it. Crosses, chains, whips, lined a wall for those with an active dungeon. I chuckled as I walked around. Vibrators and dildos, strap-ons, paddles, and ornately carved knives for blood play were proudly displayed inside glass cabinets.

A woman approached us wearing a cat suit with a tail that she held and swung around.

"Mackenzie, and you must be Alex. You are the spit of your cousin. How is Veronica? I must visit this new club of yours," she said, air kissing us both. "Oh, please accept my apologies. I'm Jodie." She held out her hand, finally letting go of her tail.

"We were hoping to find Gabriella here," Mackenzie asked.

"No, I was expecting her earlier, but she didn't show. I have some amazing new Louboutins in for her to try on."

I crumpled my brow. "She didn't show?" I asked, concern lacing my voice.

Jodie shook her head, slowly. "Is everything okay?" she asked.

"Yes, I'm sure she got distracted elsewhere," I said, offering a hopefully comforting, yet totally fake smile.

"Well, gentleman, if there is anything I can help you with, please ask or feel free to browse," she said.

Mackenzie and I thanked her but declined the offer to browse. We headed back out to the car instead.

I called Gabriella, and then left a text message asking her to return my call when it went to voicemail again. Mackenzie did the same.

"Where on earth has she gone?" I asked, more to myself.

"Let's head back to the office, in case she went there," he said.

By the time we got back, most of the office block was in darkness, only security was on patrol. We asked if Gabriella had returned to be told that she hadn't.

We decided to try her house hoping to find her in the shower without realising she'd set us off into a panic.

Although there were one or two lights on, the house was mostly in darkness. I opened the front door and called out. Her bag wasn't in its usual place on a bench in the hallway. We walked around each room knowing she wasn't there but needing to check. We walked upstairs and into the master bedroom. Something was off.

"There's been a struggle," I said.

"Huh?"

My heart began to pound at my chest. "Her perfume bottle is on the floor. That cushion is always on that chair, not the other one. The curtain is off its hook. Trust me, something has happened in this room and someone has tidied up but not well enough."

Mackenzie pulled out his phone and called Detective Burrows. He gave a report of a potential missing person and detailed what we had done to find her. Burrows finished the conversation by saying he was on his way.

We paced, we called and texted. We argued about whether to call her mother. I had wanted to, just in case there had been an accident at home and Gabriella was mid-flight without being able to tell us she had left.

Mackenzie insisted that wouldn't have happened. First, Mrs. Collingsworth would never have just called Gabriella to give bad news, she would have called him first so he could be with her when the bad news was delivered. Second, she would have had time to call one of us before getting onto a plane.

I opened the closet, her luggage was on the top shelf, where it normally lived.

I walked around the garden, although not big enough

to hide in, I wanted to see if there was any evidence of someone breaking in, for example. Could she have disturbed an intruder and...?

I ran back inside. "Call the local hospitals," I said.

"Shit, yes," Mackenzie replied.

While I Googled, he called, asking if a blonde had been brought in, maybe unconscious and unable to give her name. He received a lot of resistance initially, until he said that he had filed a missing persons report. Each hospital either told us they had no one of that description or name or offered to call us back, something I doubted they'd do.

Half an hour later Detective Burrows arrived. I explained how we were meant to meet, where we had gone to look for her, and the items in the bedroom that were displaced. He seemed reluctant to agree there had been a struggle in the bedroom initially.

My voice rose in anger and frustration. "Listen, we're talking about a southern American woman. She is precise, very house proud to the point of not trusting a cleaner to keep her house the way she wants it. That perfume can only be sourced from one place so she's very precious about it, and if I left that pillow on the *wrong* fucking chair, I'd be paying hell for it. Something has happened in this house."

Burrows held up his hand to stop my flow of anger. "Okay, let's calm down. I've put a call through to see if we can track her phone but I'm going to need some more details. You know I can't put this in as a missing person, not with her age and the short time she has been missing. But considering what we've read in the paper this morning, I am going to take this seriously."

I deflated, as did Mackenzie. The thought had certainly crossed my mind but I'd pushed it to one side not wanting to voice my concern for fear of being correct.

"You don't think..." I started but couldn't finish.

"We don't know anything just yet. She might have gotten caught up with friends," Mackenzie replied, unconvincingly.

Detective Burrows asked lots of questions, most of which Mackenzie answered. I showed him a photograph I'd taken on my phone and he asked for a copy of it. She was laughing at something I'd said. I stared at her face and my heart ached.

I love you, please be okay, I thought over and over.

An hour passed, and then another. More police arrived, a thorough search of the house was undertaken, and Mackenzie and I sat in the garden.

"I can't just sit here any longer. I feel totally useless," I said. Mackenzie nodded.

I called security at my apartment block; they'd accessed my flat with the master key to see if she was there. She wasn't but I wanted to look for myself, I needed something to do.

"We're going to check my apartment again. I doubt she's there, but we can't sit here anymore," I said.

"Okay, but someone is going to have to stay while we finish up here," Burrows said.

I looked at my watch. "How long do you think that will be?"

"No more than half an hour."

We agreed to wait, as frustrating as it was. We couldn't just leave the police in her house, hoping they'd set the alarm and lock up after themselves. I paced, Mackenzie drank endless cups of black coffee and I was sure the handshaking was a combination of fear and caffeine overdose.

I scrolled through my contacts. "Mother, I'm sorry it's late and this is a rather strange question, but Gabriella hasn't visited you, has she?" I asked. It was a long shot but that's all I had left.

"No, darling. How is she? Is everything okay? I'll tell you who has, Duncan! He came by just a few hours ago."

I wasn't interested in Duncan in that moment. "I'm sure it was lovely to see him, but I need to go. I'll call tomorrow." I cut off the call without waiting for a goodbye from her. I then texted in case she worried all evening.

Sorry the call was cut off rather abruptly. I'll call tomorrow to explain but if Gabriella does make contact in any way, could you let me know? Alex.

She was quick with her reply.

Of course, darling. I hope nothing is wrong with you both. She's a lovely girl.

The police started to pack up. It seemed there had been a partial print found on the perfume bottle. When they'd left and we set the alarm and locked up, it was gone midnight.

"Are you okay?" Mackenzie asked.

I shook my head. "I couldn't tell her that I loved her. Now, if something has happened..."

Mackenzie placed his hand on my shoulder. "Nothing has happened, Alex. We can't think that way. Let's get going."

We took a taxi back to my apartment. The lift seemed to take forever, and it was with some trepidation that I opened the apartment door. Nothing had changed since I'd left it, and, of course, Gabriella wasn't to be found.

"Anything out of place?" Mackenzie asked. He picked up a shirt of Gabriella's.

"No, well, not that I can tell. That shirt was there this morning."

I opened wardrobe doors, she had shoes and work clothes, a couple of casual outfits all hanging. Her toiletries were in the bathroom, her hairbrushes and styling products on the dressing table. My stomach started to physically ache. I sat heavily on the bed and covered my face with my hands. I felt exhausted and so very scared. I'd never felt fear like it. It gnawed away at my insides. Mackenzie sat beside me; he placed his arm around my shoulders. Before I realised, a tear dripped through my fingers.

We were beyond the, *she'd forgotten the time,* or *she'd met up with friends and forgot to call* stage. It was early hours of the morning and there was no doubt something had happened to her. We went back to the office, checked with the pool car manager again to be told, for the second time, she hadn't taken a car that day. We walked from the office door and in the direction of the store, knowing she'd never have walked that distance. We stopped a couple of taxi drivers to ask if there was a central system to track a missing person that may have used a taxi. He offered to share her photograph, but I was reluctant. I did agree to take his details and we'd have the police share anything necessary.

Eventually we just sat on a bench watching the river.

"Now what?" I asked.

"Now I think we go back to her house and we wait," he said.

If she was going to go anywhere, I would have hoped it would be home, but I wasn't sure. I sighed, feeling all the anguish knotting my insides. "Don't you think, if she's in trouble, she would come to me or you?"

"I don't know. I'm not thinking straight. Let's go to mine. You have security, if she shows up they can contact you."

We drove to Mackenzie's house and we watched the sun rise.

CHAPTER SIXTEEN

I must have been dozing when Mackenzie took a call on my phone. I sat bolt upright in the chair in the living room when I heard his voice.

"We're on our way, did you call the police?" he asked with a sense of urgency. He cut off the call straight away. "She's at the club, that was Veronica," he said.

"What?"

We rushed from the house and into my car. There was a debate about which was the fastest, his Aston or my Bentley but since his car was in a garage, I couldn't be arsed to wait even the short time it would take to raise the garage doors. I sped down the streets and through London ignoring every red light and speed limit.

When we were on the motorway, Mackenzie took a call from Detective Burrows. "Yes, Veronica called, we're on our way there now," he said. "Not going to happen," he added, and I suspected he was told we should stay away.

"Let's see who gets there first," was his last comment before he shut down the call.

"Why the club?" I asked, confused.

"All Veronica said was they'd had a little trouble but Gabriella is safe."

"They'd had a little trouble?" I stared at him with a brow so furrowed it hurt.

He shrugged his shoulders. "Coming from your cousin that could mean someone was rude, or someone is dead. Fuck knows what she meant, Alex."

Veronica often *had a little trouble* and I remembered one time having to deal with the family lawyers to get her released from a police cell somewhere after being, probably correctly, accused of smoking dope in a public place. Mackenzie was correct, of course, it could be very little or very large!

I punched in my code for the gates and they swung open. Gravel flew as my tyres spun on the driveway and we left the car running with the doors open when we arrived. The front door was locked and the house in darkness. In that moment, I wished our approach hadn't been so loud.

"I know a way in," I said, remembering a route from childhood.

Mackenzie followed me as we ran around the side of the house. There was an outbuilding and in the floor was a hatch. It was an escape route that led from the house when it was built centuries ago and an exciting playground for Veronica and me as children. I pulled back the rug to expose the hatch. Clearly it hadn't been used in years and I waved my way through the spider webs as I climbed down. I had to crouch low and scuttle along the small corridor. When we reached the end, I put up my hand.

"We don't know there isn't still someone here, do we?" I asked. Although I couldn't see clearly, I just caught Mackenzie shake his head.

A thought had run through my mind, Veronica could have been forced to call us. We could be walking into a trap.

"Where the fuck are the security guards?" he whispered.

"They have a room they use, cameras all over the place. I assume they've been incapacitated in some way," I said, having no idea what had happened to them.

I gently turned the old metal doorknob and the door creaked open. It would lead us into the pantry, which was off the kitchen. What I didn't anticipate was that racking had been placed in front of the door. It wobbled and a can fell to the floor. I pulled the door closed quickly in case the noise alerted anyone. We waited and, hearing nothing, I gently pushed the door open again. We squeezed our way out and waited for our eyes to adjust to the dim light coming from under the door leading to the kitchen.

I placed my ear to the door to listen, it was quiet and, although the club would cater for overnight stays, that side hadn't opened up as yet. There was no staff preparing breakfast. Our problem was, once we left the kitchen we would be in the hallway with nowhere to hide.

Neither of us was prepared to wait, though. I opened the door and we made our way, as quietly as we could, through the kitchen and into the hall. No one was to be seen. The bar door was open and the room empty. It was as we stood at the bottom of the stairs that we heard a sound, the noise a piece of furniture would make as it was dragged across the floor. We raced up the carpeted stairs and followed the sound.

It appeared to come from one of the attic playrooms. One set aside mostly for Veronica. Just as we approached the door, it was pulled open.

"Fucking hell," Mackenzie said.

Veronica stood in front of us. Her hair was knotted and messy. She had a black eye with her upper lid partially closed, bruises and cuts to her face, neck, and shoulders. Her shirt was torn and spotted with blood. She had been crying, clean tracks ran through her grubby, bloodied cheeks. Her lip was split, and dried blood had crusted. The gash opened when she tried to speak.

"We heard you come," she said, her voice very hoarse and I guessed she had been choked.

Mackenzie wrapped her in his arms and pulled her to one side. I rushed into the room. Gabriella was curled up on a sofa, she wasn't in as bad a condition as Veronica, but it was clear she had been attacked. She cried and held out her arms to me.

"Oh, baby, baby, I love you. My God, what happened? I love you," I said, peppering her face with kisses.

She hiccuped as she tried to speak. When she couldn't she looked over my shoulder. I turned to follow her gaze.

Tied to the wall was Stanton. He was clothed although it was clear he'd fought with someone and I began to suspect it was Veronica. He also sported cuts and bruises. He breathed hard, unable to speak because silver gaffer tape covered his mouth. His eyes were wide with fright and it was as I approached that I noticed something in his side. An arrowhead of some kind, it was attached to a wire.

I followed the wire to a black object. When I picked it up, he shook his head from side to side violently, he screamed into the tape, I pushed the button and I held the fucking thing down. He convulsed, screaming, rattling the restraints that held him to the wall.

Mackenzie had rushed into the room and was holding both Gabriella and Veronica. When he saw what I'd done, he walked over to me. He reached for the taser and I gave it to him. I didn't want Stanton fucking electrocuted, I wanted him able to answer in court. I did however, beat the fuck out of him.

It wasn't satisfying, beating a man tied to a wall, but I couldn't stop. I punched his face, broke his nose, felt his blood splatter over mine and drip down my knuckles. I was desperate to hurt him. I continued my assault until I heard Gabriella call me. Seconds later, the police barged into the room.

Ambulances were called to take away the guards, although the police didn't tell us why, and all the time, I held Gabriella. I wasn't letting her go. She cried, as did Veronica who recounted what happened to the police and us.

Between the women, they managed to tell us what had happened.

"I was in my office; we had no guests booked in for last night so I wasn't expecting anyone. I gave a couple of the guys the night off," she said, glancing at Mackenzie who had his mouth open in annoyance and shock. "Stanton came in, I didn't see him at first. He sprayed some kind of gas into the guards' room, I don't know if they're alive or dead," she said, crying harder at the thought.

"He followed me home, I'd popped back to grab a coat.

I don't remember much other than he held a cloth over my face, and I was so woozy," Gabriella said.

He'd used some kind of chemical to incapacitate the guards, and on Gabriella before bringing her to the club. He'd held a knife to her throat to scare Veronica enough to open a playroom door and then lock it behind her. What he hadn't anticipated was her fight instinct. He, stupidly, thought he could overpower them both, he told them he wanted to leave them stripped for us to find. When I heard that, it took four policemen to hold me back from chasing after the ambulance that had taken him away.

Veronica had fought well and between the women they had overpowered him.

"I don't think I'll ask where you got this police issue taser," Detective Burrows said with a cringe.

Knowing there were some high-ranking members of the police force that frequented the club, I wasn't sure what her response would be.

"Some of my clients like the thrill," she said, then shrugged her shoulders as if being tasered as part of your sexual activities was perfectly normal.

Gabriella and Veronica were taken to the local hospital to be checked over. Both were advised to stay in, both refused although they stayed long enough for their wounds to be photographed and nails scraped. We headed back to mine while the police dealt with the aftermath of the club. Veronica had called in the lads' off duty to manage things.

"I need to shower," Gabriella said. I nodded and helped her into the bedroom.

She cried gently while I undressed her, and my anger intensified when I saw bruises to her side.

"What did he do to you?" I asked quietly while gently removing the band from her ponytail.

"He hit me, mostly. He tried to... He didn't, though. Veronica was like a demon, Alex. She protected me, she fought him like a man would and I couldn't do anything to help."

She cried harder as I led her to the shower. I waited until the water had soaked her body then I stepped in, fully dressed, behind her. I poured gel on a sponge and I cleaned her body. She shook, she sobbed, she closed her eyes, and she winced in pain. I was as gentle as I could be, and I blessed the water cascading from the showerhead for concealing my tears.

I dried her as she stood there, limp with her head bowed. I cupped her chin and raised her face.

"I'm so tired, Alex."

I nodded and then kissed her lips gently so as not to hurt her. "I want to take all the pain away, Gabriella. I love you so much," I said. She simply nodded before I carried her to bed.

Whether she actually fell asleep as quickly as it appeared, or whether she'd closed her eyes to lead me to believe she had, I let her be alone for a while. I was sure she'd need company at some point, maybe therapy to get over what had happened to her. I walked back into the bathroom to strip out of my wet clothes. Leaving them in a pile, I put on a clean t-shirt and jeans then walked into the living room.

Mackenzie was sitting on the sofa, he swirled whisky in a glass, and I decided, despite it being morning, to have one myself. It was our way to control our anger and emotions.

"How is she?" he asked. His eyes were as red as I suspected mine were.

"He didn't rape her; I think she was telling me that he tried but Veronica stopped him. That's why, I believe, she took most of his beating." Bile rose to my throat and Mackenzie nodded.

"Veronica said the same. Jesus, Alex, I...I don't know what to say or how to feel other than I want to murder that bastard." He spat the words, such was his anger.

"Where's Veronica?" I asked without answering him because we both felt the same.

"Sleeping. I guess that's their way, sleep off trauma, shut down until they're able to cope with it all. Burrows called, Stanton has a punctured lung, broken ribs, a broken nose, and cheek bone. He's under *protective custody* in the hospital."

"He fucking ought to be because if I could get in there, I'd finish him off," I said. I felt sick to my stomach, useless, and still scared. I wasn't letting Gabriella out of my sight for the foreseeable future.

"I'm going to take her back to America, Mackenzie, just for a while. I'll do all the consolidation work out there," I said.

He nodded. "Good, I'm pleased you've made that decision. I want her out of this place as well. Now, if I could only persuade your cousin to do the same."

I chuckled even knowing the situation was dire. "She sure beat his arse, didn't she?"

"I don't think I'd like to upset her," he replied.

"I guess that comes from years of travelling alone and learning to take care of herself, and her *unusual* sexual appetite. I mean, who the fuck wants to be tasered?"

I sipped on my whisky and we both chuckled.

It was a couple of hours later that the police visited again. Gabriella and Veronica were sitting on the same bed having both eaten a little. A doctor had been to check them over and prescribed pain relief. He was concerned about Veronica's neck, but she refused to attend Accident & Emergency again, stating that she'd make an appointment if she felt she needed to.

Mackenzie and I were ushered from the room while both women gave more statements. Gabriella confirmed that although he had attempted to, he hadn't raped her. They were made to state exactly what happened to them, again, and although I got angry at that, I understood. The police needed an airtight case that time, any slight difference in wording would give cause for the defence to pounce. I dreaded the thought that Gabriella would be put on the stand and prayed that he pleaded guilty beforehand.

"Should we call her mother?" I asked, while we were waiting for the police to join us.

"She said not to," Mackenzie replied.

I nodded. There was no point in having her upset while miles away. I guess we still felt that we wanted to do something, be proactive. Watching the woman I loved cry, call out in her sleep, and look so sad and beaten was eating me up inside.

"I don't know what to do," I whispered.

"Love her," came a reply. Veronica had left the bedroom and came and sat on the edge of my chair. She placed her arm around my shoulders. "She knows you love her, Alex, she just needs to hear the words leave your lips."

"I don't want to ask if you're okay because it's such a daft question," I said.

She smiled at me. "I've had worse days, I can assure you." A tear streaked down her cheek.

Mackenzie rose to wipe the tear away and as much as she was grateful, she covered his hand with hers, I didn't detect anything other than a friendship there.

"Oh, fuck, Mother must be going nuts," I said, picking up my mobile and seeing a few missed called from her.

"Let me speak to her. I'll explain that Gabriella and I got a little tipsy and forgot she was meeting you," Veronica said. I handed her my phone. I didn't necessarily want to lie to my mother, but I didn't need her worrying about Gabriella as well.

Veronica walked away while talking to my mother. The police returned from the bedroom and I replaced them in there. Gabriella was shuffling up the bed and I fluffed the pillows behind her.

"Are you up for more talking?" I asked. She patted the bed beside her and I sat. "What happened when he got into your house?"

"I left the front door open; I was just going to run upstairs to grab a coat. He must have followed me. He tried to grab me, and I ran around the bedroom but there was really nowhere to go. He was shouting at me not to touch anything, which I thought was odd. I grabbed a cushion and I threw it on a chair, I knew, if you saw it, you'd think something was off. He didn't want any evidence that I'd been taken, I think."

I sighed. "When I spoke to the police I told them

someone had been in the bedroom because of the damn cushion. It was a brilliant idea, baby," I said. I wrapped my arm around her, and she snuggled into my side.

"I have something else to say. I want you here, in this apartment, it's more secure and I won't take any arguments over it. Also, Mackenzie wants me to move to the US to deal with some of the businesses there that he wants to consolidate. I think it's a good idea and I want you to come with me." I looked down at her.

She blinked a few times and I couldn't read her reaction. "Stay with you, yes, but can we talk some more about moving to the US? That's rather dramatic," she said, gently.

"No, what's dramatic is you nearly getting raped because of me. You getting beaten because of me. I'm, ultimately, the cause of this. It was my quest to bring down Stanton because of what he did to my father. And yet, what happened to my father was my fault as well."

The more I spoke, the words tumbled from that locked up box in my mind. Pandora had truly been unleashed. I spewed years of grief, anguish, and hurt. I had no idea how long I spoke for, but I know I also cried with both release from the pent up issues I had, and the relief of sharing it all with her. She kissed my cheeks, my eyelids, and my lips.

I wiped at my face. "What the fuck happened there?" I asked, chuckling. We had been sitting silently for a few minutes.

She shrugged. "Fear makes you search inside yourself, I guess. Makes you reanalyse your life. I know I am with mine. I was terrified, not for my life, I didn't think he'd go that far, but...I don't know if I could survive being so brutally violated by him."

"And I thank God that you don't have to."

"I want to go to court, Alex. I want the opportunity to stand in front of him and tell the jury what he did."

I didn't respond that I hoped she'd never have to. I'd witnessed the British judicial system and it wasn't always the finest.

"We'll deal with that when the time comes. But you'll move in here, yes? At least grant me that for now. I can't be away from you, Gabriella. I'd move in with you but…" I stopped, I didn't want to remind her that Stanton had been in there and knew where she lived. If he did, so did his *friends*.

"I'll move in with you on one proviso," she said, looking up at me. "I get to redecorate."

"You get to do whatever the fuck you want, my Lady," I replied.

CHAPTER SEVENTEEN

On her insistence, Mackenzie borrowed my car to take Veronica home. There was nothing more the police could do, and she wanted to be in her own surroundings. He was glad to, he wanted to *chat* with the security team. An overhaul was needed there, for sure. Since it was now his business, it was something he told her he was doing with immediate effect. He didn't care for her feelings towards them, how long she'd known them, they had proven to be ineffective. It had taken a long conversation to calm him down, of course. In the end it was decided a more sophisticated security system was to be installed and a better monitoring system linked to the gate. Stanton's code to get in should have been deactivated long before it was used.

I called for takeout from my favourite Italian and set the table for two. Gabriella had complained that two days in bed was long enough and she was starting to ache. I was convinced that was the bruising coming out more than being in bed for too long. We had agreed to disagree on that.

She tried to keep up good spirits while we dined but her hands shook, and she pushed more of the food around her plate than she ate.

I reached over to take her hand. "Leave the food, eat when you feel like it. Come, let's just sit for a while," I said. We sat on the sofa and although the television was on, she clearly wasn't watching. I turned it off. "Look outside," I said. The London skyline looked magnificent with the sun lowering behind it.

"I love London," she replied.

"Enough to not want to leave?" I asked, nuzzling the side of her head.

"For now. I know what Mackenzie has offered is so very tempting and I'm utterly thrilled for you. I just don't know if it's right for me."

"Then I'll turn down his offer," I said.

"But I don't want you to do that."

"I will be wherever you are. So, for now, it's a done deal. I'm not going, I can do what he wants from here although you and I might have to go visit your mother for a few days a month."

I was determined. I also knew that Mackenzie would understand. If Gabriella was adamant she didn't want to leave, then neither would I.

"Now I feel terrible. Maybe you just delay for a few months. Let me get my head around what's happened."

"Okay. It was just an idea, one decided in panic to keep you safe. Let's forget about it for now, shall we?" I asked, smiling at her as she looked up at me.

She smiled back and it wasn't one that reached her

eyes. I was serious, I would call Mackenzie in the morning and we'd make a new arrangement.

"I'm not going anywhere without you," I added.

That night we made love. I was gentle and tender and surprised that she had instigated it. She was the one that had reached for me as we lay naked in bed. She was the one that whispered how much she needed me in that moment and then, she was the one that controlled what happened. I kissed her cuts and bruises and while silent tears tracked down her cheeks, I hovered over her, claiming her as mine. Perhaps she needed the vision of me above her, or the feeling of me bringing her to orgasm to remove the horror of what could have been.

"I love you, Gabriella," I whispered when I came. She wrapped her arms around me and we slept.

A couple of days later, although I'm not sure how, the newspapers were full of Stanton's attack on Gabriella and Veronica. A consequence, according to Veronica, was that applications for the membership to the club had soared. She was asked for interviews, all of which she declined, but a statement about the club was sent out. It was important that it wasn't seen as some strip club or whore house, the local authorities wouldn't be pleased with that, we decided. Veronica said, at the rate money was flowing is, she might be able to pay Mackenzie back for the renovation loan much quicker than she anticipated.

Stanton was still in hospital and the protection he was afforded, we were told, was because there had been a credible threat to his life. We were not allowed to know by who, but Burrows pointed towards the Russians.

"Let's hope they do us all a favour and get to him before the taxpayer has to fork out thousands," I said. Mackenzie chuckled and agreed.

At first, Stanton had said that he'd visited the club and Gabriella was a willing partner. It had gotten heated and he was trying to play the *rough sex* card, something that seemed to allow scumbags to walk from a rape charge. I vowed to take up my inherited place in the House of Lords and debate that *loophole*.

When the evidence was put to him, the photographs, and a video recording of him dragging Gabriella to the playroom, he backed down and pleaded guilty.

"He will be offered a deal," Burrows said. And before I could give my angry response, he explained. "I know this is hard to take, and believe me, it sickens me as well. There are bigger players here that he is willing to give up for a deal. The CPS want those players. I want him convicted of attempted rape, assault, kidnapping, and attempted murder, trust me. But it won't be up to me anymore."

"If that deal means he's on the streets, you better pay for his security," Mackenzie said.

Burrows held up his hand. "I didn't hear that, but I don't blame you for feeling that way."

I shook my head. "I don't want Gabriella knowing that," I said. It would devastate her to know her assault was just a means to another end.

Burrows left and I recalled Gabriella's concerns about moving back to America.

"I can't go yet, Mackenzie, and leave her here. Not at the moment," I said. I then outlined plans to work on both

Trymast and the consolidation. "When she's had time to heal, I'll discuss it again with her."

"I agree, please, Alex, don't think any more about it. Right now, we'll just carry on as normal and if things change, we can make a new plan." I nodded. He asked, "How is she?" We were in the boardroom and Gabriella still hadn't returned to work.

"I think she needs to speak to someone. I'm going to contact an old friend, a psychiatric consultant and see what he suggests."

"Has she agreed to that?" he asked, scepticism was clear in his voice.

"I haven't told her. But surely, you Americans are huge fans of therapy, aren't you?" I chuckled, knowing it was a cliché. "She needs to speak to someone other than me."

"You really do love her, don't you?" he said, quietly.

"I do."

"I'm glad. It's nice to know she has you to look after her. I feel like I need to step back a little. Like the father of the bride handing over his daughter at her wedding." He laughed at his analogy.

"Steady up, I love her. No talk of weddings. It's taken this long and *that* event to get me to admit my feelings."

I gave a pretend shudder but we both knew I'd marry her tomorrow if there was an opportunity. Or, maybe I needed some time to get my head around that one.

Before I left to return to my own office a call came through to Mary. "Some bloke called Duncan Wilson is after you," she shouted across the room.

"Which one of us," Mackenzie asked.

"Him." She pointed to me. "He's downstairs."

I looked at Mackenzie and frowned. "Can you let them know to show him up here?"

She huffed as she did, even though it was part of what she was supposed to do for him. Mary wasn't in the best of moods that day and we didn't want to ask why.

The man that strode across the room, accompanied by another, barely resembled the Duncan that had played tennis with my mother. I stood to *greet* him.

"Duncan, this is a surprise. May I introduce Mackenzie Miller?"

They shook hands and there was no introduction of his friend.

He chuckled when he sat. "You probably know my name isn't Duncan Wilson, or Windsor. And I am terribly sorry for deceiving your mother. I am truly fond of her, which is partly why I'm here." He looked to his friend who opened a briefcase and slid out a piece of paper. "This will run in all the mainstream news in a couple of days. I wanted you to see it before it did." He slid the paper over to us.

It was a news piece that detailed the suicide of Lord Stanton. Apparently, he was able to take his own life while in hospital under protective custody.

I shook my head. "Who is going to believe that?" I asked.

"It doesn't matter if they do, that's the decision. He's disposable."

"Who are you?" Mackenzie asked.

He pursed his lips and breathed heavily out of his nose. Before he could speak, I did. "Don't tell us, if you do, you have to kill us, right?" I was being sarcastic, but it did break the tension.

"Mackenzie, we've actually met. Only the once and briefly. I work for an agency within the government that oversees military contracts and the people involved in those contracts. Got to make sure it's all on the straight, haven't we?" He chuckled, we didn't find it remotely funny. "Anyway, it appears that Stanton here has angered some very influential people and more so, has been stealing contract details to give to competitors, mostly foreign."

"And killing him is the punishment for espionage in the UK? Seems a trifle harsh," Mackenzie said.

"Espionage with the Russian mafia when we've just got down to controlling some of their activities in the UK is," he replied. He looked at his friend. "Of course, you didn't hear that from us. I just wanted to give you a heads-up. I know what he did to your friends, and I understand their need for justice, something they won't get. I'm sorry about that."

"Yeah, bigger things at play," I said, bitterly.

He slowly nodded. "I would also like to ask something of you. I am genuinely fond of your mother and I've been to see her a couple of times. My name is Don, but she still knows me as Duncan—"

"You want me to keep your secret?" I said, spitting out the words. He nodded and I rolled my eyes. "Fine, but I want one assurance from you and whatever department you work for, because it sure isn't *just* a government agency overseeing contracts. You wouldn't have access to that if it were true. If anyone else comes after Gabriella, Veronica, or anyone else close to us, I call you."

He reached into his jacket, pulled out a business card and handed it to me. There was nothing to suggest where, or for whom, he worked. It was just his name and a mobile number. I showed it to Mackenzie.

I turned back to Duncan. "Before you go, another thing. Why did you move into my mother's complex? And how the fuck could you ever take a lady such as my mother to dinner and forget your wallet?"

He screwed his nose and winced. "Yeah, that was, seriously, rather unfortunate and embarrassing, for sure. I can't tell you all the details but moving into that complex was just a stopgap. The government own lots of properties in the strangest of places. I fully intend to reimburse your mother."

Duncan, or Don, stood. He reached out and I did take his hand to shake it. I needed to leave the bitterness at the door from now on. Gabriella wasn't going to get her day in court, and I was pleased, but knew she wouldn't be.

When they'd left Mackenzie poured us both a coffee. "A right little double O seven, isn't he?"

"More like a fucking three and a half," Mary piped up, peering over her glasses at us.

For the first time in a few days, I laughed. Mackenzie laughed, and Mary just called us eejits.

"What is an eejit?" Mackenzie asked.

"Honestly, you don't want to know," I answered to save her calling him an eejit for not knowing what an eejit was.

She packed up her oversized handbag, the one she told us she kept a brick in, just in case she needed to swing it at someone. She also picked up a couple of boxes of chocolates. She placed them on the boardroom table before she left.

"Give those to the ladies, won't you?" she said.

"Thanks, Mary, that's a lovely thing to do. I'm sure

they'll be thrilled," I replied. She smiled at me and, I was sure, that was the first time she ever had.

"Wonders will never cease," Mackenzie said, Mary raised her two fingers to him just as the lift doors closed taking her downstairs.

"I might need to sack her," he said.

"Good luck with that!"

Mackenzie laughed. "Have you heard from Veronica today?" he asked.

"I spoke to her earlier. She and Gabriella have developed a friendship," I replied. I guessed that was because they'd experienced the trauma together.

"She's seemed *too* jolly when I spoke to her. I know about this stiff upper lip British thing but, I'm worried," Mackenzie said.

"I guess it's her way of coping. She's spent years *punishing* men," I said, with a chuckle. "Kept her in good stead for Stanton, so we should be thankful."

"I've seen what she does. Not my cup of *coffee* at all," he said, substituting the correct word, tea, for his choice of poison.

In her late teens, many years ago, Veronica had travelled the world. She had been raped in Thailand. She'd fallen pregnant from that experience and vowed to keep the baby. I remember her saying that it wasn't the child's fault. The police weren't interested, she was another backpacker drunk and high at a Full Moon party and *what did she expect?* She'd continued her travels, ending up in Micronesia. She'd call me and send me photographs of the most amazing places. Her bump was growing, and I remember asking her to come home, give birth in the UK where it was safer. She'd refused. Something she'd regret for the rest of her life, she said.

When Veronica went into labour she'd taken herself to the hospital. She called me on her way, and I wished her well. She seemed so happy, in pain, but so very excited. I didn't get to hear from her for a few days and when I did, it broke my heart. Something had gone terribly wrong and the baby had died. Veronica was wretched, yet she still refused to come home. She told me that she placed most of her baby's ashes in the most beautiful place on the planet. It was somewhere she vowed never to return. She wore a tiny glass vial around her neck, and she carried a small amount of ashes wherever she went.

I was the only other person who knew that, and I didn't tell Mackenzie, of course. I would never betray her confidence. What drove Veronica, what I was close to when I said she was punishing men, was the fact that she was unable to ever have another child. When she was raped she'd also contracted herpes. As the baby developed, and because she hadn't received the usual medical care, it wasn't detected. She vowed never to forgive herself for that and her punishment was to never have a *real* relationship. She chose to have a hysterectomy, privately of course, because she never wanted to run that risk again.

When she had said to Mackenzie that 'she'd had worse' she'd really meant it.

CHAPTER EIGHTEEN

A week later Gabriella returned to work. She would have returned earlier, I was sure, it was only that her make-up hadn't covered her bruises until then and she was conscious of them.

"I don't want to be asked questions, or stared at, Alex," she'd said as she'd attempted to blend foundation over her skin.

"You need to do whatever you are comfortable with. What time are you seeing Alison?" I asked. Alison was the trauma therapist that had been recommended by my old friend and surprisingly, Gabriella was very keen.

"This afternoon at three. You'll collect me after?" she said.

I'd been standing behind her while she did her eyes, as she'd call it. I kissed her neck not wanting a mouthful of foundation. "I certainly will. We also have dinner with my mother. Are you up for that?"

She smiled at me through the mirror. "You bet. I can't wait."

Mother knew some of what had happened. She didn't buy the 'girls got tipsy and forgot' from Veronica. Moreso because that would be the absolute least amount of trouble Veronica could get herself in and something she would expect from her in her teens. Oh no. My mother was astute and peppered me for information until she rang Gabriella herself. She then read the papers.

My punishment for not telling her immediately was dinner at her favourite, and very costly, restaurant in London.

Gabriella and I left for work and she was welcomed back immediately as she stepped into the reception area. It wasn't going to be easy to deny what had happened since it had been splashed all over the newspapers and was still an ongoing story considering the perpetrator had managed to kill himself with a substance not generally found in the hospital but was a nerve agent found in Russia.

The conspiracy theorists were having a blast. Russian influence, money laundering, killing off Lords while under guard, sex clubs, and influential businessmen made for some amazing stories. Even I had been engrossed in one.

"Have you read this?" I asked Mackenzie as I sat in his office. "Apparently this is another Umbrella Poisoning situation. Stanton was really a Russian spy."

I slowed down as I came to the end of my statement and lowered the paper. I looked up at Mackenzie who wasn't smiling back. "What are you talking about?" he asked.

"1978, a dissident was poked with an umbrella that had a spike on the end and was filled with a drug that killed him. The Russians were blamed. He was just getting on a bus, I think."

Mackenzie scowled at me. "He was getting on a bus? He was poked with an umbrella? Fuck me, Alex, that's about as fucking British as it gets! But, you might have a point."

I widened my eyes. "Who did Don say he worked for? Some government agency and then he mentioned they had got deals done with the Russians, or something?" I said.

Mackenzie nodded. "Maybe that's not too far from the truth. If Stanton was divulging information to the Russians and then got himself in trouble to the magnitude that he has, I'm sure they'd want him *disposed* of. And old Don might be involved in that."

I folded the newspaper and placed it in the bin. "Let's not read anymore," I said. The last thing I wanted was to know my mother was dating someone with Russian connections and I couldn't warn her off.

"What's on the agenda today?" he asked.

I picked up the file on a manufacturing company that Mackenzie owned in the US. "I'm sorting out a trip to finalise the sale of Andore."

Andore was a small, but very profitable, company Mackenzie had owned that needed to expand. A factory and warehouse in the docks was the ideal location for them, so we'd encouraged them to merge with the company his ex-father-in-law had recently been kicked out of.

"Will Gabriella go with you?" he asked.

"Yes, she's called her mother, and we're staying there."

"If it gets too much, you know where the key to my house is, don't you?" he asked, and I nodded. When we'd stayed there before he'd shown me a key safe should I ever have to get in myself.

I left his office and returned to my own. For the rest of the day I got on with work until I received a call from reception to notify me my car was waiting. I'd lost track of time and panicked thinking that Gabriella would be waiting for me

I rushed downstairs, dragging on my coat as I did, and slid into the back of the car. We arrived at the destination just as she came through the door. She held a tissue to one eye, wiping a tear.

I left the car and walked towards her. "Hey, are you crying?" I asked, gently.

"It was tough. Luckily, I have my make-up bag with me. Now, that has left me ravenous."

I smiled and chuckled with her even though I knew laughter wasn't what she felt inside but what she needed to hear. I helped her into the car, and we drove out of London to collect my mother, only to return to eat.

Rules was the oldest restaurant in London. Set in a small pedestrianised street, it was just what we all needed. Mother had spent the whole journey holding Gabriella's hand while Gabriella unloaded. I believed Mother was likely a better therapist than the one she had just visited. My mum was so tender, and she wiped Gabriella's cheeks of tears as if she were dealing with her own child. I looked out the side window so they wouldn't see any of my own.

By the time we arrived, make-up had been reapplied and we were back to how Gabriella was going to refurnish the apartment.

"You really should buy a house, Alex. Outdoor space and fresh air are what this girl needs," Mother said.

"Maybe," I replied, distracted by the doorman.

The problem with somewhere like Rules was one often bumped into acquaintances or friends. Len and Pete were dining, and both rose to greet me warmly. I introduced Gabriella and she was hugged, as was Mother. It took an age to get to our table.

"I really don't know why those two don't just come out of their wardrobe," Mother said, fussing with her napkin.

"Closet, Henrietta," Gabriella corrected her. "Are they gay?" she asked me.

"I have absolutely no idea and since they've never said, I don't presume to think so," I replied, looking pointedly at my mum.

She laughed, and that was good to see. She reached over to take my hand. "I owe you such an apology, my darling," she said. I frowned, confused and she continued, "For way too long I buried myself in my grief and anger over your father. I was so bitter that he chose, what I believed, was a coward's way out. I don't believe that now, of course, but I neglected you and I must have been awful to be around. I'm just so glad that I managed to find my way out of that depression before it damaged our relationship too much."

I didn't really do public displays of emotion. It made me feel uncomfortable which was why both Mother and Gabriella often forced me to. According to my delightful girlfriend, it was another one of those *sticks up my ass* that I had to remove. I pushed back my chair and stood then scuttled around the table, careful not to bump into the very close neighbouring one, and gave my mother a hug.

Gabriella looked at me wide-eyed.

I laughed and asked her, "How many sticks are left to

be removed?" She laughed and it was Mother's turn to look confused.

"We're off to the states in a couple of days, Alex has to work. Why don't you come with us? My mom is desperate to meet you," Gabriella said.

As much as I loved my mum, the thought of both her and Gabriella's mum was the stuff of nightmares. We'd never get anything done because I knew both mothers would spend the entire time arranging things for us all to do.

"I'd love to," Mother replied. "I haven't been abroad for years. I'm sure my passport is still valid. If not, you can sort it for me darling, can't you?"

"No, Mother, I can't just *magic* you up a valid passport. Check when we get you home," I replied. I glared at Gabriella who smiled so very sweetly back at me.

The meal was wonderful, and it was lovely to hear the tinkle of laughter from Gabriella. I cringed the whole time while my mother shared horror stories from my childhood. Short of bringing out a family photo album, Gabriella got to know *everything* there was about my upbringing.

I was very glad to not only drop Mother off home, but to find out her passport was indeed expired.

"Another time, Henry. I'm sure we'll need to head back in another month or so, won't we?" Gabriella said, nudging me.

"Yes. Get that renewed and we'll book a holiday. How does that sound?" I replied.

Both Mother and Gabriella nodded enthusiastically.

Once we were back in the car, I pulled Gabriella close and nuzzled into her neck. "You deserve a spanking for your behaviour this evening, my Lady," I said.

She pulled back to look up at me. "A spanking. Why, my Lord?"

"You made me behave like a real son and a decent human being." I chuckled as I spoke.

"And that deserves a spanking?" she asked, purring as she spoke.

"It most certainly does."

I kissed her deeply, biting at her tongue and giving her a taste of what was to come. I planned a night of pleasure and smiled at the secret box that had arrived from her favourite shoe store.

Except the box didn't contain shoes.

Gabriella broke the lease on her house and moved in with me. We had decided that, although we would sell the apartment and buy a house, she could still redecorate. I thought it a total waste, but it made my lady happy so I let is pass.

For the first couple of weeks I spent more time with Mackenzie than I did in my own home. The decorators and designers were driving me nuts and for the first time, Gabriella and I argued. It was because I wasn't showing as much interest in what fucking shade of blue the blue wall was going to be. I didn't care for blue paint, I didn't care which shade of blue, and when she put her hands on her hips and gave that *look,* I took action.

I grabbed her and pushed her against the wall. I kissed the complaints from her mouth that the wall was still wet until she sighed and kissed me back just as hard. I unfaste-nend my jeans and reached inside for my cock. At the same time, she wriggled out of her panties. I pulled her skirt to her hips, grabbed one thigh and raised her leg, placing it around my waist.

I pushed into her. "I. Don't. Care. What. Fucking. Colour. The. Wall. Is." I grunted out each word matching my thrusts. She laughed and dug her nails into my skin.

I bit down on her shoulder and her neck. She moaned out loud, tangling my hair in her fingers.

I fucked her hard and fast. Her body scraped against the freshly painted wall, and paint smudged onto her cheek.

She came, tightening her body around mine. Muscles inside clamped, milking my cock as I joined her in release. My feet tangled in the protective material that had been laid on the floor and we heard the crash as a paint pot toppled over.

I started to laugh, and she joined in. "Baby, paint the walls whatever fucking colour you want, okay?" I whispered as I kissed her neck and released her from my grip.

"If that's the reaction I get when I try to have a conversation with you about paint, I'm gonna do that for every room in this house. There are, what? Six?" Gabriella smiled so fucking sweetly at me that she made my insides knot and my knees go weak.

"You'll be the death of me," I said, tucking my now blue paint covered cock inside my jeans.

I took her hand and led her to the master bedroom for a shower together.

"I love you," I said, as I shampooed her hair.

"I know, and I love you more," she replied.

We both laughed as we watched the blue coloured water swirl away down the drain.

The End

Gabriella and Alex feature in the erotic romance, The Facilitator and The Facilitator, part 2. You'll find Mackenzie Miller and Lauren Perry are the main stars in those books.

If you haven't read The Facilitator, then you can start that journey here: mybook.to/TheFacilitator
If you have, you might like to think about adding the CEO Series to you naughty collection: mybook.to/CEOJanuary

ACKNOWLEDGMENTS

Thank you to Francessca Wingfield from Francessca Wingfield PR & Design for yet another wonderful cover.

I'd also like to give a huge thank you to my editor, Lisa Hobman, and proofreader, Joanne Thompson.

A big hug goes to the ladies in my team. These ladies give up their time to support and promote my books. Alison 'Awesome' Parkins, Karen Atkinson-Lingham, Ann Batty, Elaine Turner, Kerry-Ann Bell, Lou Dixon, and Louise White – otherwise known as the Twisted Angels.

My amazing PA, Alison Parkins keeps me on the straight and narrow, she's the boss! So amazing, I call her Awesome Alison. You can contact her on AlisonParkinsPA@gmail.com

To all the wonderful bloggers that have been involved in promoting my books and joining tours, thank you and I appreciate your support. There are too many to name individually – you know who you are.

ABOUT THE AUTHOR

Tracie Podger currently lives in Kent, UK with her husband and a rather obnoxious cat called George. She's a Padi Scuba Diving Instructor with a passion for writing. Tracie has been fortunate to have dived some of the wonderful oceans of the world where she can indulge in another hobby, underwater photography. She likes getting up close and personal with sharks.

Tracie likes to write in different genres. Her Fallen Angel series and its accompanying books are mafia romance and full of suspense. A Virtual Affair, Letters to Lincoln and Jackson are angsty, contemporary romance, and Gabriel, A Deadly Sin and Harlot are thriller/suspense. The Facilitator books are erotic romance. Just for a change, Tracie also decided to write a couple of romcoms and a paranormal suspense! All can be found at: author.to/TraciePodger

ALSO BY TRACIE PODGER

Fallen Angel, Part 1

Fallen Angel, Part 2

Fallen Angel, Part 3

Fallen Angel, Part 4

Fallen Angel, Part 5

Fallen Angel, Part 6

The Fallen Angel Box Set

Evelyn - A novella to accompany the Fallen Angel Series

Rocco – A novella to accompany the Fallen Angel Series

Robert – To accompany the Fallen Angel Series

Travis – To accompany the Fallen Angel Series

Taylor & Mack – To accompany the Fallen Angel Series

Angelica – To accompany the Fallen Angel Series

A Virtual Affair – A standalone

Gabriel – A standalone

The Facilitator

The Facilitator, part 2

The Facilitator, part 3

A Deadly Sin – A standalone

Harlot – A standalone

Letters to Lincoln – A standalone

Jackson – A standalone

The Freedom Diamond – A novella

Limp Dicks & Saggy Tits

Cold Nips & Frosty Bits

Posh Frocks & Peacocks

My Lord – a standalone

STALKER LINKS

https://www.facebook.com/TraciePodgerAuthor/

http://www.TraciePodger.com

https://www.instagram.com/traciepodger/

Printed in Great Britain
by Amazon

42140037R00169